Unclay

Unclay

T. F. POWYS

A NEW DIRECTIONS PAPERBOOK

Published by arrangement with the Estate of T. F. Powys, represented by Peters, Frasers & Dunlop, Ltd., London

Manufactured in the United States of America
New Directions Books are printed on acid-free paper
First published as a New Directions Paperbook (NDP1427) in 2018

Library of Congress Cataloging-in-Publication Data
Names: Powys, Theodore Francis, 1875–1953, author.
Title: Unclay / by T. F. Powys.
Description: New York, NY : New Directions Publishing, 2018.
Identifiers: LCCN 2018025667 (print) | LCCN 2018040839 (ebook) | ISBN 9780811228206 (ebook) | ISBN 9780811228190 (alk. paper)
Subjects: LCSH: Death (Personification)—Fiction. | LCGFT: Novels.
Classification: LCC PR6031.O873 (ebook) | LCC PR6031.O873 U43 2018 (print) | DDC 823/.912—dc23
LC record available at https://lccn.loc.gov/2018025667

10 9 8 7 6 5 4 3 2 1

New Directions Books are published for James Laughlin
by New Directions Publishing Corporation
80 Eighth Avenue, New York 10011

CONTENTS

CONTENTS CONTINUED

UNCLAY

Daisies

THERE was a hedge in the way and, behind the hedge, a very narrow lane.

A fox, who was hidden in the meadow amongst some high rushes, intending to sleep until the evening came, and then to take a roosting fowl from a cartshed nearby, being smelt out by the hounds, sneaked to the hedge, crept through a little hole between the thorns—the way he had come—and, giving his tail a determined whisk to rid it of a dead bramble, ran nimbly up the lane.

He was an old dog-fox who had been hunted many times before. He understood the ways of hounds as well as any kitchen cat, and though—according to an established custom in his family—he always ran away from them, yet he by no means feared them. His cunning had always outwitted their blundering onslaughts, and he never failed to reach his earth safely, that went deep into a rocky hill.

The fox belonged to the country party in politics and always praised the landed gentry to his cubs, but all the farmers he wished dead because, having no manners, they sometimes shot or trapped the foxes.

When the fox slunk away, the hounds—not being accustomed to use their eyes—took him for a weasel. However, they soon discovered the scent and, making their usual sound, wagged their tails, rushed, pushed, and scrambled, and at last found a way through the hedge, and followed the fox.

If the hounds were surprised at the sudden appearance of

what they had intended all the day to look for, the hunt—
as the riders and runners after such a proceeding are called—
were far more so, and all looked excitedly for a gate.

The chief whip, who was steward to the estate, and whose
name was Mr. Pix, being called for by the company, pointed
out to his master where the gate was which led into the lane.

Mr. Pix's master, who was also master of the hunt, was
Lord Bullman. His Lordship had been even more astonished
than the hounds at the fox being discovered so near to the
Hall, for he had not expected a find any nearer to home than
Madder Hill. He blamed his ill-luck that the find should be
made in a small meadow surrounded by high hedges. The
fox, he believed, must have had a personal grudge against
him, and had chosen this very spot in order to trap the whole
hunt, and make the Master look foolish.

Even though that was not the direction in which the fox
had gone, Lord Bullman—giving a very modest "Halloo!"
—rode directly to the gate that had been pointed out to him.
He even made his horse gallop, giving the beast a sharp stab
with his spurs, and, coming quickly to the gate, he endeavoured to open it.

All who know his kind can truly say that, if a great man
tries to do any self-imposed task, it's best to leave him alone
to do it. Seeing Lord Bullman ride up to the gate, his mounted
servants and the rest of the hunt held back a little.

It is well known in all the countryside near West Dodder
Hall that his Lordship's tenants are advised to fasten all the
gates through which the hunt may wish to ride so that they
may open easily, or else they may incur his displeasure.

This order—that Mr. Pix never forgot to give to a new-
comer—was, in most cases, obeyed, but in the meadow where
the fox had been found it had often happened in the summer
months that young people—happy in one another's company

—would wander in upon a Sunday and lie down upon the grass, making less room—it was supposed—for Farmer Mere's cows. Thus it came about that Farmer Mere had fastened this particular gate, that led into the lane, with barbed wire.

There is always—as religious teachers in the last century knew—mischief ready for idle hands or for idle mouths. Lord Bullman grew impatient.

A fine gentleman, who had recently made a fortune by trading in picture-halls and had bought an estate near to Dodder, wishing to show his general unconcern about all common events—as well as to call attention to his good horsemanship—took a golden case out of his red coat and lit a cigarette. He hoped and expected that his horse would caper. But, instead of showing off the proficiency of his master as a rider, to all who might see, the horse—observing that the green grass looked tempting to one fed only on oats and beans—suddenly lowered its head and began to bite. The young man, in a hurry to chastise the unmannerly beast, dropped his gold case.

A woman laughed.

Lord Bullman pulled at the gate.

The remainder of the field sat idly upon their horses and chatted with one another. They had come into the meadow by one gate, and they intended to go out by another, and at least they sat safe and would not get dirtied if they remained where they were.

In every part of the British Empire, and in other places, too, of less repute, it is well known that an English gentleman never likes to be beaten. Neither does he care to commence a task that he is unable to finish. Lord Bullman might easily have called to his mounted lackeys, or else have delivered a command to Mr. Pix that the gate should be pulled down.

But he did not do so. He had his own character to think of—his own honour.

There were strangers present, onlookers from the village, and the rest of the hunt. Amongst the riders there were a few who were as well-bred and as rich as himself. To show these that he could not open a paltry gate, made of wood, would be an insult to his own noble ancestry.

Mr. Pix looked worried. He leaned down to get the ear of a friend who was walking, and whispered that they would soon hear something. And so they did—Lord Bullman was beginning to swear.

He swore first at Farmer Mere—who unfortunately was not there to hear him—for shutting the gate so tight, and then damned the gate to Hell because it would not open, and after that, gave his horse to the Devil because it would not stand still. But, for all his loud words, the gate remained closed.

Though some may argue otherwise, wealthy people, we affirm, are bad idlers. They do not like to be kept waiting. When matters grow dull and things come to a standstill, people of quality soon begin to fret. When the rich—and there is no mob like that mob—see a house a-burning, they like the flames to rise high; if the fire slackens and only black smoke appears, they begin to lose faith in the gaiety of the elements, and in themselves too. Even at a funeral fine people often become impatient, for they do not like any restraint.

But others, besides the gentry in'the meadow, soon grew dissatisfied with the entertainment. Three little children, who had walked from Dodder village that was two miles away, considered that they were being cheated of their sport. They had hoped at least to see a man or two thrown or a woman's leg broken. That was what they had come out to see. One of them, Winnie Huddy—for want of anything better to do—suggested a game by themselves. They soon forgot all about the hunt and Lord Bullman, and began to play touch in a corner of the field.

Besides this disrespectful gesture made by the children towards the noblest of country sports, there were other signs, too, that the kingdom of England was fast going to the Devil, or, what would be far worse for the landowners, to God. Two young and beautiful ladies, well-mounted, the daughters of an honourable knight, slipped—shameless hussies— from their horses, and began to gather daisies, their wish being that, during these moments when there was nothing doing in the way of murder, they might make a daisy-chain. The field was a sunny one, and the daisies plentiful, and the young ladies, with an entire disregard for what went on about them, picked greedily.

They might have accomplished their object, and decorated one another like two goddesses, if some one had not appeared to help Lord Bullman to open the gate.

It was certainly high time that he received assistance. My lord had a large income, and his oaths were like his guineas. He was justly and properly incensed against the gate.

The gate reminded him of his wife. She was the only other thing in the world that had ever withstood his will, and, seeing the gate in that fashion, he became more angry.

Lord Bullman had already broken his crop and torn his gloves, and his curses could have been heard upon Madder Hill, but the only one who seemed to heed them at all was Mr. Pix—a man religiously minded—who was forced to console himself, at a little distance away, with a flask of brandy.

II

Mr. Hayhoe Opens the Gate

THE gentleman who stepped forward from the lane to help so usefully was a poor clergyman—the Reverend Francis Hayhoe—who had recently been taking the duty at Dodder, because the late incumbent, Canon Dibben, had been preferred, being a man most zealous in forward works, to the town of Stonebridge.

Coming from Dodder, that was about two miles from West Dodder Hall, Mr. Hayhoe, walking softly along the lane, heard the buzz of horrid oaths, like hornets swarming; and, being sure that a devil had escaped out of Hell and was doing some one a mischief, he began to run.

Arriving quickly at the spot from whence the sounds came, he found Lord Bullman struggling in unequal combat with the five-barred gate.

Mr. Hayhoe hoped to be of use. That, he childishly thought, was the reason why he existed in the world. Indeed, he never went out a-walking without the wish being quick in his heart that he might, with God's help, be the means of assisting some one in distress. Once he had been more kind than wise. He had found a flock of sheep all clamouring to enter a field of rich clover ready to be mown. Mr. Hayhoe had opened the hurdles for them.

In the present emergency, wire was the trouble. Whenever Mr. Hayhoe saw barbed wire it reminded him of sin. Sin, he knew, has ugly spikes and twists itself round the heart of man to his eternal hurt.

8

Lord Bullman swore at Mr. Hayhoe. The clergyman, noticing where the knot was, unbound the wire, and the gate opened easily.

As Lord Bullman rode through the gate, he nodded gratefully to Mr. Hayhoe and, addressing him as though he were a poor dog who had earned a piece of liver, he called out, "As Dibben has gone to Stonebridge, if you want Dodder you may have the living."

Mr. Hayhoe raised his hat, and replied thankfully that he was very pleased with the gift. He had always wished, he said, to live at Dodder. His young child was buried in the Dodder churchyard, and his wife—Priscilla—never liked to be far away from the small grave. And never had a village, he believed, a clearer air, nor was there one anywhere better suited for peaceful reading.

Before Mr. Hayhoe had finished his thanks to his patron and his praise of Dodder, Lord Bullman had ridden out of sight, and the rest of the field was gone too, including the two graceless young ladies, who had been forced to mount and follow the others before they had finished the daisy-chain, which they dropped near to the clergyman. In a moment the lane was utterly deserted, except for Mr. Hayhoe, a blackbird, a wren, a mouse, and the first swallow.

In a northerly climate, every human being is gladly surprised and not a little relieved when the cold winter days change into warm spring ones. For who can tell when the winter creeps round him what his fate will be? Those last days in September, when the blue summer sky gives a caressing farewell, are sad and ominous, and appear like days that one has already lived, and are but come again to tantalize us with their sweet warmth, and so vanish in mist.

With the October rains, there comes a sad doubt. Who can tell what will happen? The next year may bring again the vernal glory, but we may not see it. Those holy scents of a July evening, that add so much to the beauty of the green hills, will another summer bring them to us?

In the autumn, sickness gathers like the clouds, and many troubles, that the warmth of the summer has laid to sleep, revive again. Out of the damp places in the earth, out of the hollow tree in the wood, where the night-bird broods, stepping upon pale and stricken leaves, there come the imps of darkness to harvest their winter carrion. And, as each winter day becomes more sodden and weary, so man's heart saddens and faints. Upon every side, when our own vitality is lessened by the want of sunshine, signs are heard and seen of what our own fate may be.

The church bell tolls: some one has been raised up for the last time, to be laid low. A coffin is being put into the ground.

Though a man does see each autumn as a season that he has already lived through, the spring is always a new birth. And Mr. Hayhoe—no less than we—could be glad in it.

The spring had come early to Dodder and, even though the day was only the last of March, bees were already busy in the soft flowers of the willow. The swallows had come, and a cuckoo had called.

The sun was more than usually kind for the time of year —its warmth could be felt—and Mr. Solly, who lived at Madder, and was an enemy to love, had seen signs already that the year would be good for nuts.

Winter troubles are soon forgotten when the sun rises with healing in its wings, bidding the hopes of a new summer enter the heart of man.

The Reverend Francis Hayhoe, though he shaved every morning, and read and preached, had never really understood worldly manners. He still held the oddest of ideas. He believed that men had souls, that men sinned, and that all men might be saved if they repented of their sins and believed in Jesus. "Jane," he sometimes said first, but fortunately he always corrected himself just in time and named Jesus.

Mr. Hayhoe was poor; his God had not given him any money, and what estate he had once possessed Farmer Beerfield had taken away from him. Mr. Hayhoe had been sold up for a debt of thirty pounds. That was how he had lost a small cure that once had been his own. When they were turned out, Mr. Beerfield had the church bells rung, and the Hayhoes, with their little son, took lodgings at Shelton.

Soon after they came there, the child died, and Mr. Hayhoe—who had begun to take the duty at Dodder—buried his son there.

Mr. Hayhoe had even odder ideas than the mere belief that mankind might be saved. All the doctrines expressed by the Church of England were true to him, and every word written by Jane Austen he believed to be almost as necessary to salvation. And so—by bringing Amos and Emma together, and considering their observations upon mankind—Mr. Hayhoe learned to love others more than himself.

He felt for those who had never known the loving-kindness of the Church of Christ, and he shook his head compassionately over those who had not read *Mansfield Park*.

From the Church, Mr. Hayhoe garnered and stowed away enough humility to last any man a lifetime; from Jane, he learned that it is better to listen than to look. The Church graciously permitted him to love God as much as he wished—which was with his whole heart—and Jane Austen allowed him to see into, and approve—though not all of them—the ways and habits of many a pleasant young lady, and more than one sober or frolicsome young gentleman.

Though a meek man, at certain times Mr. Hayhoe could do a brave thing. He was a protestant, and he once sent a sermon to the Pope. In this sermon, he pointed out—addressing the Italian gentleman as "Holy Father"—the many errors of Rome.

Every day Mr. Hayhoe expected to receive a reply, couched in the most courtly language, informing him that —led by His Holiness himself—every priest in the world would be permitted, and all in a hurry, to marry a "poor Miss Taylor."

Courage breeds courage. Soon after writing to the Pope, Mr. Hayhoe visited Daisy Huddy to read the Bible to her. . . .

Joy comes easily to the good; 'tis ever in their path; they have not to hunt or to look for it. Joy comes to them. Though Mr. Hayhoe had been astonished and troubled by the monstrous curses of Lord Bullman, yet no sooner had the man ridden off, than he forgot all about them.

Mr. Hayhoe sat down upon the grassy bank, wishing to rest a little—though first he picked up the daisy-chain that the young ladies had let fall in their eagerness to follow the chase, and he bound the gate with the daisies instead of the barbed wire, which he threw into the ditch.

He decorated the gate happily with this new bond, hoping that soon every piece of spiked iron might be removed out of man's way, together with those deep and adamantine chains that bind human souls to greed, cruelty and to all evil.

Mr. Hayhoe sighed and leant back upon the soft grass.

When he left his lodgings, he had put a book into his pocket—as he was used to do—wishing to think over a sermon when he went out, and a book may often be a useful help to encourage thought, as well as to quote from when the book is the Bible. The book that Mr. Hayhoe took from his pocket he supposed would do nearly as well; it was *Northanger Abbey*.

He read for a little and then, allowing the book to slip into the grass beside him, he began to watch the birds.

The birds were happy because the mild airs of spring made them so: Mr. Hayhoe was pleased too, because he had succeeded so easily in his mission that morning. He had certainly left his lodgings with a doubtful heart, little expecting any good to come of the attempted visit to West Dodder Hall, though he hoped that at least he would be replied to civilly, should he be bold enough to ask Lord Bullman for the gift of the Dodder living.

In order to make himself look more respectable, Mr. Hayhoe had put on his best coat, leaving his wife, Priscilla, who remained at Shelton, to darn the old one, that was very much in need of a lady's care.

Before he left, he had preached a little homily to her, observing that it was God's wish that a woman should rather sew than sorrow, "and though we may not be permitted," he said, tenderly, "to see yet, for a little while, our child in Paradise, we may be allowed to live all our lives near to his grave in Dodder churchyard."

Mr. Hayhoe then strode out, more hopeful than he had been since their sorrow, leaving his wife busy about the threadbare coat.

He had always known, he told himself—sitting contentedly upon the bank, that God's ways are most curious. For, had Lord Bullman never sworn at the gate, he, Francis Hayhoe, might never have had the offer of Dodder. Did some good come to some one whenever Lord Bullman swore? If that were so, it would be lawful to pray that Lord Bullman might swear the oftener.

Mr. Hayhoe smiled.

As a matter of fact, benefits had rarely come to him as easily as the living of Dodder, though of course, even now, there was a chance that his lordship might change his mind about the gift.

To ease his soul of this new fear, Mr. Hayhoe found his book again and began to read.

III

Mr. Hayhoe Hears Footsteps

MR. HAYHOE closed *Northanger Abbey* and lit his pipe, for he would sometimes smoke a little, as well as read, when he was out by himself.

He watched for a while the smoke of his pipe rise in little rings, that grew larger until they vanished altogether, and then, as he looked down into the lane, his attention was caught by the queer behaviour of a little mouse. This small creature, Mr. Hayhoe saw, was most dreadfully frightened, but why this was so he did not know. The mouse trembled with fear, and seemed so utterly overcome with a strange dread that it could not even run into the grass for safety.

Mr. Hayhoe watched the mouse. Perhaps the little creature had gone mad. He did not think so. What it appeared to suffer from was terror. Mr. Hayhoe wondered what ailed the thing. No cat was after it; evidently its nest was just under the bank; what was there to frighten it?

The mouse ran to Mr. Hayhoe, looking up at him piteously —as though he were a god who could save. Mr. Hayhoe took the mouse in his hand. It was plump and well. Why was it trembling?

Mr. Hayhoe gently put the mouse down upon the bank near to its hole. Its body twitched for a moment. It turned over, and was dead. Mr. Hayhoe shivered. He looked up into the sky.

The day was become very still; not a breath of wind stirred the new elder leaves in the lane. Like the mouse, all nature seemed too frightened to move. Though there was no sound, an invisible fear moved and crept in the lane. What was it? The trees listened and waited.

Mr. Hayhoe put his book into his pocket. In doing so, he noticed that his hand shook. He looked upward, wondering where the cloud had come from that so suddenly had dimmed the sun. Only a few moments before the sky had been quite clear, and now all had darkened as if a pall had fallen upon the land.

Mr. Hayhoe took out his watch. His hand shook so that he could hardly hold it—the watch was stopped.

A hare came up the lane, looking as frightened as the mouse. She paid no heed to Mr. Hayhoe and stopped within a yard of him, pricked up her ears, and listened. She stood upon her hind legs, with her fore-paws bent under her. She waited for a sound to come. She heard something, scattered the dust of the lane in her hurry to get away, and fled.

What had happened to the creatures, wondered Mr. Hayhoe. Some unseen fear had killed the mouse and made the hare scamper off. What was it that frightened them?

Mr. Hayhoe heard the sound of soft wings. Near to him, upon an elm-tree bough, sat a large owl. The owl blinked its eyes, and peered in the direction of Dodder. It cast out from its stomach a little ball of fur—the undigested portion of a rat—and blinked again.

Mr. Hayhoe shivered. He supposed that a spring thunderstorm must be coming up, and yet he heard no thunder.

As a good husband should do, whenever he is surprised at what goes on about him, Mr. Hayhoe thought of his wife. He remembered, with pleasure, that she had promised, when the coat was done, to meet him in the Dodder churchyard, so that they might eat their lunch together, near to the child's grave. But now there would be no need to do that. They could get the key of the Vicarage from old Huddy, the care-taker, for that was their own house now, and lunch in the empty dining-room, sitting on a window-sill. Then they could walk as proudly as they liked over their new house, and choose a bedroom for themselves—the bedroom that over-looked the churchyard.

Though thinking about his wife pleased him, as it always did, Mr. Hayhoe still noticed that he trembled. He felt his forehead; it was covered with cold sweat. Surely he was not going to die, like the mouse! He hoped not. But why did he feel so cold? There was nothing in the weather to account for that. Even though the sun was dimmed, the air was warm. Perhaps, he thought, he had better soon leave that bank and go home. He liked a grassy place, but his wife had told him that a bank is not always safe—ants or snakes might be hid-ing, to sting a good man. He knew he was rather too fond of staying about in country lanes.

Mr. Hayhoe was upon the point of rising, when he dis-tinctly heard the sounds of footsteps approaching from the direction of Dodder.

Near to where he was resting, the lane turned a corner, so that whoever was coming would have to arrive very near be-fore being seen.

The sound of a human footfall, though it may be approach-ing, is not likely to be much heeded until it comes very near. Though Mr. Hayhoe heard the sound, he did not regard it, except so far as it made him remain where he was for a little longer, wishing to give the footsteps a chance to go into some field or other and disappear.

He wished to think, too—before he closed the gate, that deserved his gratitude for its boldness in checking Lord Bull-man, and its kindness in allowing him to open it—of the pleasure that his tidings would give to his wife, Priscilla. Since her child had died, Priscilla had wished, more, he knew, than she liked to say, to live near to where her little boy had been laid to rest.

Priscilla had grieved very deeply at his death, and had only kept her interest in living because of a strange hope that, somehow or other, had got into her head. This was nothing less than the wish to meet Death himself.

She would often—and Mr. Hayhoe, knowing how shrewdly her sorrow pinched her heart, listened to her wild talk—tell her husband how she expected Death to look, if she did meet him.

"If I search carefully," she said, "and gaze closely upon every stranger that I meet, I shall be sure to know him when he comes to Dodder."

"He will come to Dodder," said Mr. Hayhoe sadly, "one time or another."

"And perhaps you may be the first to welcome him," said Priscilla.

"Then," said Mr. Hayhoe, with a smile, "I shall be the first to see our little Tommy."

IV

Mr. Hayhoe Makes a New Friend

AGAIN Mr. Hayhoe heard the same footsteps; they were coming nearer. He thought he knew the sound of the steps, and tried to recollect when he had heard them.

He soon remembered, for the hour during which he had last listened to them was not one that he was likely to forget. Not many weeks had passed since that unhappy time.

Dr. Jacob had shaken his head over Tommy, and had spoken rudely to every one. Whenever a child died, Dr. Jacob believed the mother was to blame—or else the father, and he always told them so. He liked children, but hated fathers and mothers, all of whom he believed to be murderers.

Dr. Jacob had just left, after informing Mr. Hayhoe that he had only himself to blame for allowing Tommy to catch measles, and Priscilla was gone to lie down for a few moments, for—worn out with constant nursing—she had hardly closed her eyes for five nights and days.

Mr. Hayhoe waited beside the child's cot. The moments passed slowly. He thought the child slept.

Soon he saw a change come over the boy's face. It was become expressionless; a pallor was there instead of a flush. The breathing was hardly noticeable. Mr. Hayhoe took up his hand. The eyes saw nothing. Tommy's week of sickness was nearly at an end.

When a man dies, Nature rages in anger: when a child's life ends, she broods silently. Perhaps she is afraid of Dr. Jacob. Anyhow, the night when Tommy died was an un-

usually mild and quiet night for February. The window of
the little room in Shelton was wide open, and the air came
in, sweet and kindly.

All the other village children were recovered of the com-
plaint, and at that time of the night were all sound asleep. It
was hard for Mr. Hayhoe to believe that his alone was the
one to be taken. Was it all his fault? Dr. Jacob had told
him that it was, and, anyhow, he would have to bear the loss.

In the morning, just before nine, he would hear all the
noise and clatter of the children going to school. His child
would remain in bed, lying very still.

"Every parent who lets a child die should be hanged," Dr.
Jacob had observed. But who was it who had sent this trouble
so suddenly upon them? What had they done to be so punished?

Mr. Hayhoe bent down over the hand that he held, and
kissed it.

The hand was cold.

He heard steps in the lane. Not hurried steps, nor the gay
going of a midnight reveller, nor were they the heavy slum-
bering steps of a labourer, returning late home. These steps
were not like that: they were the sure and certain steps of one
who has something important to do.

The footsteps came up the village street; they neither
paused nor loitered, they came on. When they arrived at the
cottage where the Hayhoes lodged, they stopped. Some one
opened the garden gate and came to the door.

Mr. Hayhoe looked at the child. He gave a low groan, a
gasp. He was dead. . . . .

The footfalls that Mr. Hayhoe heard in the lane were the
same as the ones he had heard when his son died.

It was not an ordinary field-labourer who had visited that
Shelton cottage, "but perhaps," thought Mr. Hayhoe, "it

might have been a gentleman's gardener, who had called with a gift of seed potatoes for his landlord, Mr. Thomas."

Whoever it was, Mr. Hayhoe could not be mistaken in the footsteps, that were now coming very near.

Mr. Hayhoe leant back in the hedge: the stranger turned the corner of the lane, and came into sight. He walked very slowly, keeping his eyes upon the ground, as though searching for something that he had lost.

The man was so busy searching that he did not notice Mr. Hayhoe. He stopped in the lane, and stood for a while considering deeply. Evidently he was trying to recollect whether it was really in that place, or elsewhere, that he had lost what he now sought. The stranger seemed to Mr. Hayhoe to be no one in particular—just an ordinary man.

Perhaps a tradesman? His clothes, though they did not fit him very well, were quite new, and the man's general appearance was tidy and respectable. He was certainly no idler; he had a busy look that indicated that, only a little while ago, he had had work to do.

The new-comer now turned and looked down the lane, the way he had come. He rubbed his forehead slowly with three fingers, and remained thoughtful.

Mr. Hayhoe never met a man but he looked well at him —and that for a reason—because in every human creature that he beheld he saw two goings—a falling to Hell or a rising to Salvation. Whenever he saw a new face, the thought always came to him, " 'Tis a soul to be saved or damned."

And a human soul, Mr. Hayhoe would remind himself, should be kindly led to Heaven.

Mr. Hayhoe hoped that the new-comer, if he mentioned religion to him, would take his words in a friendly way— some of them didn't. Once or twice, when he had spoken of damnation to a farmer—Mr. Mere—he had been recommended to go to Hell himself. Upon another occasion, Mr. Hayhoe had happened to name the Holy Ghost—a person of the Trinity that is hardly noticed now-a-days—to John Card of Dodder, and received as a reply that his wife "had never yet tried to make a cake out of that self-riser." Mr. Hayhoe hoped to do good to all whom he met. He watched the man, who was beginning to pry about in the hedge on the other side of the way, and to peer under the brambles.

"He may have lost his tobacco pouch," thought Mr. Hayhoe, who remembered having once walked ten miles to regain his pipe, having left it, one summer day, upon the seashore.

Mr. Hayhoe examined the appearance of the stranger, who had not yet noticed him.

The man was of medium height; he wore a small beard and moustache, already turned grey. Mr. Hayhoe could not be sure of the colour of his eyes, though when they looked his way, they shone and sparkled, then turned to darkness. He supposed them to be blue.

Although his eyes were interesting, there was nothing otherwise strange about him; he was a mere common appearance—a man neither old nor young, and certainly not one who would attract any attention from others.

It is always a pleasant diversion of an idle moment, to wonder what a person, whom one meets out a-walking in the country, does. Sometimes the profession of a man can be known at once by his gait. There is no mistaking the squire. His lordly manner of walking is a proof of the fine quality of his blood. Others are not so easy to know, and, though a country labourer is likely to show what he is, yet there are other traders, about whose business there may well be a doubt. Mr. Weston, the wine merchant, has been taken for a colporteur, and Jove for a swan.

Mr. Hayhoe considered the stranger. He might, he fancied,

have come thereabouts to sell something, or else to measure a piece of land, or discover in a church register the date of a funeral. Was he a journeyman stone-mason, or an insurance agent, or was he collecting orders for a new patent medicine, a certain cure for all the ills of mankind?

The man had by no means the look of a person who travels for pleasure. Evidently he had some duty to perform, some occupation that brought him into close contact with his fellow men.

He appeared to have, too, besides other qualities—as far as Mr. Hayhoe could judge—a social side to his character. He looked as though he would not be ill at ease in any company, and as if he might enter the palace of a king without being ashamed.

The two were alone in the lane: the hunt was gone far away. The hounds had followed the first fox, never expecting that much good would come of that journey into an earth under a great rock, and then had been called off, and all the following was gone to Madder Hill, where they hoped to find again.

The curious feeling of cold dread that Mr. Hayhoe had experienced so lately, almost as if he himself might have been at his last gasp, now completely left him. Indeed, his spirits were happier now—he had never been one to sorrow unduly —than they had been since the time of his boy's illness.

The day brightened; the dark cloud that had lowered upon the earth moved softly away in a thin mist; the sun shone warmly, and the stranger turned and saw Mr. Hayhoe.

The clergyman was the first to speak.

"If you have lost anything, my friend," he said to the man, who was now come quite close to him, "perhaps you will allow me to help you to find it?"

The man looked down anxiously at the ground; he did

not reply, but said hurriedly, as though speaking to himself, "Such an unlucky accident as this has never happened in the memory of man, no, not since that foolish girl ate of the apple. Never before have I lost an order. Every command that has been committed to me to do, that command have I done until now."

"Tell me your name," asked Mr. Hayhoe, who began to think that the poor man must have escaped from a mad-house, "so that, if I have the good fortune to discover your property, I may be able to restore to you what you have lost."

"My name is Death," answered the man.

"Suffolk family?" rejoined Mr. Hayhoe, "for I know a village in that county where your name is common, and I have seen it too written upon a tombstone in this neighbour-hood. But I trust you will not think me rude if I ask you to tell me your Christian name too?"

"I have never had one," replied Death simply, "though in coming here this morning I met a little girl who made fun of my beard and called me 'John.' "

"Oh, that must have been Winnie Huddy," cried Mr. Hayhoe, "who only likes to be happy. But, alas! good sir, have you then never been baptized? Tell me, what is your faith, your belief, your religion?"

"I belong to God," replied Death.

Mr. Hayhoe bowed his head reverently. He then looked up gladly.

It was indeed a rare thing for him to hear The Name spoken, unless in jest by the simple peasant, and, as a minister of the Gospel, he could not but commend one who spoke so truthfully.

"And, taking the matter in another way, a man," thought Mr. Hayhoe, "who has read his Bible and acknowledges to whom he belongs, might have read other books too, and have heard of Mr. Collins."

"You say well, friend," said Mr. Hayhoe, joyfully, "and, in a little while, I am sure we shall have you in our fold."

"Or you in mine," answered Death, amiably.

Mr. Hayhoe was glad to talk to some one. Besides seeing this man's name upon a Shelton tombstone, he also recollected noticing the same name in the local directory as belonging to a rag and bone merchant.

Mr. Hayhoe invited his new acquaintance to sit beside him upon the grassy bank.

V

Death Has No Memory

A GOOD man knows at once whom he likes and whom he can trust, and Mr. Hayhoe saw in his new companion one who would not betray his confidence, nor take advantage of his humble simplicity. It would be pleasant, he thought, because he had some one to talk to, to remain for a few moments more in that place now that the sun shone again.

He saw no harm in resting for a little longer. Priscilla would await him where she most liked to be, beside her little boy's grave in the Dodder churchyard. She used, each day, to go there to see if the cowslips she had planted were in flower. Perhaps they were and, at least, the primroses would be still blooming.

Spring flowers are a holy company, and Priscilla loved them. To kneel and pray beside the first celandines was no uncommon thing for her to do, and now that there were flowers upon the grave, she must needs be happy there, even if she cried a little at first.

Another reason—besides the softness of the bank—that moved Mr. Hayhoe to invite John Death to rest, was that he did not lack a very natural curiosity. His favourite author had given him a proper taste for wishing to discover what any one he met did for a living and, besides that, he was most anxious to know what it was that Mr. John Death had lost.

"Perhaps you will not mind," said Mr. Hayhoe, after

they had talked for a little about trees and flowers, "if I call you 'John,' and I trust that the hunt will return the way it came that I may show you Lord Bullman—the greatest man in the county—and even introduce you to him."

"I fear," answered Death, smiling, "that, if you were to do so, you would lose your benefice, for Lord Bullman has already heard of me, and he hates the very sound of my name."

"Perhaps he thinks," rejoined Mr. Hayhoe—who, for the moment, supposed that Death might be a farmer—"that you bind your gates with barbed wire, and drive sharpened stakes into your fences, as Mr. Mere."

"Or, rather," answered John, laughing, "he fancies that my gate opens too easily into a narrow pit."

"One certainly never knows why one is disliked," observed Mr. Hayhoe, with a sigh. "But would you be so good as to tell me what it was that you were searching for so diligently when you first approached me?"

Although Mr. Hayhoe asked this question in a careless manner, as if he did not wish to pry too nearly into another person's affairs, yet he thought that his companion was unneedfully startled by so simple a request.

John Death jumped up. He looked this way and that, fearing evidently that they might be overheard by some one, but, seeing Mr. Hayhoe looking expectantly at him as if he waited for a reply, he sat down again.

"You need not be afraid to tell me of your loss," said Mr. Hayhoe, wondering why the man did not speak.

"I have lost something of great importance," replied Death in a low tone, looking anxiously up into the sky, as if he expected a censure for his carelessness from that direction. "Indeed, I hardly like to name what I have lost, but as I know that you—as well as I—belong to God, there can be no harm in my telling you that I have dropped or mislaid a small piece of parchment.

"I have no excuse to offer," continued Death, looking again up to the sky, "unless it be that I had been idling more than I should—and, indeed, during such lovely weather any workman has a right to enjoy himself—and somehow or other, owing to my thoughtlessness, the parchment must have fallen from my pocket."

"The title-deeds, no doubt, of a small estate," suggested Mr. Hayhoe.

"Why, no," replied Death, "for this parchment, that I have so foolishly lost, gives the right of way to a wide land. There are written upon it two names only—the signature of my employer, and one other word, that is the command."

"I suppose," said Mr. Hayhoe, "that the persons named in your paper are those with whom you have some particular business." And Mr. Hayhoe looked at John a little unhappily, for he now began to think that he might be a county bailiff, and, alas, he himself still owed money to the court.

"But surely," said Mr. Hayhoe, "this little mishap cannot trouble you much, for you have only to remember the names that were written so lastingly—when any common sheet of notepaper would have done as well—in order to manage your business?"

"Alas!" cried John, "I have tried my best to recall them to my mind, but though I may appear to you as a person not altogether lacking in intelligence, yet I have the worst memory in the world. You may be surprised to hear me say so, but as soon as I have accomplished any work that I am ordered to do I forget all about it, and even the material upon which I have exercised my art seems also to be as if it had never been. My employment is a simple one—I change one thing into another."

"Perhaps he is a ladies' hairdresser," thought Mr. Hayhoe suddenly.

"It is well sometimes to change the colour of a thing," went on Death, "and my business is a most necessary one. Nothing can endure for ever in the same form. Even the mountains crumble, and the seas change their places, yet I am always being reminded by some one or other that my profession is a very unseemly one."

"I do not believe I am right," thought Mr. Hayhoe.

"It's my bad memory," said Death, "that makes me so unpopular."

"We all have our troubles," observed Mr. Hayhoe.

"My memory is one of the worst of them," remarked Death, "and knowing my lack, I have never dared to do anything for myself and only do what I am told, though perhaps—if I live a little while in Dodder, in order to find what I have lost—my memory may improve."

"But up to this moment," said Mr. Hayhoe, "your employer has always given you his commands in writing, and even as a good Christian has the right rules for his behaviour given to him in the Bible, so you have your proper labours for the day written upon paper."

"But now that I have lost my parchment," observed Death sadly, "who will trust me again with a written order? As soon as I discovered my loss, I wished myself the freedom of a certain vasty Hall that I have procured for many."

"A madhouse," ejaculated Mr. Hayhoe.

The clergyman looked anxiously at his companion.

"Do not despair," he said kindly, "for it often happens that something that is utterly gone is yet happily discovered. Though, of course, no merchant who employs a servant is pleased when that servant has mislaid his goods, yet as long as the master knows that his goods have not been applied to a wicked use, but have only been left by mistake in some wood or dell, he cannot be very aggrieved."

"You do not know my master," observed Death.

"I think I do," said Mr. Hayhoe, who had in his mind a certain wine-merchant who had once visited the neighbourhood.

"But, even though my master may not care," said Death, "—and there are some who affirm that nothing troubles him —yet my employer's clients may be very much disappointed if I do not find what I have lost. For these poor people may very soon be sorry that I did not visit them as I was ordered to do."

Mr. Hayhoe gave a little groan. "A moneylender," he murmured.

And yet it was extremely unlikely, he thought, that any one in that way of business should employ a man as an agent who not only confessed that he remembered nothing that he did, and who had the boldness to say that he belonged to God.

"Neither would his name," considered Mr. Hayhoe, "recommend him overmuch to any business man."

Death muttered something into his beard.

"I am unable to hear you," observed Mr. Hayhoe to his companion.

"I only said," replied Death, "that, though I forget most things that I do, yet sometimes certain little incidents do happen to me that I remember, and when I come to think of it, only this morning I met a kind lady who offered me a religious tract."

Mr. Hayhoe smiled gladly and rubbed his hands. He believed he knew, he said, who that lady was.

"And did you read what Priscilla gave you?" he asked eagerly.

"I certainly did," answered John, "and the first lines, set in large print, pleased me very much. I have them here." And, taking the tract out of his pocket, John read:

" 'O Death, how bitter is the remembrance of thee to a man that liveth at rest in his possessions, unto the man that hath nothing to vex him, and that hath prosperity in all things: yea, unto him that is yet able to receive meat.' "

"Mr. Mere even curses Death in the street," said Mr. Hayhoe, "when he thinks of his end. But did you not read further?"

"I read further," replied John.

" 'O Death, acceptable is thy sentence unto the needy, and unto him whose strength faileth, that is now in the last age, and is vexed with all things, and to him that despaireth and hath lost patience.' "

"I have often heard old Huddy say," observed Mr. Hayhoe, "that when his time comes, he will go gladly. But did you not tell Priscilla of your loss?"

"I never trust a woman," replied John Death, "for I have often heard them speak when they had promised to be as silent as the grave. But, hearing that her husband was the clergyman, I asked her where he could be found."

"And you read the last words of the tract, I hope?" said Mr. Hayhoe, "that were written large too?"

"Certainly," replied Death, "and excellent words they were:

" 'Earth to earth, ashes to ashes, dust to dust.' "

"Oh," cried Mr. Hayhoe, "any man—whatever his trade may be—who says that he belongs to God, must know that the Earth is God's bed as well as his own, and that to lie there is to lie with Him."

"I would rather lie with a Dodder maid," John muttered.

"And Priscilla told you where to find me?" remarked Mr. Hayhoe.

"I certainly thought that you might assist me in my search," replied Death, "for, though you may not remember the meeting, we too have met before."

"I cannot say that I remember you," answered Mr. Hayhoe, "though when I was a curate at St. John's, Weyminster, I used to see a great many people in one way or another that I have now quite forgotten. But, perhaps you were the doctor who came to see old Mrs. Dominy, but you only stepped into the room and she died?—though I have forgotten what the doctor looked like."

"I am glad that I am not the only one who forgets," said Death gaily. "And now that you are going to be the vicar of Dodder—where the very goats, as merry Sancho once said, are like white violets—you will not perhaps mind giving me a little necessary information that will help me to recover what I have lost."

"I am your servant," answered Mr. Hayhoe.

"Well, then," said Death, "I should like to know a little about some of the people who are under your charge, for one or other of them, I am sure, must have stolen my parchment, and though, of course, my master can employ others —for his state is kingly—to do my work, so that I may not be missed elsewhere, yet in Dodder I alone must perform my allotted task, and must remain there until I have found my lost command."

"Would it not be possible," asked Mr. Hayhoe, "for you to write to your employer, and ask whether a new writ, or warrant, or whatever it was that you have happened to mislay, could not be posted to you, to replace the one that you have lost?"

"Alas! no," answered John Death, "for my master is a

strange person, and will never do again what he has once done."

"Proud as well as lazy, I fear," suggested Mr. Hayhoe.

"He is indeed a determined gentleman," replied Death, "and always likes his own way."

"Perhaps he is a Scotchman?" observed Mr. Hayhoe, rising from the bank, "but we may as well walk together to Dodder, as you and I intend to live there."

"I will gladly be your companion," replied John Death, moving too, "for I am sure that there are many subjects that we can discourse upon that will be of great interest to us both. And I may certainly say that—though of course I am vastly troubled about my loss—yet I shall not be sorry to take a short holiday, for I am no liar when I tell you that, both in peace and war, I have a great deal to do."

"I have heard," observed Mr. Hayhoe slyly, "that a sanitary inspector is a very busy man."

"You have come very near to guessing my profession," answered Death, laughing, "and it is certainly true that the hurry of my occupation has never for one moment until now allowed me any time for love or friendship. There are many other experiences too, besides those two, that my busy life has prevented my knowing. Unlike my Lord of Northumberland, in the play, I have never had the leisure to be sick in such a jostling time. I have never known either sickness or pain, no, not even the scratch of a little pin has harmed me. My life has always been one of perfect health, and never have I had the time to pity the illness of others, nor yet the quick sob of one whose doom is sudden."

Mr. Hayhoe shuddered. Was John Death the hangman? They walked together down the lane.

"During my stay in Dodder, I hope to enjoy myself without pain," said Death.

"That," replied Mr. Hayhoe, "is quite impossible."

"But, at least, I mean to know love," laughed Death.

"I hope without guile?" observed Mr. Hayhoe, a little anxiously.

"You have been reading Milton," said Death, turning quickly to him.

"Only when I was at school," replied Mr. Hayhoe, "and I thought him very tedious."

"I am glad you did not like him," remarked Death, "for, though John Milton wrote some noble lines—that have never been equalled in beauty—yet he sometimes mistakes an honest man for a rogue, and surely all mothers are not so easy to tumble, nor all sons as wanton as he would have us believe?"

"Are you married?" asked Mr. Hayhoe.

"I am a bachelor," replied John Death, "and have always lived wisely."

"I honour you for it," said Mr. Hayhoe warmly.

"But, however honestly one may live," remarked Death, "there is sure to be some neighbour or other to cry out 'lecher.' And I—as well as others—have been accused of certain doings—but I can promise you that I have never been as bad as those Flemish gravediggers, who were wont to cry 'Welcome, plague!' in the city streets. . . . I now mean to enjoy myself in Dodder."

"I am sure that you will," said Mr. Hayhoe happily, "and before you have been a month with us we shall have you baptized, confirmed, and married."

"But not buried, I hope," replied Death, smiling.

VI

John Reads a Notice

THE day was now as fair as ever it had promised to be earlier in the morning. There was not a sign anywhere to be seen of the dark cloud that had so lately overshadowed the lane.

Mr. Hayhoe, pleased with his company, walked along gaily. Already, during the short time that they had been together, he had grown very fond of his companion, whose every remark seemed fresh and interesting to him.

Nothing that they passed in their walk escaped John's observant eye. He was delighted with a flock of rooks that fed in a field upon Joseph Bridle's new-sown barley, and gazed with pleasure upon their sleek black coats, clapping his hands together to see them fly. Near to Madder Hill, Death stopped to listen, and asked of Mr. Hayhoe what was the low and distant rumble that he heard, and was answered that he heard the waves of the sea.

Going down a little hill in a shady part of the lane, they came upon a hedgehog who, seeing strangers so near to him, and not being sure of their behaviour, wisely curled up into a ball—to John's vast amusement. He had often, he said, seen people straighten out when he came to them, but never before had he seen a creature turn into a ball.

As they went along, the countryside blushed like a young girl, for the spring—being a mere child—had not yet got used to the eyes of men who regarded her so warmly.

A blackthorn was fully out—a purity of bloom as white as snow—and, below the hedges, the large leaves of the lords and ladies curled amorously. In places, too, there was green in the hedges, the green of elder and honeysuckle, and everywhere there were pleasant meadows and cornlands newly tilled.

"How was it?" inquired Mr. Hayhoe, after a short pause in the conversation, "how was it, John, that you came to lose what is of so great value?"

"Because," replied John, "instead of heeding the good advice of John Bunyan in the *Pilgrim's Progress*, I must needs step into a field on my way to Dodder and rest a while. I even walked a little in this very lane; and it was while waiting in a Dodder meadow to admire the flowers that I discovered my loss.—I am one, I fear, who has always liked to wander a little in out-of-the-way places."

"Perhaps you lost your paper in the field where you lingered," suggested Mr. Hayhoe. "That, I should say, from the flowers that you mention, must have been Joseph Bridle's. It is one of the pleasantest meadows in Dodder. Whoever goes in there to rest will wish to stay the whole day. I myself have spent hours in that field, looking into the waters of the pond, that are very deep. Resting there, it is likely that the most busy man would forget how time goes, and, instead of continuing his labours, should lie down and dream of God. I do not wonder that you dropped your paper there."

"Though I am a busy man," answered Death, "time is nothing to me, for I work at all hours and know no calendar. But I do not think that I lost my order in the field which pleased my fancy, and must be the one you speak of, near to the edge of the pond."

"Where Miss Sarah Bridle keeps her ducks," observed Mr. Hayhoe.

"There was a girl's name, written with smooth pebbles, laid upon the grass. I read the name—'Susie Dawe.'"

"That must have been Joe's doing," said Mr. Hayhoe.

"Doubtless it was," observed Death, "but as I looked upon that name, a curious sensation came into my head for the first time—it is called 'pity'—and I hoped that my visit to Dodder had nothing to do with the young girl whose name was written with pebbles upon the grass. It was then that I felt in my pocket for the parchment, wishing to read the names upon it, and found that it was gone. At first I thought little of my loss, merely supposing that, in climbing the stile into the field, I had dropped the paper from my pocket, and I expected to find it at once. Finding nothing under the stile, I began to search elsewhere, and even leaned down over the pond to look, and though at the bottom I could clearly see the bones of an infant and other human remains too, yet my parchment was nowhere to be seen."

"A man may easily lose a piece of paper," said Mr. Hayhoe, plucking a primrose from the bank, "and—unless the parchment that you have lost bears upon it the signature of the chief cashier of the Bank of England—there is no need to attach so much importance to it. And, even if the order that you have lost is of great importance, yet surely upon a glad day of sunshine such as this, a business mistake should be forgotten."

"I cannot let the matter go so easily," replied Death, "even if I might wish to—and would you be so good as to tell me what sort of a man Joseph Bridle may be?"

"Only a poor man," answered Mr. Hayhoe, "though honest. He owns but one good field and a few acres of downland that yield him next to nothing, for what the rooks leave the wireworm eat. Joe is one of the most harmless of men. He neither hurts nor destroys."

"Every one to his taste," replied John, with a laugh. "But,

from what you tell me of Joseph, I do not think that he has my paper."

"Neither do I," said Mr. Hayhoe, "and for a good reason too—Joe Bridle is in love!"

"I do not understand you," observed Death.

"He loves a girl," explained Mr. Hayhoe.

"You mean," said Death, "that he wishes to reproduce his kind, with the help of a woman; but such doings must be extremely common here upon earth, as my occupation proves, for in some parts of the world there are as many children as flies."

"A clerk to a registrar," murmured Mr. Hayhoe, leaning over the bank to pluck another primrose.

"I am willing to allow," he said, smiling upon Death, "that love is common to mankind, but some are stricken more deeply with his darts than others. Joe Bridle's feelings in this matter are of no ordinary kind, and the only cure for him is the coming together—with the sanction and blessing of the Church of Christ—in Holy Matrimony.

"It is said in Dodder that, although Joe is forty years old, he has hardly ever looked upon a maid before, and has certainly never walked out with one. Joseph is a sober man. He has never been one to seek here and there for his pleasures, to pluck at all and to gather none. One has only to look at him to know that his passion for a girl—if once permitted—would be for all time, and that he would be faithful to the one that he loved unto death."

"And why not afterwards?" asked John lightly.

"A proper rebuke," rejoined Mr. Hayhoe, "for our religion teaches us that those who love truly, with the Church's blessing, will never be separated."

"And who is it, then," inquired Death, "that so strong a lover as Mr. Bridle has taken a fancy to?"

"Methinks," answered Mr. Hayhoe, "that you would answer that question well enough yourself, if you saw the young lady. Joseph loves faithfully, and wishes to marry, Susie Dawe."

"Why," answered Death, carelessly, "ever since I saw Susie's name written in pebbles beside the pond, I have intended to lie with her myself."

Mr. Hayhoe looked troubled.

"Though your words are scriptural," he said, "and far more to my liking than the vulgar expressions that are common now-a-days, yet I trust you will choose for a bride some other Dodder maid than she whom Mr. Bridle wishes to marry."

"Perhaps," replied Death, stooping to pick up a flint that showed signs of having been worked, "Joseph Bridle may one day give her to me of his own free will. Has not this poor man any one who can tell him of the dangers of loving too faithfully, for even the very gods have discovered that true love is often a very doubtful happiness. Surely some one should tell Joe of the sorrows of loving."

"He has Mr. Solly," replied the clergyman, "a gentleman older than himself, who lives at Madder, and is his closest friend. Mr. Solly regards women as a kind of wurzel."

"Ha!" exclaimed Death, "then he must consider that they are best buried."

"That is exactly what he does think," replied Mr. Hayhoe, "but I, for one, very much disapprove of his views."

"A mere matter of taste," said John. "But how, I pray, does Mr. Solly express himself about women?"

"He says," observed Mr. Hayhoe, a little hesitatingly, "that when they are not required for cooking or cleaning, they ought to be kept in a grave, covered first with straw and then with earth."

"This worthy Solly," replied John Death, "must be a true friend to Bridle, who, if only he gave heed to him, would live always happily. And I—like Solly—think poorly of love. But, tell me, has Joseph no relation living with him, who might have picked up my paper?"

"There is only his aunt," answered Mr. Hayhoe, "Sarah Bridle, who, when she was a child, had a fright that left her with a strange delusion. She is now a middle-aged woman, a hard worker, very gentle and willing, but she has a fancy that those who do not know her may consider a little curious; she thinks she is a camel."

"She might have eaten my paper," said John, "though I fear the signature thereon would be a little hard to digest. But tell me, Mr. Hayhoe, is there no harlot in Dodder? for he that keepeth company with harlots spendeth his substance, and I know well enough that my parchment may be sold for a good price."

"Alas!" answered Mr. Hayhoe, with a sigh, "there is Daisy Huddy."

Death laughed loudly.

Mr. Hayhoe looked very sad.

"I assure you, John," he said, "that Daisy is no thief, she keeps nothing—that is even her own. She sells herself so cheaply to Farmer Mere that what he gives her hardly pays for old Huddy's tobacco."

"I will go in to her," said Death, readily.

"You mean that you will visit her," observed Mr. Hayhoe, "to advise her to lock her door to Mr. Mere. But you had better be careful, John. Farmer Mere is a very rich man, and all-powerful in Dodder."

"I will remember his name," said Death, quietly. "And is there no one else," he asked, "who might find and keep something that is a little out of the common?"

"There are Dillar, old Huddy, and Mr. Dady, who go to the Inn," replied Mr. Hayhoe. "There is also Mr. Titball—the tavern landlord—who has the highest respect for the great of the land, and can never praise Lord Bullman enough. There is also the rich landowner and farmer—Mr. Mere—whose wife is dead."

John nodded.

"But I have forgotten James Dawe," said Mr. Hayhoe.

"Who is he?" inquired John Death.

"An old man," replied Mr. Hayhoe, "who is said to be a great miser. But he not only hoards all he can, he also likes to sell what has cost him nothing—he will sell the skin from a dead dog even. He is the father of Susie, and is a widower."

Death smiled.

"You mention pretty Susie," he observed, "as though you like her too, and perhaps you have given her a Bible?"

"I gave her *Sense and Sensibility*," answered Mr. Hayhoe, blushing deeply.

"You love her," said Death.

"I respect her very much," replied Mr. Hayhoe, "and I also admire her. No young creature of seventeen could possibly be more charming. Susie sits next to me in the choir at church and often, when I stand up to pronounce the absolution, I look down at her as she kneels beside me."

"You had much better keep your eyes upon your book," said John, "or perhaps you do not know the danger of looking at a maid?"

"You must not think ill of me," replied Mr. Hayhoe, "but surely, a thing of beauty ought to be admired! All the poets say so, and Susie must delight all who see her. She has the sweetest voice that ever man heard, and no father could wish for a better child. I have heard it said by Mrs. Moggs—who lives at the Dodder shop, and sells ink sometimes—that Susie's mother was exactly like her, and evil rumour says that James Dawe only married his wife in order to sell her for money. He was an old man when he married. But she was not allowed to sin, for God prevented it."

"You mean she died?" said John.

"Death is often kind," observed Mr. Hayhoe, in a low tone.

"I am glad you think so," said John, "though, of course, good—as well as evil—is prevented by him."

"Goodness is never destroyed, only evil ends," remarked Mr. Hayhoe. "But I have now, I think, mentioned every one into whose hands your property might have fallen."

"My paper might have been pawned for beer," suggested John, "by one of those who, you say, go to the Inn?"

"Had that happened," replied Mr. Hayhoe, "Mr. Titball—noticing the signature that must be, from what you tell me of your master, a determined one—would have at once carried the paper to West Dodder Hall, and given it into the hands of Lord Bullman, who is, as all know, the chairman of the Maidenbridge bench.

"Mr. Titball would be the last man in the world to keep anything that he thought ought to be given to a great man. He honours Lord Bullman above all, and I have had the utmost difficulty in explaining to him that the creator of the world is as important. I remember remarking—in order to show where true worship should be rendered—that God has the larger family. But to that argument Mr. Titball replied that Lord Bullman—were his wishes and rights properly allowed—would have the greater number, and after all, the world is only one village, and Dodder another."

"An honest gentleman!" said John gaily.

They were now near to Dodder, and approached an old shed that, when every gale came, expected to be blown over, yet remained standing. Going up to this shed, Death stopped to read a police notice, that the Shelton officer had just pinned upon it.

The notice, that was written in a large hand, asked for any information about a man—a description of him was not given—who had robbed of his clothes the corpse of a poor suicide. The notice explained that a man who had hanged himself in his best clothes in Merly Wood had been found by his wife, stark naked. The colour and the size of the clothes were given, and a small reward offered for the apprehension of the thief.

John Death read this notice, with the greatest care, two or three times, and, smiling for a moment or two at his trousers, he brushed them carefully, and then returned to Mr. Hayhoe who was admiring a coloured butterfly that had settled upon a flower in the hedge.

The pair walked on in silence. Mr. Hayhoe was considering how he might bring his new friend into the loving arms of the Church, knowing him as one who would be likely to give close attention to a good sermon.

Walking thus, they soon reached Dodder village, and were noticed by a lady who, leaving the churchyard where she had been waiting, came to meet her husband.

VII

Priscilla Answers a Question

MR. HAYHOE stepped gladly to his wife. Evidently he had only to be away from her for a very little while in order to return to her joyously.

"This is Mr. John Death," he said, presenting his new-made friend, "a gentleman that I was fortunate to meet soon after seeing Lord Bullman. But I must not let you wait longer for the news—the living of Dodder is ours."

Priscilla was looking at Death.

"John has had the misfortune," explained Mr. Hayhoe, "to lose something hereabouts that he very much values, and he wishes to live a while in this village until he finds what he has lost."

Priscilla regarded her husband with anxiety; something, evidently, had troubled her. Though she had looked at her husband's companion, she had not noticed his name, and even the news that Lord Bullman had offered the living did not appear to please her as much as Mr. Hayhoe expected.

Her husband wondered why she was not more glad. All the way, in coming along the lane, he had looked forward to the pleasure of telling her that now they might leave the dingy lodgings at Shelton, where everything reminded them of the death of their child. Something unpleasing to his wife, he feared, must have happened while he was away.

Priscilla had not welcomed John very kindly. This was strange, for, usually, she welcomed any friend of his—however poor—with the greatest friendliness. Only a week before, he remembered how gladly she had received a travelling tinker, Mr. Jar, at their lodgings, giving him all there was in the cupboard to eat—but now she seemed disinclined to speak to Death.

"I hope that Mr. Mere's fierce dog has not sprung out at you," Mr. Hayhoe asked of his wife, looking at her with concern. "That dog ought never to be allowed so much liberty; one day it will do some one a hurt."

"No dog has frightened me," answered Priscilla, "and if you did not find me as pleased as you expected at the good news, it is only that I fear sometimes that what we do here is not always for the good of the people, for, in passing along the street on my way to the church, I saw something that made me wonder."

"You saw nothing that I have lost?" inquired Death, eagerly.

"No, sir," replied Priscilla. "I am quite sure that what I saw—and blushed to see—had nothing to do with you. It was merely a scarlet thread hanging out of Daisy Huddy's bedroom window."

Mr. Hayhoe coloured deeply.

"Alas!" he said, "I am altogether to blame, for before reading the Bible to Daisy, I ought to have explained to her that all scriptural doings are not meant for us to copy. I called a few days ago upon the young woman and, knowing nothing then of her way of living, I read all the way through the book of Joshua. I shall never trust myself again; I put the Bible into my pocket instead of *Persuasion*! Never was a poor clergyman more unlucky than I! Only the other day I advised Mr. Solly, who despises love, to read the Song of Songs. I am always showing people the way to go wrong, and when I tell them to do right they hate me. I advised Mr. Mere to give all that he had to the poor, in order to save his soul, and he set his dog upon me. Even Mr. Jar, the tinker, looked at me with surprise, when I told him he was the chief of sinners. And now I have caused poor Daisy to own publicly to all the world that she is a harlot."

"Never mind, my dear," said Mrs. Hayhoe, looking at her husband with the greatest affection, "God knows your mistake and also, that in reading His word to Daisy, you hoped to do good. Before long I am sure that she will learn where true happiness is to be found."

"Be so good, madam," inquired John Death, who had listened with interest to the lady, "as to tell me where true happiness is to be found?"

"In plain sewing," replied Priscilla.

VIII

An Old Woman's Eye

EVERY village, whose buildings were first made of mud, has the soul of an old woman. Her spirit is everywhere. She is never seen, and yet she guides all the doings that go on. If one stands upon Madder Hill and looks down upon Dodder her lineaments may be discovered.

Her forehead is the green and her nose is the church tower: she is neither Miss Pettifer nor Mrs. Fancy, and yet she is a person. When she laughs, a horse runs away with a wagon, crashes through a gate, and frightens every one—and when she smiles, a man is lowered into a grave.

The old woman's soul has but one eye, which is Joe Bridle's pond. When she winks there is a flash of lightning, and when she sleeps the waterweeds close over the pond. It has been said that all the worlds are tiny cells in the brain of God, and so why should not all Dodder dwell in one old woman?

No one can escape her tittle-tattle. When the church bell rings, calling the people to their prayers, all know that 'tis to the old woman's gossip that they are going to listen. Even the fox-hunting squire—Lord Bullman—cannot escape her, and is interested in the doings of Daisy Huddy, reported to him very soberly by Mr. Pix, who said that he once found Daisy lying in the rushes over Madder Hill.

"Alone?" asked Lord Bullman excitedly.

"Why, no," Mr. Pix replied, "for I believe that Tinker Jar was with her. . . ."

No one who ever comes to Dodder escapes the old spider,

whose invisible web binds him tightly, a web not altogether
unholy, which holds a man to the earth, that at the last—and
let us gather no more sorrow than we can bear—unravels the
web and delivers man to Death.

At the first house in Dodder Mr. Hayhoe met his wife, and
together they showed John Death the village. This was easy
to do, for the Vicarage was near to the green, and the cottages
by the side of the lane.

Going a little farther along the street, they waited beside
a gate that led into a little garden close by the village green.

Here a removal was taking place. A man, named John
Card, was leaving Dodder to return to Tadnol whence he
had come, and was leaving his cottage empty. This man had
been useful to the late vicar, Mr. Dibben, in many little ways,
and when Canon Dibben left for Stonebridge, Card wished
to move too. He obtained a place at Tadnol, where, besides
his usual occupation of chimney-sweeping, he might also trap
rabbits for Farmer Spenke.

Mr. Card was leaving Dodder sooner than he intended.
When he came there, Canon Dibben had promised to pay
his rent for a twelvemonth, and so Card had hired a cottage
for that period. But now Dibben was gone and would pay
nothing, and John Card was left with a house in one place
and a house in another, which would mean two rents.

John Card decided to leave Dodder—though in an ill-
temper. He would have to pay two landlords each week, and
Mr. Mere was not the kind of man to forgive a debtor.
"Houses," Card considered, "were not like wives." During
his life he had married two wives—one in one place, and one
in another—and each had presented him with money before
he buried her. Two giving wives were one thing, two houses
were another.

When Mr. Card was cross, he always complained to the

clergy. Seeing Mr. Hayhoe beside his garden gate, he told him his trouble, and John Death was left with Priscilla.

Priscilla asked John where it was that he met her husband. John answered her gladly. He told her that they had met in the lane, and that Mr. Hayhoe had been very kind to him and had never for one moment wished him away as most people did.

Priscilla looked towards her husband, and then at the churchyard.

While they waited, the village children came—as children will—to gaze upon the stranger, the foremost amongst them being Winnie Huddy, who was returned from the hunt, where nothing interesting had happened.

No sooner did Miss Winnie see John, and know him to be the same man that she had met in the lane, than she began to mock him—though at a safe distance—calling out "Moppet John," and pulling at her own little chin as if she wore a goat's beard like his.

Unnoticed by Priscilla, John turned to Winnie and made certain country gestures with his fingers—that the Devil uses when he meets a witch—and set all the girls a-laughing. The noise troubled Mrs. Hayhoe, who chid the children for being so rude and sent them away.

When they were gone, John Death started suddenly and looked extremely dismayed.

"Of all the fools," he cried out, "I believe I am the greatest."

"Why, what's the matter?" asked Priscilla, a little frightened.

"It's my scythe," exclaimed John. "I left my precious scythe in Merly Wood. This countryside must be bewitched! I dropped my parchment, which has been stolen, and now I discover that I have left my scythe in the wood. Though my memory is so bad, I have never yet forgotten to carry my scythe with me when I go upon a journey. What a fool was I to loiter so long in the wood!"

"If you were in Merly Wood," said Priscilla, moving a step backwards, "perhaps you may have seen the thief who stole the poor suicide's clothes?"

"I trust that my scythe was not stolen too," replied Death anxiously, "for I believe I hung it upon the very tree where the man swung."

"How came you," Priscilla asked, in an altered tone, "to leave your scythe there, and so near to where a poor man was hanged?"

"One cannot remember everything when one is busy," replied Death, "and I have lately had a great deal of young grass to cut near Maidenbridge, and did not I know that, when the grass is grown, it would be sure to be trodden down by heavy beasts, I might have felt sorry to mow it so young. But I cannot work without my scythe, and I ought to go back at once to the wood and see if it is still there—the scythe might be a danger to any who touched it."

"Your scythe is very sharp, then?" inquired Priscilla, in a low tone.

"Not so sharp as it ought to be," replied Death, "and I fear if it hangs long idle it may grow rusty. It's really surprising how easily a scythe can be blunted, and I hate to bungle a good cut."

Mr. Hayhoe stepped near.

"I think," he said, smiling at his friend John and speaking to his wife, "that if Mr. Death means to stay for a while in Dodder, he may, if he wishes, hire this cottage from Mr. Card, who is most anxious to obtain a little rent for it. Mr. Card tells me that he is willing to leave in the house a small bed and a few other necessary things for the use of the new tenant. A week's notice to be given by either of the parties, and the rent to be paid in advance."

"Nothing could have fallen out better," exclaimed John, "for, whenever I have entered a cottage, I have been treated with reverence, and so I am sure I shall live in one happily. A lowly place, perhaps, but far better than a mansion!"

Death stepped briskly to the little gate and looked into the garden, where his new landlord was pulling up by its roots a small plant. John Death watched him admiringly.

"You did that as well as I could have done it," he cried, watching Card place the shrub in his cart. "But you must know, friend, that every flower is not a Rose of Jericho."

"Neither be every woman a whore," replied John Card angrily, for though Mr. Hayhoe had recommended Death to him as an honest man, Card did not like his looks.

Death smiled.

"I wish to have your cottage," he said winningly.

"Cottage be to let," replied John Card slyly, "to any who mid pay a good rent."

John Death felt in his pockets; he found nothing. Card laughed. Evidently the man had no money.

Death looked glum. But presently his face brightened, and he hurried into the churchyard and disappeared amongst the tombs.

"He be looking for money," cried John Card.

Almost as he was speaking, Death returned.

"I have not, at the moment, any current coin to pay you with," he said, "but if this gold ring will content you, so that I may have the cottage, you are welcome to whatever you can make of it."

Death rubbed the ring on his coat, and handed it to Mr. Card.

"Thee didn't steal 'en, I hope?" asked Card suspiciously,

taking the ring into his hand—it looked a valuable one—
and holding it tightly.

"Oh no," answered Death carelessly, "it's mine if it's any
one's, though once I think it belonged to a Lady Bullman;
but you must know that I have often to act as a residuary
legatee."

"What be 'en worth?" asked John Card, looking greedily
at the ring.

"Enough to buy more than you can drink in a month,
though you open your mouth never so widely," replied Death.

Mr. Card edged himself away. He was afraid that his
tenant might ask for the ring again, and he wished to get off
quietly. He walked softly to the horse, that began to move,
and without saying good-bye to the company he started his
journey, leaving the cottage open for Death.

The arrival of John Death and the departure of Card
had been watched with interest by the neighbours. Every
one had noticed the discomfiture of the stranger when he
felt in his pockets and found nothing, and wondered why it
was he had run in such a hurry into the churchyard, returned again so quickly, and received the cottage key in exchange for something that he handed to his landlord.

Even Mrs. Moggs, who sold notepaper and clothes-pegs
as well as ink at the little shop, moved a window-flower so
that she could have a better view of what was happening.
She noticed that Mr. Card never looked back once when
he left the village.

As soon as Card was gone, John Death entered into possession. He locked the cottage door and put the key into his
pocket. He then bid good-bye to Mr. and Mrs. Hayhoe, and
started off at a brisk pace toward Merly Wood.

Mr. Hayhoe looked at his wife a little wonderingly.

"He is a strange man," he said. "He went off in a hurry."

"He is a mower," replied Mrs. Hayhoe, "and has left his scythe behind him in a wood, where I suppose he spent the night. Perhaps he comes from Ireland?"

"He will be the more welcome in Heaven," replied Mr. Hayhoe, smiling. "But come, my dear, we will go to the Vicarage, and choose a bedroom from which we can see Tommy's grave."

IX

Joseph Bridle

MR. JOSEPH BRIDLE was often in difficulties. He could not help himself; the fates were against him.

If a cow slipped its calf or broke a leg, it was Joe's. If the wireworm were hungry and wished for a dinner, they ate the green shoots off Mr. Bridle's young corn. If a milk-dealer or a corn-merchant went bankrupt, it was always the one who owed Joe Bridle money. His uncle had robbed him. He was Farmer Bridle of Shelton—a very ill-tempered man —who kept for himself certain monies that had been left to his nephew, Joe. When asked for them, Mr. Bridle replied that his man, Tapper, had stolen them. This, Joe could hardly believe. When he left the house, after asking for his money, he had heard his uncle wish him to Hell.

But, for all his disappointment, Joe returned happily enough to his cottage and forgot about the money. And after tea he took out his knife, found a piece of wood, and cut out a large toad for a Noah's Ark, with a head like his uncle's.

Joe had a friendly disposition; he disliked fighting. If a champion in a grand cause had to be chosen, no one would have thought of choosing Joe Bridle. He preferred to enjoy himself in other ways. In drink or riot he saw no pleasure; he preferred to watch the tadpoles in his pond. He was the kind of man who could be merry for nothing; he could also be serious. His looks were reliable, he wore a moustache, had the kindest of eyes, and could cut anything out of a block of wood—except Dodder church.

Often the greatest misfortune that a poor man can have is

to look rich. This was another trouble for Joseph. If a man looks well-to-do, yet has nothing, he is the more tormented.

If anything was needed at Dodder—if a subscription was required—Mr. Bridle was always the first to be asked to give. He was always at home, always easy to find, and never tried to hide out of the way. No tramp passed by his gate without going in, and though no beggar would call at rich Mr. Mere's or Miser Dawe's, yet all in want visited Bridle.

Joe liked conversation, and so every one would speak to him and hinder his work, so that at times—when he met many on his way to the down—he would never get there at all. Joseph enjoyed a glass—though he rarely took one, because his pockets were nearly always empty—he could sing a song and tell a merry story as well as another.

If any stranger saw him leaning over the little bridge that led to his field and watching the water that flowed under, he regarded him as a friendly man from whom he might inquire the nearest way to Maidenbridge. And be told no lie.

He would do any one a good turn, though without thinking the better of himself for doing it. He dug Mrs. Moggs's garden for nothing, only because she claimed him as a distant relation—through Adam. He admired Madder Hill, and lived to be happy. That was Joseph.

But perhaps Bridle was too simple. There was nothing unpleasant about him, and so he did not get on. He had no real eye to his own advantage; he merely worked. He might have done better—so the people said in Dodder—if he kept more pigs, sold milk instead of butter, and harnessed his aunt to the plough, instead of a horse.

But, even with these omissions, Joseph Bridle succeeded well enough in being merry, until one day. That one day comes to all; before then the river of life flows smoothly, and all is well.

Then the change comes. The first change—the forerunner of Death—is Love. When the sun of Love rises, and a man walks in its glory, he may be sure that a shadow approaches him—Death.

Love creates and separates; Death destroys and heals. A dead thistle-stalk, a fallen ash-leaf are the same thing. Man, alone, is separate and different from nature. Love has bewitched, bewildered him. Love comes up in the dark, and, before a man knows what has happened, he is pricked by an arrow. That stab is a sign. The man will soon sleep again in an unknowing consciousness: he will die. He will be like the thistle-stalk and the dead leaf. Let the young years be long, there is no trouble in them, let them last: "Be thou as little children."

But to be so is not easy. The day comes, the mine explodes, the man is blinded, Joe Bridle loves.

At first the fierce explosion took him off his feet and cast him into the sun. Then he fell headlong. Where there had been quiet and content, all was become unrest, longing, and a burning fire. An altar had been set up, and Bridle was the victim. Love held the knife to his throat.

He believed, his feelings were true, he was confident in his power.

No sooner did he love Susie than he felt her presence always near to him. She was his spouse, his fair one, and from her he knew he could never be parted. His love for her could not be defeated, nor turned into any other channel.

The breath of longing that burned so hot in him must draw her with the power of that longing to him. She was a young creature—lively—a being of flesh that wished and desired, and her flesh covered the heart of a woman, glad and faithful. God had planned her out, He had made her a wanting thing, an eager wish, a soft hope. She was something that wished to receive, in order that she might give again in full measure.

When Joseph was cast up into the sun, he caught a-fire. That fire became his heart, and burned with furious joy. His heart—that was well alight—set fire to all that he did.

At first he was riotous, a spendthrift of his days. His joy leaped and danced with him; he hardly trod upon the earth; he walked the hills with disdain. His Aunt Sarah looked at him with terror; the light in his eyes frightened her, and she began to fear him.

She was but a tame beast: he looked wild. Was he changed? Would he devour her? Was he hungry? And she was more careful than ever to cook plenty of food for him.

Where things had been ordinary, Joe saw now only wonders. A heart that lives in the fields remains very youthful. No day now was too long for him. The hours passed curiously; they were coloured hours, and made music; they seemed to kiss with a woman's lips as they went by. Where there had only been a mild pale light—enough to show a man the way to do his common tasks—there now burnt a fierce radiance. Joe Bridle breathed deep. He was like a runner in a race, where every movement spurs him to stronger exertion. He must win—no idea of defeat could enter his head.

And so Bridle lived for the first days of his new being, but gradually more sober thoughts conquered his early outbreak of the fever of love. He settled down again to work; everything that needed doing upon his small farm, that he did. He rose early and performed all his tasks with vigour; he worked late and nothing seemed too hard for him to do.

He had fine hopes about his one good meadow; perhaps this meadow would provide him with the means to marry Susie. There was nothing he had that he would not part with for the sake of her. He might even sell the first cut of the

field grass, and later the field itself. For, when he married
Susie, his own hands and her loving care would see that they
did not want.

He had only three cows now—the down grass would be
enough for them until the meadow was cut, and then they
could feed there for a while. Somehow he must get money,
but that would be easy, and then Susie would be his. Her
laughter was everywhere, and at night her eyes shone in the
sky. The air he breathed was Susie; whatever he touched was
her too.

He passed people in the lane without even seeing them. In
the rustle of the wind, in the trees, he heard Susie's voice, and
when he saw her, he was bewitched by love.

At the moment when Mr. Hayhoe was unfastening the
gate for Lord Bullman, Joe Bridle—full of his plans for the
betterment of his farm—went to roll his meadow. He had
but one horse, and this horse he harnessed to the roller. On
the way to the field he went by James Dawe's cottage and
saw Susie. She was trying to catch a broody hen that had
deserted its eggs. Joseph stopped his horse, and watched her.
The hen bustled out into the lane through a hole in the fence,
and ran towards Joe. He joined in the chase, and very soon
the hen was captured.

Susie allowed him to stroke its feathers, while she held it
in her arms as if it were her babe.

The sun shone warmly, and the hen opened and shut its
fierce little eyes. Upon the Dodder green there were children
laughing, a sheep's bell tinkled from the down, and a dog
barked. Susie began to fondle and to croon over the hen,
holding it closer to her breasts. Then she began to talk merrily, gossiping about Dodder.

"Oh!" she cried, "Winnie Huddy met a stranger in the
lane this morning, and asked him for a penny. She called

him 'John'—there never was such a naughty girl! She talks to any man she meets, and no wonder, when her sister, Daisy, has a red string tied to her bed, taken from the Bible, and let out of the window!'"

Susie smiled coyly and stroked the hen. Joseph Bridle had little to say; he could only look at her. Her girl's body appeared a lively, a loving grace. He saw, for the first time, the whole of her beauty. Nothing escaped him; she was his dish to love. He breathed deep; before him, and so near that he could have touched her, was this being—a maid, created for his enjoyment. Her hair was a brown gold. She was the darkness and the light of his desire.

Joe Bridle stood silent before her. She began to talk to the hen, chiding it for having left its eggs, and calling it a wicked mother. Then she turned and ran into the garden because her father had called her.

He watched her as she went. Her movements filled his heart with longing. She bore about her the simple seductive beauty that can bite and tear the entrails of a man. To see her made sadness come. Without knowing what she did, she called up storms and dark clouds, hailstones and fire. She waited, asking to be culled. But by whom? Joseph answered the question boldly—himself. No one should touch her, only he.

And why should he not have her as well as another? She was a maid proper to marry, a little young maybe, but eager and loving. Her eyes told him so. She could be trusted to know whom she liked, and a village maiden can be a very faithful creature. Bridle knew that; he also knew that Susie was fond of him. She had once kissed him all of a sudden, when he had least expected it.

Joseph had made no secret of his love. He had told Mr. Hayhoe, who had shaken him strongly by the hand, and wished him all happiness, as if they were to be married the next day.

Joe was sure of her. He might live many years with Susie as his loving wife.

In the country, married joy can still be found. Life can be merry and happy where keen winter blasts and the smoke of autumn bonfires keep the devil away. Two straws, blown into a corner, hold together; the dark night keeps them near each other. One never knows when Madder Hill may begin to talk; and when fear creeps in under the stairs, two are better than one.

Joseph also told Mr. Solly that he loved Susie. Mr. Solly only blew his nose hard.

The Name

JOE BRIDLE led the horse into the field. But he did not begin to roll the meadow at once, he wished first to go and look into the pond. He felt impelled to do so, though he did not know why.

Sometimes a man's feet behave oddly; they wish to walk, the mind wonders why. For no reason at all, a man will step out of the path, and will pick a flower as if that were what he had meant to do.

Joseph's pond was in the middle of his field; it was said to have no bottom. In Dodder a story used to be told of a greedy farmer who, in a time of scarcity, kept all his grain from the poor and then, to tantalize the people, drove a wagon-load of wheat into the pond. And neither the wagon nor the horses were ever seen again.

The water in the pond—where there were no lily-leaves— was black. Mournful flowers grew about the edge, and there were places in the pond where large bull-rushes grew. And some said the water smelt strangely.

There was a reason for that, for if any poor creature was lost in the neighbourhood, the country people knew well enough that he might be found—if any one cared to look for him—in Joe Bridle's pond.

The pond had a curious existence; it tempted, it fascinated. It was said that to drown oneself there gave no pain. One only had to step in, and sink at once. Drowning there was thought to be a pleasure. Little children, in times past, had ventured, and old men. The pond pitied all men's sorrows, and the relief that it gave was death.

Before Joe Bridle went to the pond, he looked at his horse. The beast trembled. Something had frightened it. Joe patted the horse, and went to the pond.

The day began to darken strangely. Joe stopped and looked back at the horse—for some reason or other he did not care to gaze at once into the pond. The horse looked at him, still frightened. Its eyes begged him to return; then it bowed its head low.

Joe Bridle looked from the horse to a great elm-tree that grew nearby. What was happening to the tree? Though no wind blew, the whole tree bowed towards the pond, as if a great tempest had blown upon it. Above the field certain rooks were flying. The rooks behaved wildly, rushing downward with a fierce sound, then flying off in fear.

Joe Bridle looked into the pond.

Where the waters were black—though near to the edge of the pond—he saw something floating. What was it? The thing looked like thick paper, or parchment, and Joe Bridle could see that there were words written upon it.

Then a strange thing happened to the paper; it began to flame. Though floating upon the water, it was on fire. A marvellous tongue of flame rose from it, golden at first and then scarlet. The paper burned in the water and yet it was not consumed. Joe Bridle knew that he was near a dreadful thing. He might have fled, and yet he did not do so. The parchment, that had the power to burn and yet could not be consumed, held him in his place.

Joe Bridle was not without strength, he had power—love. He was on fire, too. He burnt, and yet was not destroyed. And he alone might take the paper out of the water, without being harmed by it.

Joe Bridle leaned over the pond; he stretched out his hand, and took the paper.

At the moment when he touched it, the tongue of flame that rose from it vanished. Joe Bridle held in his hand only a piece of parchment. As soon as he had touched this, there came a low mutter of thunder. Clouds gathered in the sky and all grew dark.

Though he held the paper in his hand, Joe Bridle dared not look at it, but he looked into the pond, the waters of which had grown very clear.

As Joe Bridle bent over the pond, two dead corpses rose up, but, when he thought he knew their sodden dead faces, the waters thickened and the faces vanished.

Joseph gazed into the sky. That a spring morning that had looked fair should turn so dismal was very strange. But often clouds come unexpectedly, and when they drop suddenly from nowhere and the sun is hid, the country people say that a blight is come.

Joe Bridle held the parchment firmly. He wondered why, but he soon knew. A sudden tempest rising, it seemed, out of the pond, rushed by him and tried to tear the paper away. A few weeks ago—before he had spoken to Susie—he would have let it go, but now he held tightly to what he had found, for the power upholding him was love. Though a quiet and peace-loving man, he had now the strength and fury of a god.

When the wind grew still, other things happened. Horrid creatures—great pond beasts—newts and vipers, swarmed about him in the darkness. A year-old corpse crawled out of the water and clutched at the paper with foul dripping fingers.

Then the light of many little burning candles shone over the pond, and a lovely nymph, with tangled hair in which water-flowers were entwined, came to Joseph, out of the pond. She begged him to ease her desire, to embrace her. She lay

near to him, looking up at him with soft eyes, then suddenly
she sprang up and tried to snatch the paper from his hand.
Then she vanished.

After the nymph, there came a beautiful naked boy, who
knelt down beside the pond, in order to see his own loveliness reflected in the water. He gazed for a while as though
ravished by the sight, and then, coming to Joe Bridle and
kneeling down again, begged for the paper with soft words,
in a strange tongue. He wept and stretched out his hands,
but Joe Bridle held the parchment firmly and would not let
it go.

Next, a huge toad with splendid glowing eyes, like coals
of fire, crept out of the pond and, pressing his great soft body
against Bridle's, tried to force him into the water. The monster was covered with slime and stank foully, but Joe Bridle
held the paper and did not move. Love makes a man stub-
born; whatever the paper was, Joe Bridle did not mean to
let it go.

Joe looked boldly about him. He believed he had a right
to keep what he had found.

Soon he heard sounds like dying groans, and from the
bottom of the pond there rose up a mass of decayed carrion.
What he had seen before was as nothing to this new horror.
The pond was changed. It was become a charnel-yard, full
of cadavers, all visible. A hideous stench surrounded him.
Fleshly corruption, in its most revolting and dreadful forms,
clung to him. A snake, crawling out of the body of a child,
raised its head and hissed at him; pond newts swarmed over
the breasts of a woman who was newly drowned. Fingers,
soiled with grave-mould, tried to pluck the paper away, but
all in vain—for Joe Bridle would not let it go.

Then the cloud lifted, the pond looked as usual, the sun
shone again, and a lark rose up from the green meadow to

sing. Joe Bridle felt bolder; he even dared to look at the paper that he held in his hand. It was quite dry, and appeared neither to have been burnt by the fire, nor soiled by the water.

Upon the top of the paper was written a command, and underneath that word two names—

UNCLAY
SUSIE DAWE
JOSEPH BRIDLE

Joseph Bridle read the names, but quickly held the paper away from his eyes, and only just in time. Had he looked longer, he would have been blinded.

The order was signed. Scrawled unevenly below the names, and across the bottom of the parchment, there was the signature. The name twisted like a serpent. Who could see it and live? Joe Bridle saw that the paper was signed, then he shut his eyes tight.

What had he looked at? Something that in the same moment could Unclay a man, let a star fade into nothingness, turn a city into a wilderness, and create a fair garden of life in empty space. A name that could hurl a sun across the firmament, and make an emmet hurry across a lane upon Shelton Heath.

The field faded. Dodder, Madder, the whole world were gone too. Only that name remained. . . .

Joseph Bridle hid the parchment in his bosom, and returned to his horse. What he had found concerned himself very nearly—and one other. He must keep the paper, for neither Susie nor himself could be harmed while the parchment was his.

Joe Bridle began to roll the field, and completed the labour sooner than he expected. When he had finished he looked at the grass. The grass of the field appeared richer and more green than he had ever known it before, and a sweet scent rose from the meadow.

When Joe Bridle, leaving the roller in the field, entered the lane in order to lead his horse home, he was surprised to see that the sun was nearly setting. How long he had been in the meadow he did not know, but all the time he had spent there had seemed to be but a few moments. He waited, allowing the horse to feed in the lane.

The sun rested—a great golden ball—on the top of Madder Hill. Never had a Dodder evening seemed so lovely! The spring, new-risen from its winter sleep, and yet unspoilt by summer idleness, had awaked singing. Never had Joe Bridle felt a greater desire for life. No air could be sweeter than that which he breathed, blowing from the wide seas over Madder Hill. Scented by the sweet earth and the newly-rolled meadow, the air tasted like honey. The old horse ate the grass gladly. Never had there seemed to be a better prospect for the blessed fruits of the earth to grow. And where better could a man be in the spring than in a country lane in a green land?

All was quiet in the village; there was no human sound. Joe Bridle was content to wait there for ever, watching his horse feed.

But presently he turned very cold. In the Dodder village he had heard a cottage door shut. Some one had come out of John Card's cottage. Joe Bridle saw this man walking in the lane. He knew who he was. Though he walked in so ordinary a manner, he knew that he was a great king.

A merry one, too, for he borrowed Jackie Dillar's hoop and trundled it into a ditch, then he chased and caught Winnie Huddy, who had put out her tongue at him.—A king on holiday at Dodder, but being there as an ordinary man, a friend of Mr. Hayhoe's, and one who hoped to be happy, a king who liked to play. Joe Bridle watched him.

A group of little children surrounded Death; he was telling them a long story. Dairyman Dady came by and tried to drive the children away. "Who wants to be pestered by these little devils?" he said. But John Death invited the children to come near to him; he even took little Jackie in his arms. He laughed as a man would who has cast away a burden and means to live carelessly, forgetting all labour.

Joe Bridle knew him: he was Death.

XI

A Queer Mistake

A HUMAN being can be mocked into madness, as well as into sense.

From what one is told by churchmen, God Almighty does not like to be teased, nor did Sarah Bridle, who had been mocked into believing a rather odd idea.

Country people like oddities; there would be no pleasure for them if all their neighbours were ordinary. They are always ready to forgive those who have caused the trouble; they even approve them. To drop a baby, so that its nose is flattened out is an amusing pastime; when the child grows it will be a subject for laughter. To drive any one into madness is a fine fancy. Every one is pleased. In November, when the rain splashes in the puddles, and the trees shiver, there will be some fun, for the doings of an innocent are always pleasant to tell of.

Perhaps the most entertaining madness in the world is religion. Those who destroy religion will destroy merriment too. It is a crazedness to believe, but also a happy fancy.

Though good cannot come from evil, laughter can. Mrs. Fancy, who had lived in Dodder for many years—though now dead—once shut up her child, while she went to the Inn, in a dark cupboard where a rat lived. When she let the boy out he would only crawl upon the floor. He had escaped his terror by believing himself to be a rat with a long tail.

Sarah Bridle had always been a good girl, and good girls get fat. Having no wickedness to exercise their thoughts, they grow comely, too—and perhaps a little stupid. Sarah believed everything that she was told.

In every village there is some young man who frightens the girls about their bodies. In Dodder there was young Mere, but Sarah would not have heeded him had it not been for her own mother. Mrs. Bridle was a religious woman; she was strict; she believed that the human body is a very wicked thing. From every point of view it looked bad. The breath of life should have been breathed into a deal table. Mrs. Bridle covered up her child, and laced her tight.

Mrs. Bridle also filled her head with terror. When Sarah's breasts were like walnuts, her mother bid her beware of them and hide them. "They would not have been there at all," she said, "had the world been good."

Sarah believed her mother. She became fearful and tried to prevent herself from growing properly. But Nature, who likes to laugh at such unnatural folly, caused Sarah to grow plumper than ever. This made her more frightened. She thought that her body, being unregenerate, had become deformed, and she looked everywhere to see an animal that resembled herself. About that time Sarah went to a circus, and saw a camel.

The day after going to the circus, her mother sent her into the village to post a letter. It was the summer-time, the meadows were lovely; coloured flowers were everywhere, and the sun shone warm. As Sarah went out of the door, her mother cursed her.

It often happens that a mother's tender care is transformed into hate. Sarah's mother was jealous of her child. Though religious, Mrs. Bridle was flat-chested, but she still wanted the men to look at her—the chapel elders. There was one man, Mr. Perrot the blacksmith, who wore sidewhiskers and grew the finest pumpkins in all Shelton. But, instead of looking at Mrs. Bridle in chapel, Mr. Perrot looked at Sarah. He looked at her with pleasure, as if she grew in his garden and might one day win a prize at a fête.

Mrs. Bridle sent her daughter off, and hoped that she would come to some harm. Sarah posted her letter, and then she returned by the footpath that crossed a pleasant field.

The path was a sheltered one; high hedges upon either side hid the meadow from sight. In the middle of this field, Sarah met young Farmer Mere.

No one in any country of the world disputes the right of a rich young farmer to do as he chooses. For any girl to have complained about Mr. Mere would have been the height of folly.

Young Mere took hold of Sarah, but he did not rape her. He had other ends in view. Every one knew of Sarah's fears for herself and of her mother's warnings. The young man examined her with his hands, and shook his head dubiously; he evidently supposed her to be a very curious animal.

"They be grow'd wrong," he said, "they two humps." And, leaving her, he went his way.

After that Sarah hid herself, and for many months she was seen by no one. When she appeared again, she was mad. She told whoever came to her home, that she was a camel. Not like the one at the circus, but different—deformed.

When Sarah's parents died, Joseph Bridle, her nephew, took her to live with him. Except for his uncle, Joe was alone in the world too, and needed a housekeeper. Certainly, no one better could have been found for him than his Aunt Sarah. Mr. Solly used to say that it was a pity that all women were not crazed.

If a woman thinks of herself as a camel, her pride must be humbled. Then each woman would think of herself as merely a burden-bearing creature, and be happy at work.

A camel only wants to drink water. Sarah Bridle loved her master and served him faithfully. Her only fear was that he would drive her to the market-place at Aleppo, and sell her for gold.

At first when she came to Joseph, her behaviour was a little strange. She would go out into his field, and try to drink all the water in the pond. Once she fell in, but Joseph —hearing a splash—pulled her out. After that day, she began to drink tea.

Kindness is the best teacher, and Joe Bridle soon got his aunt into better habits. Besides giving her plenty to do in the house, there were other ways in which he amused her. Joseph was very clever with his hands. He could use a knife cunningly; he made a fine Noah's Ark for his aunt to play with. All the animals were there—and some insects, too—but there was only one camel, so that Sarah herself made up the pair.

Sarah grew quieter; she began to behave like an ordinary person, and no one—unless he were told of it—would have thought her mad. It was only when a word was said about the marketing or sale of beasts, that she would show her strange delusion. Then she would lean her head upon the tea-table, expecting some one to come and put a rope round her neck and lead her away to Persia. And all that Joseph could do was to pat and make much of her, and take her into her bedroom, that she thought was her stable.

When something like this had happened that upset her, Joe Bridle would hear her talking to herself in the night. She would turn heavily in her bed, give a groan, and begin to talk. She would lament and cry out that she was but a brute beast, that had no soul to be saved.

"I shall never go to Heaven," she used to moan, "where mother be"—Sarah had loved her mother. She would then call upon Jesus to pity her. "Though I be but a beast, I do love 'Ee," she would say, and begin to moan and weep.

XII

Mr. Solly Is Polite to Turnips

BESIDES his Aunt Sarah, who thought herself a camel, and lived in his house, Mr. Bridle had a particular friend, who came there too. This was Mr. Solly, who was called in Dodder— "Joseph's Sunday companion."

If poor Sarah was regarded by some people as being a little queer, others thought that Mr. Solly was not much better. Mr. Solly had sworn always to despise Love; he hated the very name of the god, and so he must have been more mad than a poor woman, who only fancied herself a beast.

Mr. Solly had lived at Madder, in a quiet sort of way, and he could not help growing older there, for the four seasons that are harnessed to the chariot of a man's days never stop to rest.

Madder Hill lay between Joe Bridle's house and Mr. Solly's and, when Mr. Solly came to Dodder, he would often climb the hill.

Love loiters in hedgerows and small grassy pits. If one hears a sort of scuffle with gasps and sighs in those places, then Love is there. Mr. Solly avoided such places. He might meet Death upon Madder Hill, but Love's doings were not suited to so high a place, where the winds blew shrewdly. Mr. Solly considered that Death was the lesser evil of the two.

He knew that—however much Love may pester mankind —Death always makes full amends. Death must come in the end, but Love can always be left out. In order to protect himself against Love, Mr. Solly planted a grove of nut-trees round his house.

But that was not all that he did to protect himself, for he knew that Love is very sly, and that young women are everywhere. Others had fallen; Solomon and David had been taken, and so he might be caught too. In every direction there was sure to be danger. Suppose that he walked quietly in Madder, tapping with his stick upon the road, or went round by the main thoroughfare to Shelton, he might meet a girl.

To keep his eyes shut would not help matters, for the girl might shut hers too, and then they would walk into one another. And what, after that had happened, could they do unless be married? So Mr. Solly thought of another way to protect himself from Love.

All appearances deceive; when one sees one thing, it may be another. If that is so, one only has to stare a little to see something quite different from the object one looks at. "A green skirt," thought Mr. Solly, "might be a leaf, and though leaves are generally green, they are not always so—nor are frocks all one colour."

Mr. Solly opened his eyes, and saw all women and young girls as turnips, mangold-wurzels, and other vegetables.

They walked out sometimes, or rode bicycles, but that did not prevent him from being certain that their roots were still in the mud. They were probably tossed and flung about by some earthquake, or the mad shaking of the planet by some god, but, as long as he kept them out of his garden, they would do him no harm. Mr. Solly's idea was really a very humane one. For what man is there living, who is always, in every act and fancy, as kind to women as he would wish to be?

In Mr. Solly's case he found it easy to be polite. He knew that it was altogether an impossible thing to quarrel with——

or to be rude to—roots. A sharp word, an oath, or even a blow, could do them no good. They would be no better for cattle after such usage. The sheep would not nibble, nor pigs munch them easier for unkindness.

But, even with these precautions, Mr. Solly could not be quite sure of his safety. He knew that Love, when put to it, has odd tricks. Love, if left by himself, has strange imaginations. He was afraid of young turnips, and had more than once climbed a bank to get out of their way. He was very careful how he walked, for if he tripped over a carrot, something unpleasant might happen.

In Madder few people heeded Mr. Solly. He was but regarded as a poor gentleman, who appeared—for some reason —to be a little ashamed of himself. That was because he always looked upon the ground. He walked quietly, and his clothes were never untidy, and so he was not much to stare at.

It was only when Mr. Solly planted his nut-bushes that he received a little more notice. That any one should grow nuts, instead of potatoes, was a strange thing. It showed a tendency to madness, or else was it that Mr. Solly thought to live upon nut pudding? He had once been seen reading a cookery book —the Madder people looked at him more suspiciously.

When Joe Bridle first brought Mr. Solly to his home, his one fear was that his aunt might regard him as a camel-merchant. So that she might not think so, Joseph had told her about him, and of what he had planted in his garden to defend himself from Love.

When Solly arrived, Miss Bridle looked at him curiously, and shook her head. Mr. Solly behaved with the utmost politeness, but she only looked at him the more curiously, because she thought that he fancied that she was a nut-tree and wished to crack the buttons of her blouse, believing them to be nuts. That was why she shook her head at him, trying to explain that she was only a camel.

Solly always liked Miss Bridle; he would sit beside her and arrange the animals upon the tablecloth with the greatest solemnity. He was particularly fond of the beetles. He would put them behind, allowing these two to go last into the Ark, for fear the others might tread upon them.

Miss Bridle would watch him with interest. As Joseph had only made animals, she supposed—at first—that Solly must be Noah, then, looking at him again, she believed that he was a Persian cat. She must make sure; so she found a little bird in the garden—that had broken its wing—and brought it to him, in order to see what he did with it. But when Solly stroked and tamed the bird, and fed it with crumbs, she was sure that he was no cat, but Noah, the man whom God loved.

Every Sunday, Mr. Solly would come over Madder Hill, to walk out with Joseph Bridle. He used to arrive at three, and they would go off together, like two friends whom no calamity could separate.

No one who lived in Dodder, and saw these two, could forget how they looked. They always walked slowly. Mr. Solly carried his hat in his hand and—in almost every kind of weather—wore an overcoat. Joe Bridle, the taller of the two, walked with his hands in his pockets. Joe's voice was easy to be heard; Mr. Solly talked quietly.

They never varied their ways, but first they would bid farewell to Miss Bridle, as though they were starting off to Peking. They always began their walk by going into Joseph's field, and looking into the pond. Then they would be silent for a while and gaze into the water.

Mr. Solly had often observed that cool, still water is the best sanctifier of human thought, and that to look for only a few moments into a deep pond, must calm and ease all those wayward flutterings of a man's folly, and give to him instead the holy and blessed thought of an everlasting peace.

After staying for a while upon the bank of the pond, they would traverse the lane that led to the down, in order to visit the two other little fields that belonged to Bridle.

When one walks out upon a Sunday, at always the same time, one generally meets the same people.

Mr. Solly and Joseph usually met James Dawe and Farmer Mere.

Mr. Dawe Likes to See

A MAN is often hated without knowing why. As one begets a child, so one begets an enemy—unknowingly. The more harmless and docile a nature may be, the more easy to dislike.

James Dawe, as well as Farmer Mere, hated Joe Bridle. Joe never boasted, his ideas were humble, and his crops—with the exception of his one good meadow—were always worse than other people's. No one would have thought of Joe as being a man who was important enough to be disliked. His bad luck, every one knew; but his cleverness in cutting out of wood so many creatures with a mere knife, no one talked of—and yet James Dawe and Mr. Mere hated him.

Of the two Mr. Mere hated him the most, but perhaps that was because Joe Bridle was always the first to help Mr. Mere. For when one of the farmer's cows fell into a ditch, Joe would bring a rope to pull it out, and when all Mere's sheep—with a great clamour of voices—broke pasture in the night, Joseph roused himself, dressed, and drove them safely to the fold.

It was said at Dodder that to curse a man at one spot upon the downs, where a fairy circle always was, would mean his death. In this magic spot, Mr. Mere—as well as James Dawe—had often cursed Bridle, and both hoped to see him buried while they yet lived.

A part of the down belonged to Mr. Mere. He would often go there upon a Sunday afternoon, in order to try and catch the Dodder children, who would sometimes in fine weather run up and down a tumulus. When he caught them, he would beat them with his stick.

When the children were not there, he would hunt the rabbits with his dog. When he caught a rabbit, he would watch his dog gnaw and devour it. Mere was a cunning hunter. He would appear when you least expected to see him. When the children were all happy playing, he would run suddenly upon them, with his fierce dog at his heels. He would have killed the children, as well as the rabbits, had he dared. To hurt was his pleasure, it was an act that he liked. He liked to see a creature in torment.

James Dawe was different. He did not go to the down to hurt, but only to find. He moved like his schemes—a slow, steady pace—always looking for something. If the children were there, he would watch until they ran away, then he would search the grass where they had been—hoping to find a penny. He would also look out for a rabbit in a snare, in order to carry it home under his coat.

Sometimes James Dawe and Mere would be on the down together. They would only pass one another, and rarely spoke. From a distance, they looked like beasts. Mere crawled upon the earth—he always seemed to be stooping in order that he might not be seen. James Dawe grovelled; he moved upon the ground, as if he wished to sink into it.

When Joseph and Mr. Solly passed either of these men, they knew that they cursed them. Had not Mr. Bridle been a very trustful and simple man, he would have feared James Dawe, even more than Mr. Mere.

Nothing was ever hidden from the miser; he was aware of all that went on in Dodder. He had a hawk's eye for anything of value, and often—for a few pence—purchased what was worth pounds. If one man hates another, nothing that the hated one does escapes notice. His every movement is known. James Dawe knew the exact moment when Joe Bridle first thought of Susie. He also knew when Joe first spoke to her.

To bring Joe Bridle to sorrow was his hope. For a while, he considered how that could be done, and then he knew. He learned from the Bible what it was that brought sorrow into the world. God could set a gin, as well as he. God had given a fine apple as a bait, and Dawe knew a trick worth two of that.

If a woman likes an apple, a man likes a woman. Though Dawe hated Bridle, he spoke to him now and again, in a friendly manner. He hoped that Susie might marry a good man. "Some folk," he said, "do only think of money, but I bain't like that." He saw hope in Joe's eyes.

Nothing escaped James Dawe. He knew his own cottage, as well as he knew other people's. He knew the spyhole that, from his own bedroom, looked into his child's. This hole was behind a large photograph of Susie's mother, that had no frame—a wedding photograph. The hole, that a nail had torn out, was behind the woman's eye. And through this hole it was easy to see into Susie's bedroom.

Mr. Dawe was a father; he was also a man who liked to see.

XIV

Hidden Treasure

SOME say that a miser is an odd contortion—that his mind is twisted. That is not so. A miser is a mathematical figure, an exact computation. But he always counts in low numbers. He likes to begin to gain and never to finish. He will say to his money, "Lie down, oddity!"

He believes in unity; if he holds one penny in his hand, it is all that he thinks he has. He hoards only units. He believes that his belly is a bank, and his guts hiding-places for gold. What passes from him, he regards as lost. His most constant fear is that his store may go into the belly of another. When he has lent anything, he would like to rip up his neighbour's body and find his gold again.

A miser is aware of certain great truths. However far he runs forward, he always knows that he never really leaves the same spot. Nowhere does he see anything that he can call his own. He is altogether an unbeliever in concrete fact. If he does not take care to save more, he will have nothing. Of all earthly pleasures, a miser's are the most sure. He is certain of earthly content, for he has only to gain one penny in order to be happy.

To take—in order to hide—is his wish. He hides his money by putting it out to breed.

A miser's joys never fail him; he pretends he has little, then he counts his bags. From every man's estate he takes something. From not spending himself, he gains by the waste of others.

He not only hoards money, but saves days and years too. A miser usually lives to be very old.

Where another would see nothing, he sees a great deal. A little coaldust in a shed, a despised heap of small sticks—these he sees as a fine estate. Nothing escapes his wary eye. He will not pass by the smallest nail, or piece of string. What other people throw away, he could live upon. He lives by adding one to one. He is a fine leveller.

He goes from one sale to another. He buys at one, a great house; at another, a rotten mattress. He sees these two purchases as the same, but the mattress pleases him the best. A bug in it is a good omen; when he rips up the mattress, he finds money. . . .

As James Dawe spent so little and saved so much, it was hard to understand how Susie could have grown so prettily. Perhaps she was loved by Madder Hill. One would like to know what the ground thinks when a girl steps upon it. Sometimes Madder Hill smiles like the Pope.

But, whoever else smiled, James Dawe never did. He did not smile, but he liked to see. Some possessions are worth looking at. When Susie had a bath, Mr. Dawe would watch her through his spyhole.

What he owned, he liked to see grow into money. For some years James Dawe had looked at her. He saw now that the apple was ripe. What price could he ask?

Mr. Dawe examined the market. He looked out for a buyer. Having a girl to part with, Mr. Dawe became all at once interested in the behaviour of men. He regretted that all men were not chaste. If men were allowed to misbehave with women, then Susie's price would be lowered. With women common, a girl would go cheap. James Dawe hated a harlot.

Mr. Mere went to see Daisy Huddy, and it was Mr.

Mere that James Dawe had thought of as a husband for Susie.

But Mr. Mere was the one to cheapen other folk's goods. He did that and Daisy Huddy did more. She sold herself for a mere nothing, and people said that it took seven visits from Mr. Mere to provide Daisy with a thin summer frock.

But James Dawe was sly, and he watched Mr. Mere. Even though Daisy had lowered prices, there were ways of raising them. The human mind has many an odd fancy. A man's enjoyments are manifold. Mr. Mere's favourite entertainment was cruelty. For such a mystery, Daisy had not been a good subject. To use a fine art upon her had been only a waste of time. When Daisy was badly treated, or hurt unpleasantly, she would only cry, and she would go on crying until Mr. Mere let her alone. James Dawe knew that Susie had more spirit.

A good thing is often thrown away upon an object unworthy of it: pearls are cast to swine. Daisy Huddy was only a harmless village creature, like a sow; indeed, she was more docile than such a beast often is. If one ill-uses a sow, it squeals; Daisy did the same.

Susie was different. She might even show fight, and then Mr. Mere could enjoy himself. James Dawe made up his mind what to ask for his girl. He believed that a lucky, unlooked-for chance had come. He thought he knew where there was a hidden treasure.

A new-comer to Dodder never escaped his eyes. He had seen John Death.

John searched for something. Was that pretence? At first John had spent a long time in Joe Bridle's field, then he searched everywhere about the village, and in the lanes. Dawe thought he did so only to draw people away from where he had really hidden his treasure. The truth was that John Death had hidden his gold in Mr. Bridle's field.

When John had wished to find something of value with which to pay his rent, he had pretended to look for gold in the churchyard. That was only his trick. The treasure was hid in Bridle's field.

James Dawe never missed a piece of news. John Death paid his landlord a rich weekly rent. What exactly he received John Card never said, though it was known at Tadnol that he gave a five-pound note for a pot of beer.

Greed and Hatred are two pretty sisters; they are often invited to the same party. When a man takes one by the hand, he must take the other too.

Dawe wished to have Bridle's field.

Joe wished to get money, and why? James Dawe knew. He would sell his daughter to Mere, and the price would be Joe Bridle's field.

XV

Joe Bridle Sees a Shadow

JOE BRIDLE was a man who loved his friend. But his acceptance of Mr. Solly as a Sunday companion had led him into deeper waters than mere friendship. Joe loved a girl. Had Mr. Solly talked more about women, Joe might never have loved one, but though Mr. Solly used to speak of curly kale, he never mentioned girls.

Joe had not expected to love. He did not know what had moved him to love Susie. He had always thought himself safe. He might have lived on without worry, going always the same, even pace. He had always lived easily, and had never been raised high to fall low. In all innocence, he had taken one day with another, rain or shine, as they chose to show themselves.

His world had been real. He sowed for himself and reaped. The soil that he trod upon never vanished. His plough handles were wood, and all stones were stones.

Solly had much to say when he knew of his friend's love for Susie, and Bridle listened to him respectfully. He agreed with him when he could.

Solly began by observing that perhaps, on the whole, taking everything into account, it is better to go on living than to die. Though there are, he explained, many reasons why a man should destroy himself, yet, for those very reasons, it is perhaps better to live for a little.

"An enemy," said Mr. Solly, "who is sure to win in the end, is really no enemy, and may as well be regarded as a friend."

It is proper to be polite, and when Death lays you along,

you should say "thank you." One might even address Death as "squire." It is best to treat every one well—and Death, too. No one knows his real nature; he may be a good fellow, one who knows his friends. . . .

"Though Death," said Mr. Solly, one Sunday afternoon, "sometimes likes a good man, he has always been the sworn enemy to Love. Between these two a battle always goes on. They fight in the field and in the parlour. Though Death is not Love's spouse, yet they disagree as if they were married. Death does not like the way that Love combs his hair, and Love says that Death ought not to wipe his feet upon the best front-room rug. When two people quarrel, it's best not to try to part them. Let all kings and cardinals go by in the road; never call after them. When you call attention to yourself, by taking one king's part against another, you are the one who will suffer. Learn to eat nuts."

Solly showed by his example that he was a careful man. On his way over Madder Hill, he had met two bulls fighting, one red and one black. He watched them for a moment, and then turned aside out of the path. He was aware that one bull would soon defeat the other, and then the winner, in the excitement of victory, would turn and gore him. Solly came down the hill by another way. . . .

Mr. Solly was visiting his friend. They were standing by Bridle's pond. Joe Bridle felt gloomy. What Solly had said to him, he knew to be true. He did not tell his friend the terrible secret that he hid in his bosom.

The paper was there, and as long as he had it safe, he could keep himself and Susie from Death. That was all that he could do. There were some things, he knew, that were worse than death, that could happen to a girl. Perhaps Susie would have none of his protection, perhaps she might prefer to be harmed, then what could he do to save her?

Since Joe had been in love, he had observed how wilful and how changeable a girl's ways can be. Susie had not been the same since the stranger, Mr. John Death, had come into the village. She had grown to be quite different. She would torment Joe one hour and love him the next. All in a moment, Susie had become a creature of fancies, a wayward wanton—though not wickedly so. Often she turned angrily upon her lover, and sent him away.

Joe Bridle and Solly left the pondside, and stood upon a little mound that overlooked the village. From this mound nearly every cottage could be seen, and Susie's too.

They had not been there long before Susie ran out to her gate. She was in a gay mood. She wore a yellow frock, and began to play with Winnie Huddy, who was in the lane.

Winnie was nine years old—a mere child, but a merry one. Her eyes always sparkled with fun. Her hair was light-coloured—always a mop. She could toss it anywhere. Her hair looked like a bunch of yellow guineas. Winnie used to tease every one; she never cared what she did. She even laughed at Mr. Mere, and she often made Daisy cry. She would wander off alone, and no one knew where she went to. When any one met and chid her for being so far from home, she would reply saucily that she was looking for a husband.

Solly and Joe Bridle watched the two girls; they could easily hear what they said. Winnie began to tease Susie.

"Oh!" she said, "you will never guess what I know about you, Susie Dawe."

Susie chased Winnie, meaning to chastise her for her naughty words. She caught her near to Joseph's field. Winnie, who had noticed the two men upon the mound, gave an indelicate pull to Susie's frock. Susie pushed down her frock, and shook Winnie by her shoulders.

But Winnie's naughtiness was hard to lay. She began to

push Susie about, and to tickle her with her small, quick hands. And, all at once, she began to kiss her as if she never would stop.

Joe Bridle watched them gladly; he was pleased to see the girls so happy, but, looking a little further down the lane, he saw something more, something that he had taken to be a shadow. He thought that he had seen the shadow of a tree-stump. The kind of shadow that appears sometimes at night when the moonlight is in the room. At first it is a draped figure, with hand outstretched; then slowly it vanishes when true consciousness returns.

What Bridle saw in the lane had been but a shadow at first, then it became a man. Though the girls were quite near to him, they had not seen John, but when they did notice him, Winnie—as became her sex—ran to him at once and teased him, as she had teased Susie. Susie, left to herself, began to toy with a little yellow cat, that matched her frock.

While she stroked the cat, something that John Death tried to do to her frightened Winnie who, though she had but pretended to before, this time really ran away.

Then John Death went to Susie. They began to talk together and, being near to one another, it appeared to Joe that Death touched her.

The paper that Joe carried in his bosom burned him. Should he give it up? Should he go down, take Susie in his arms, pulling her from Death and holding her close, give the parchment into Death's hands? He could then kill them instantly and together.

A sudden flash of lightning could do that simple work. In a moment God can call up a storm to work His purpose. But Death left Susie, and walked quickly up the lane towards Bridle's own cottage.

XVI

A Laugh from a Camel

OFTEN the two friends stood silent for a long while; they were silent now. The summer evening had grown very still. Perhaps Mr. Bridle's pond helped to make things cold. Sometimes a heavy dampness rose up from the pond, and circled slowly about Joseph's field. The fog crept now around the little mound where the friends stood. It rose steadily, and they breathed its clammy moisture. It was a shroud come to envelop them.

The mist rose higher; only the top of the great elm escaped its enveloping folds. Bridle wished himself that tall tree. The tree had never known a woman's love. It had neither known Love nor Death.

Mr. Solly was the first to speak. Since he had seen Winnie Huddy teasing Susie, he had not said one word. Now he sighed heavily.

"Spring cabbages should never be planted," he said mournfully. "They are too pretty to be good. Their outer leaves are deceitful; who can know what there is underneath? A round, well-grown field beet is a harmless thing," continued Solly, "there is nothing hidden about it. Even the red variety is no fraud, and the yellow ones are not painted. A white turnip, too, is very proper for the pot; it can be boiled until it is tender, and then placed in the marriage bed, in a dish with mutton and a well-steamed carrot.

"A turnip only grows; it has implanted in its nature a proper decorum. There is pretty Susie; she would make any man a good wife. But I ought to have shut my eyes and never have looked at Winnie Huddy.

"She may like nuts. One never knows what a small cabbage does like. Often it has no heart. It develops lying leaves. You may think that they enclose a plump heart, you expect a fine dinner on Whitsunday, but you are sure to be sadly disappointed. You squeeze the leaves, and there is nothing inside. Your dinner vanishes.

"But that is not all that happens—the cabbage laughs at you. No one likes to be mocked by a vegetable."

Mr. Solly became very thoughtful. He had never expected to find danger in a Dodder lane. Had he planted his nut-trees thick enough? What had made him look at Winnie? He knew Love was very cunning; one has to be very wideawake to keep a god out. If he cannot get in at the front, he will try the back door.

Mr. Solly felt in his pocket for the key of his garden gate. He was always afraid that an unlucky day might come when he would forget to lock his gate, and that Love— in the habit of a young maid—would find a way into his house. He trusted to his wall of nut-bushes, and to the garden gate, to keep out the foe. He never locked his cottage door. He thought it of no use to do that, for, when Love knocks so near, all doors must open. But with Love outside his grove, Solly felt safe.

Mr. Solly found the key in his pocket.

Joe Bridle said nothing; ugly doubts had entered his head. Did Susie really care for him? Had he a rival in John Death? Might there be others too, he wished to know. That same day, he had seen James Dawe speak to Mr. Mere —and those two did not usually address one another. Was there an evil plot being made to take Susie away from him? He wished to know.

In the lane, on their way to Joseph's house, he asked a favour of Mr. Solly. He begged him to go to the Inn that evening. He asked this favour of his friend because he wished to know what was being said about Susie. He had heard an unpleasant whisper that James Dawe intended to sell his girl to Farmer Mere, as his wife. Joe wished to know whether there was any truth in this report. If he visited the Inn—an unusual thing for him to do—he knew that no one would mention the matter. All tongues would be tied, for all Dodder knew that Joe Bridle looked upon Susie as his own sweetheart.

Solly promised to go. He was aware that a Sunday evening was a fine time for gossip, and that at the Inn everything would be talked of.

Besides serving his friend, Solly had another reason for wishing to go to the Inn. There was something in the look of Winnie Huddy that made him, for the first time in his life, doubt the strength of his fortification. He knew Love to be a savage—the very worst of them—and Winnie had smiled at him. He feared her, but he might forget her at the Inn. Mr. Solly liked gin.

The evening mist, rising up from Bridle's pond, had thickened. All Dodder lay hid in a bath of white vapour, only Madder Hill raised itself above the cloud. They reached Joseph's cottage without being seen by any one, and were surprised, while still in the garden, to hear merry sounds in the parlour. Besides Miss Sarah Bridle, some one else was there.

Joseph was astonished. He had never heard his aunt laugh before; she had only worked. Thinking of herself as only a beast of burden, she had laboured like one; she did all with patience, she served a good master. The parlour was an oasis, the kitchen a small grove of palms, the pantry a caravanserai. The passage between these places was a sandy desert, the bedrooms a plateau upon a mountain.

Sarah would labour with her head bowed. Only when she took the clothes from the garden-line would she raise herself a little. Then it would seem to her that some one called her by name, and she, being frightened, would hurry indoors again.

Joe Bridle waited in the garden, near to the parlour window, and wondered what could have happened to his aunt. Had she become worse, more crazed, or had she—by some strange fancy—recovered her senses? Joe Bridle and Mr. Solly waited and listened.

Sarah's laughter had ceased, but instead of laughing, she now made low sounds of delight—from the sofa. Evidently some kind of amusement was being enacted there that pleased Sarah.

Hearing these sounds, Mr. Solly began to smile. From suchlike folly his nut-bushes prevented him; being wise himself, he was pleased to hear that others could still be fools. Mr. Solly went softly to the window and peeped in. What he saw going on made him nod his head violently, and wink back at Joe. Mr. Solly had his own ideas about medicine. He believed that a learned doctor was performing a necessary cure upon Miss Bridle. He advised Joe to wait a few moments before he interrupted the cure.

Joe, who had not gone to the window, was rather alarmed; he did not know who was indoors with his aunt and felt anxious. But Mr. Solly assured him that nothing unnatural was happening in the parlour.

After waiting a few moments, Joe Bridle and Mr. Solly entered the house, Mr. Solly observing as he went in, that the best way to preserve a good swede was to put it in a grave.

Inside the parlour they found Sarah, resting contentedly upon the sofa, and smoothing her skirts. John Death was sitting next to her, with his arm round her, and was asking her to take him to Bagdad. He informed her, proudly, that he believed that General Gordon was not the only one who could ride a camel.

Death was in the highest spirits, and Sarah looked at him lovingly. Mr. Solly shook hands with them both in high glee. He called Death "doctor."

"My dear doctor," he said, "your treatment has been excellent; no king's physician could have acted with more propriety. You doctors are knowing fellows. But perhaps you have been in practice for some while."

"Only with Daisy Huddy," replied John, a little disappointedly.

Sarah blushed and looked affectionately at her nephew, who was delighted to see her looking so different.

"I declare," she said joyfully, "that Mr. Solly was not so very much mistaken in thinking that I am a woman, and no nut-tree. Mr. Death could never have behaved so lovingly to me, had I been a mere bush. Neither would he have liked me so well, had I been a camel."

"I must grow my trees higher," cried Solly, in alarm.

Miss Bridle smoothed her frock, blushed coyly, and invited Death to tea.

But John Death excused himself and withdrew.

XVII

One as High as the Almighty

WHEN Mr. Solly entered the Bullman Arms and sat down quietly in a corner, no one seemed to notice him.

Mr. Dady, who managed Farmer Mere's large dairy of cows, was there, Dillar the labourer, and Thomas Huddy. As Solly entered, Mr. Huddy was explaining to the company why it was that his daughter, Daisy, behaved so naughtily.

" 'Twas she's mother who first taught her," observed Mr. Huddy.—Dillar looked surprised at this news.—"She were religious, I do know," said Huddy, "and died good, but she always taught Daisy to do what she was told."

"And how could that have done the harm?" inquired Mr. Titball.

" 'Tain't always good that a maid be told to do," answered Huddy meaningly.

Though the company had not noticed Mr. Solly, Mr. Titball now observed him. No new customer ever escaped the landlord's eye, but it was not only the hope of gain that made Mr. Titball like to see a new face. He had another, and a more lofty reason than that—he wished to show him a book.

Before he came to the Dodder tavern, Mr. Titball had been, for many years, in service with Lord Bullman as butler, and from his nearness to so great a man he had come to regard my lord as an equal to—or even greater than—God Almighty.

Mr. Titball had served Lord Bullman so long and so faithfully that, as a reward for his service, when he left the Hall, Lord Bullman presented him with a second-hand picture-book, together with the second housemaid.

Mr. Titball married the one, and admired the other.

At the Bullman Arms, he always kept his wife in the kitchen and the picture-book in the parlour. He was ashamed of his wife, and for this reason. It had been Mary's privilege to make my lord and my lady's bed, but once the housekeeper discovered that she had not turned the mattress in my lord's room—and so, in Mr. Titball's opinion, she was shamed for ever.

Mr. Titball considered his wife to be a common slut, a mere drudge, a betrayer of her former master.

The picture-book was different. It contained all the houses of the great, beginning with Arundel Castle, and ending with the king's residence in Norfolk. Exactly in the middle, where a large marker taken from a family Bible had been placed, was a fine picture of West Dodder Hall.

As soon as Mr. Solly was settled in his place, Mr. Titball, treading noiselessly, took the book in his hands, carried it to Solly—as if it were an infant—and placed it gently upon his knees.

Mr. Solly, who did not know the ways of the place, and felt the book a weighty burden, rose quietly and returned it to the table from whence it had been taken. Mr. Titball who, even with his back turned, noticed everything, saw what Solly had done.

The landlord was a stout little man, with a mottled complexion and a fiery eye; he could forgive everything in the world except an insult to his former master. He had thought his wife a slut, and now he believed that Solly was an atheist, and so he brought him the worst gin—for he considered that only those who opened and enjoyed his fine book deserved the best.

Though Mr. Titball's book did not interest Solly, he liked the smell of Mr. Titball's parlour. Smells change according to the seasons indoors as well as out-of-doors. Each visitor who enters an inn brings with him an odour from outside. About Mr. Huddy there was always the scent of damp clay, together with the smell that comes out of the ground when the furrow is newly turned. Dillar stank of the stable and Mr. Dady of cow dung, and by such mixtures did the Dodder Inn parlour get its summer scent.

Mr. Solly sipped his gin and decided that he preferred cows to horses. No one heeded his presence. He had chosen a corner to sit in that was rarely occupied by any one, unless it were Tinker Jar, who used sometimes to enter the inn to drink a pint of sixes.

Mr. Solly might as well have been Jar for all the notice that was taken of him.

Presently the tavern door opened and Mr. Mere appeared, and took the chief seat upon a stool that was only left for the gentry.

Mr. Mere spoke to Dady. He asked whether a cow that was being fattened was ready for the butcher. He needed money, he said, for a new purchase.

"I have bought Joe Bridle's grass," he said, "to cut and to carry. The grass is growing thick and green, and 'twill make a fine stack."

"Master be the woon for a bargain," cried out Dillar.

"The field is a strange one," observed Mr. Mere thoughtfully. "Besides the pond and the elm tree, there are mounds here and there, and deep hidden places that prevent a hay-cutter from being used. When the grass grows a little more, I must hire a mower for it."

" 'Tis said that Bridle is a bankrupt," observed the landlord, who filled Mr. Mere's glass. "I trust that he does not owe anything to my lord, who has not bought a pipe of port wine since I lived at the Hall. And who deserves more wine than he?"

"If 'twere beer," said Mr. Dillar, with a wink, " 'tis I who deserve it."

Mr. Titball frowned; the joke was ill-timed.

"Folk do say," remarked Mr. Dillar, thinking it best to change the subject, "that Joe Bridle be the one to want money, and maybe 'e have a mind to a furry doe-rabbit to keep company wi' wold ca.nel in 's house."

" 'Tis a rabbit that others do want as well as he," said Mr. Dady, looking at Mere.

"Master be a knowing one," cried old Huddy. " 'E do like to take all; 'e be the one to fancy folk's fields and houses, and where a pretty maid be, there will Mr. Mere be also." Mr. Huddy was the church clerk.

Dillar grinned. All wished to please Mere and to minister to his wants. Mr. Dady sat near to the inn window; he liked that place best because he could enjoy himself there, killing flies.

Thus he enjoyed life; for by killing he always obtained pleasure, sometimes profit. Whenever he killed a pig— though it was Mr. Mere's—he was always able to get something for himself. Besides meat in an animal, there is blood, and Mr. Dady liked a blood pudding.

Mr. Dady believed in art—the art of killing. He liked to kill slowly. He would approach a fly, with his thumb going nearer and yet nearer, and the fly supposed that all was well. Then Mr. Dady would squeeze the insect against the pane.

When he had killed all the flies that were there, Mr. Dady happened to notice James Dawe, leaning against the bank, near to the inn. Dawe appeared to be there for no purpose other than to look at the inn signboard that was in front of him.

Though he seemed to rest so innocently amongst the daisies, all Dodder knew why he was there. He was a merchant who waited. When Mr. Dawe waited like that, all knew that he had something to sell.

That was his gait, his manner, when he had goods to part with. Even when his wife was alive, he offered to sell her in the same way. He would wait until a man spoke to him, and then, after speaking of the weather, he would talk of women.

"In these lean times, a poor farmer do want a bit of fun," he would observe. "And there be something at home to please 'ee."

Mr. Dawe was a cunning one; he never spoke first, but he liked to hear what was being said. Village tales that had no meaning to others had a meaning to him.

Mr. Dawe was a man who looked underneath appearances.

XVIII

A Tale Told to Mr. Dawe

EVEN the most unfriendly people are fond of something. Mr. Mere of the Dodder Manor Farm was fond of his dog. His dog's name was Tom. He was a great shaggy brute, half lurcher and half wolf-hound.

Tom was extremely fierce. There were many stories told about Mr. Mere's dog, and one of them particularly interested James Dawe. This story was about something that happened in the fields. The shepherd had told of it.

While the lambs were being tailed and castrated, one of them—a ewe—whose tail had not yet been cut off, escaped from the fold and galloped away. Mr. Mere, leaving the shepherd to go on with his work, followed the lamb with his dog.

Sport is kingly; a great many people of quality enjoy it, besides numbers of the lower orders. A fine gentleman, who has all that he can need for this world and the next, will walk out in peculiar clothes, to kill a little fluffy rabbit. Why should not Mr. Mere enjoy a little fun, too? He liked young meat.

He drove the lamb into a corner and set his dog to worry it.

Once having learned to be amused, a man may be amused at everything. There are people who shake with laughter when they see a coffin. Others will laugh at the most horrible cruelty. They point out the fun. To hunt is a pretty pastime. Set fire to the bushes, see the burnt rabbits run, set the dogs at them.

The lamb Mr. Mere was after was soon caught. Tom was in a merry mood, Mere was delighted. When the dog began to bite and torment the lamb, he was yet more pleased. The shepherd, even, left his work, came nearer and watched. A man can do what he likes with his own.

The story reached James Dawe. It was the sort of tale that he liked to hear; it gave him food for reflection. Here was rich Mr. Mere—a man who never missed the chance to gain a penny—willing to see, and even aiding in the destruction of one of his own lambs—a ewe. Dawe became thoughtful. Perhaps what his dog did, Mr. Mere might wish to do, too. And even the meanest of men will sometimes like to pay for their pleasures. There were other tales, too, to hear.

When the farmer went to the down upon a Sunday, he would sometimes set his dog at the children. Mr. Mere saw a difference between the Dodder brats; some were boys, some girls. And 'twas the girls that he sent Tom after. Even when she played upon the green, Winnie Huddy often had to run for her life, and sometimes left a piece of her frock in Tom's mouth.

Mr. Dawe liked such stories.

Once he had overheard Mere call Susie "a little bitch," which, though a compliment from a man of Mere's merit, might be misunderstood by the vulgar.

James Dawe knew that the way to get what one wants in this world, is always to sift, as it comes in, the chaff from the true corn. All goodness that he heard of, he quickly forgot; in such things he saw no profit for himself. Only by famine, pestilence, and war do people grow rich.

Evil doings are a rich field for gain; out of pitifulness and loving-kindness nothing can be got.

Mr. Dawe thought the matter out. He opined that Mr. Mere set his dog at a prey that he wished to bite himself. Even though his dog's teeth had gnawed the lamb, Mere had what remained of it roasted for his dinner.

Mr. Mere had old-fashioned table manners. When the woman who cooked for him was out of the way, he would growl savagely like a brute beast, and then begin to tear the meat apart with his nails, as well as his teeth. But what of that? Children, who follow the hounds to the death, have to be blooded, and why should not Mr. Mere enjoy blood as well as little Jessica Bullman? . . .

As soon as Mr. Mere heard that James Dawe was outside, he sent Mr. Titball out to call him in. He wished to talk with him, he said, and to give him something to drink.

James Dawe crept lowlily into the inn. His scent came with him. He entered crouchingly, as though the door were very low. But his eyes looked craftily as he entered, and the first thing that he saw was a halfpenny under the table.

He stooped a little lower and picked up the coin. Then he looked up and showed his face that was covered with soft, dirty hair. His little blinking eyes—full of cunning— looked at the company. His wish was to put the money that he had found into his pocket—without being noticed.

He cursed Solly, who alone saw what he did. Dawe did not like Solly any better than he liked Bridle; he hated the pair of them. For a man to go about calling a kind of saleable goods merely parsnips might lower prices.

To lower the price of anything—except what he wished to buy himself—was, according to Mr. Dawe, a sin against the Holy Ghost. Why then was not Solly sent to Hell, together with his nut-trees? Dawe wished him burnt.

After putting the coin he had found into his pocket, James Dawe moved towards Mr. Mere.

So a jackal might have gone to a hyena, willing to become friends—until a carcass is found.

Mere called for some drink, and Dawe watched what was put into his glass. Mr. Titball began to talk—Mere had treated the landlord, too—and at once began to drink to all the sons and daughters of Lord Bullman, as though they were the children of the king. He drank to each and every one of them. "Percy!" he called out, "Mona, Rupert, Jessica, Dorothea, Edward, Monica!

"I know them all, even the baby," cried Mr. Titball. He drank to each three times. "An' 'tis a strange coincident," he said, with a low bow, "that at the Hall, every child's birthday comes in August."

"I do know why that be," said Mr. Dady who, having a large family, was interested in birthdays. " 'Tis they Christmas doings that be all the mischief. 'Tis the time of year that be to blame."

Mr. Dady quickly killed another fly.

"In they merry times," he observed, looking admiringly at the fly, "married folk be forgetful, and the nights be long. 'Tain't always the beer neither—a cold night do need warm work. And many a poor toad be born in consequence of a snowstorm."

Solly wished to hear all that was said. Mr. Mere and James Dawe were beginning to talk together in low tones. Solly appeared to be interested in Dawe's boots; he moved nearer to them.

Greed and Malice, together with unholy Lust, make a pretty trinity. One the Son, one the Father, and one the Spirit. To count by three is in the fashion.

Solly looked at Dawe's boots. They were hobnailed, and the upper leather was dry and warped. They looked as though they had been picked up out of some ditch, thrown off, perhaps, by a drunken fellow who thought he was an angel in heaven and had no need of them.

Mere opened his mouth to speak, and showed two ugly teeth.

Those who hunt heed only one thing. Summer days and winter days are alike to them. Mountains and valleys are the same. All cities and all country places provide a like sport. In darkness or in light they seek the same—the prey to devour.

In every gesture of Mr. Mere's, there was the certainty that he could never be overreached. Each word of James Dawe's was as subtle as a serpent's glide. Greed drew near to Cunning, and Mischief winked.

Those who play with loaded dice know who will win. Good is easy to destroy, but evil has as many lives as a cat. Trample it down upon one side, and it will grow up upon the other. It was said by one man that it is best to let evil grow together with good and wait until the harvest time comes, until both are reaped together and gathered into the barn. Then a sifting will begin.

In every sack of seed that comes from the great storehouse, there is a mixture of good corn and bad. Only a white dove can tell the difference, and that dove is always being caught and killed by an old cat—God.

In the Bullman Arms James Dawe talked close. He was explaining what he had to sell, in natural words; he was telling in detail exactly what his girl was like. He appeared to know all about her. He described the roundness of her form, her young breasts, the pleasing look of her naked body, her hair—all. James Dawe was a good salesman; he left nothing out, and the words that he used were common and ordinary.

A good seller need be no poet, in order to dispose of what

he has in stock. James Dawe was no polite talker; he did not trouble himself to say that "beauty is a joy for ever," nor did he say, "there is a garden in her face, where roses and white lilies blow." He said other things than that.

"She be an idle lambkin," he told Mr. Mere, "an innocent chit, a foolish maid, who could give a man some pretty sport."

Then he began to whisper. Solly drew words from their lips.

They shook hands. They must have come to some kind of agreement. Mr. Mere called for more drink.

XIX

Mr. Dawe Names His Price

To DRINK one opens one's mouth. When the drink is swallowed, the tongue is loosened. After taking more liquor, James Dawe and Mr. Mere unthinkingly raised their voices.

Though they seemed to have come to terms, there was much yet to arrange and, having once agreed together—kite and crow—they did not care so much who heard what they said.

So far, Mr. Solly had been the only one to hear, but now the others listened. No one likes to be left outside some merry parlour talk. From a word or two spoken by Mere, Mr. Dady caught the drift of their conversation.

This was not hard to follow when once the key was given. A laugh, or a look even, will disclose the secret. There is a kind of smile that a man uses sometimes, that tells what he is thinking of. There are also a man's eyes that betray him.

Mr. Titball had just drunk the health of the Dowager Lady Bullman and her cat, Tib, when Dady and Tom Huddy cried out together, " 'Tis Susie they be telling of! 'Tis a small furred coney; they do say she be to fondle and to kiss. And she bain't got no mother to tell she what to do wi' they men!"

All laughed, and Farmer Mere laughed the loudest.

After this was said, there was no need to whisper. Whatever woman is named at an inn is the common property of all. Mere was not the one to be ashamed. He knew the law—money. He had a right to his bargain. Most of those

in the room were his servants, and now Shepherd Brine—
a silent man—came in too. If Dawe asked too much for
his goods, Mere was sure that the company would side with
him in beating the miser down.

"And the price?" shouted Mr. Mere. "What price be
she to do with as I choose?"

James Dawe blinked and shook his head. All at once he
seemed to become a different being. Only a few moments
before, he was saying, with glee, how Susie might hold back
a little from the marriage encounter, and how merry Mere
could be with her then. Now James Dawe became a cautious
parent.

" 'Tis me poor young maid," he observed, turning to
Dady, "that 'e do want to marry, but she be but a tender
chick to give to an old man. He bain't always kind neither,
bain't farmer; 'is breath do stink, and maiden be faint-hearted
at night-time. She do hide out of the way when a bull do
bellow. No father do like 'is small girl to be hurt, and wedded
ways bain't all orange-blossom. 'Tis a weak young child to
be put to bed to an old man, neighbours."

"Tell me the price," shouted Mere angrily, whose lusts
had been more than ever inflamed by Mr. Dawe's quiet talk.

"Name a price for the girl!"

"Oh, don't 'ee talk so fierce," replied Mr. Dawe, "for I
be feared thee mid do harm to the poor maid. 'Tain't much
that I do ask in exchange for all they beauties that me child
do have."

Mere raised his fist as though to strike.

" 'Tis only Bridle's field that I do ask in exchange for
she," said Dawe plaintively.

Mere looked at him sharply. Besides the purchase of the
growing grass, unknown to any one—so he supposed—Mere
had arranged with Bridle to buy the field too. The property

to become his in two months' time, Bridle's field going then into his possession, and to his heirs for ever.

"How did you know," asked Mr. Mere sternly of Dawe, "that Joe's field, as well as the growing grass, will soon be mine own?"

"Because I was nearby, hidden under the churchyard wall, when you made the deal," answered Dawe, "and I heard Joe Bridle say that he wanted the money to pay off his debts, before he was married."

Mere became thoughtful. In his lecher's heart he had decided to give even more for Susie than the price of Bridle's field. Why had not the miser asked more? Presently he thought he understood.

"Ha!" he cried out, "I believe I know now why you wish for that field. You have read the notice in the shop-window that a treasure has been lost, and you think that you know where the treasure is."

"No, no," answered Dawe, in a conciliatory tone and with a sly wink at the company, " 'tain't for no treasure-seeking that I do want the field, but only that I mid bury me child in thik deep pond when thee 've done she to death."

Dady laughed loudly.

"Farmer will be a rare one at 's work," he called out, "and will thrash finely with his flail, but most like 'twill be only 'is old joints that are shaken when wedding night do come."

Every man now clamoured to speak and all spoke at once. Only Solly remained silent. Each man knew Susie. Each saw her now. All that was foul in man was cast upon her. Her breasts were spat upon, and loathsome slime poured out upon her. Each man saw her as his, to ravish brutally. Even Solly saw her as a young lettuce that he was cutting for his dinner, and shook his head nervously.

Could thoughts and words harm, Susie's state would indeed have been desperate. Out of the Dodder mud much can be said. All that a beast can do can be done there. Once the game is begun, who can stop its continuance? Only the dead can escape notice.

Mr. Solly became more and more astonished and surprised at what he heard. He had no idea that a mere bunch of endive, even surrounded by the most luxuriant hog's dung, could make so much talk. Evidently his friend, Joseph Bridle, had got himself into a difficult position. Joseph had much better have loved a hollow tree than a yellow beet, about whom so many words could be used—so many odd expressions.

When quiet came again, all began to wonder how it was that Mere should have offered so high a price as a whole field for a girl. He had always—until John Death came into the village—been able to do all he wished with Daisy, for a mere nothing. What had happened to the careful farmer? Why was Susie so much thought of? She was only a girl. Why was all this fuss being made about her?

Mr. Solly was astonished, too. He had advised his friend to be cautious, but as Susie didn't look maggot-eaten, he thought she would make a good, wholesome wife. He only expected a simple country wedding to come of it. A few cheap cakes, a barrel of beer, and Daisy Huddy to entertain those guests who might wish to be initiated into wedded doings. All the talk made about a poor root—that must one day rot in the earth—he thought very unseemly.

In a field of swedes, considered Mr. Solly, all are nearly equal. All grow together and, in the spring, throw up green sprouts. Why should one be regarded as sweeter than the rest, when all look the same? Mr. Solly sighed dismally.

"A poor man," he decided, "should never look too long at a spring cabbage."

XX

Mr. Dady Opens the Window

WHEN lust is shut up in a small narrow room, it begins to breed. Such a room is the body of a man; lust breeds in him quicker than fleas in a country tavern.

In a room, from which all pure air is kept out, little lewd devils may spawn and multiply. Sometimes they make mistakes and enter a room where they are not at their ease. When they get into the wrong man, they escape at his ears.

Mr. Solly thought they were bugs. He scratched his neck and gave his head a shake to get rid of the trouble. He looked suspiciously at Mr. Dillar, who had come nearer to him. Perhaps he was lousy?

Lewd thoughts, Mr. Solly knew, if they have any encouragement given to them, become lice in the head. He had often seen gentlemen and ladies scratch, and knew what was the matter. The life-history of a louse is an ordinary affair—a simple transformation.

The parlour became noisy again; mugs clattered, all the company shouted. Solly alone did not shout, but, wishing for some more gin, he was forced to raise his voice a little in order to obtain it.

After drinking that glass, he fancied that a large louse fell from Mr. Dillar's head upon the table, and became a female demon called Peg, a succuba. Solly grew frightened; the demon reminded him of Winnie Huddy; she was eating his nuts. Mr. Solly called for more gin.

Even Mr. Titball was tormented by the frolics of the

imp, but, being a faithful servant, it was not for himself that he wanted the fun, but for his master. He, a loyal man, desired all that was best in the world for his lord's comfort. The imp danced, more appeared, and Mr. Titball wished to provide dancing girls for my lord.

Besides such a proper desire, Mr. Titball, having been much impressed by all that had been said of Susie, felt that no farmer should take possession of so much beauty, but that my lord's great curtained bed should have its lawful share.

He knew that the great of the land deserved sometimes a little relaxation from their more arduous duties. To ride after a fox appeared to Mr. Titball to be the hardest of labours. In all kindness and secrecy he had more than once opened a side door for a young lady, who said that she brought a private message to my lord from his cousin, the Bishop of Portstown.

Mr. Titball had never asked her to give her name.

Mr. Titball had a generous mind. He would give all to a lord, and would only wish to keep for himself his picture-book of the homes of England.

Mr. Dady pursued with his thumb the last fly upon the window; he had killed all the rest. This particular fly did not wish to be killed. It wished to live and multiply. But Dady meant to have him. He followed it with his thumb, up and down the pane. The fly was driven into a corner, and Mr. Dady killed it slowly. Then, hoping that more flies would come in, he opened the window.

This was an unusual action; no one had ever done so before. Whether winter or summer, the parlour window at the Bullman Arms had always been kept tight shut.

But now that the window was opened a change came upon the room.

Those who drank so noisily a few moments before, now became as silent as the grave. The only sound that could be heard was the drip, drip, of a little puddle of spilt beer, falling from the table to the floor.

Mr. Mere sat in silence, and, instead of thinking what he would do with Susie when he got her for his wife, he began to listen.

When a sudden silence comes, a man's ears are opened. He waits for something, for a sound to come to him. He wonders what the sound will be.

The puddle of beer had run away; the dripping had ceased. Mr. Dady leaned nearer to the window and listened too. The little lewd imps hearkened; something had quieted their obscene frolics. Was it the sweet wind that came from the sea?

In the common lives of people, one power is always waiting ready to drive out another, in order to rule in its place. There is always a stronger one coming. Each guardian of the temple is slain in his turn, then the victor becomes priest in his stead. Power that conquers power is the order of all our lives, but who is it that dare name the last power to kill? What will He do, when the fatal blow is struck, and He becomes lord of the temple, with no rival to challenge His victory?

With no power above Him, with no power higher than Himself, what can He do? Will He—in order to complete the conquest—slay Himself? Will He listen too, like our poor drunkards—for in all that temple there will be silence? Shall He hear again the many trampling feet of a new generation of men, or will the last enemy destroy Him too? Will God die? . . .

Dillar and old Huddy moved nearer to the open window

and listened, but it was not the sound of the aspen leaves, softly stirred, that they heard.

The usual, the ordinary village sounds, were quieted. The new summer that was come to Dodder brooded silently, thinking of her own loveliness. The fruitful sun had warmed the green earth. There was no hedge, no wayside place, that had not drunk a cup of the new life. The winds moved softly over the downs; the daytime flowers slept without dreams.

Mr. Hayhoe stood, with his wife Priscilla, at the Vicarage door, taking together a loving farewell of the summer day before they retired to rest. A holy love moved in the garden and they—being simple, childlike people—felt its presence. Love moved for a while in the Vicarage garden, and then passed into the churchyard and lingered beside the grave of Priscilla's child.

Mr. Hayhoe kissed his wife's hand. A feeling, he knew not what, brought tears into his eyes. They both looked towards the grave.

His Will be done. . . .

All thought in Dodder was quieted. Still waters covered all motion, and no mental webs were being spun there that bring false hope to man. To grow like the field flowers, what else could man do? To bloom in the summer, to eat of the season's joy and then drink the dark wine of the sadness of the earth during the fall. To breathe deep again, perhaps, when the winter's sleep is ended. To awake like a leaf to the new season. To exist as a creature of the earth for a moment, what more should be needed?

The evening gnats quivered and danced in the warm air, unmindful of danger. The swallows caught them and they heeded not the act. The tiny pigslouse that lived in the grass upon Madder Hill ate its prey. Then it rolled up into a ball to sleep near an anthill, and was eaten itself. A frog, seeking amusement, hopped out of Joe Bridle's pond, only to find a grave in the cold body of a snake.

Life and death do not quarrel in the fields. They are always changing places in the slow dance. Alive here and dead there. So the evening is devoured by the night, and the dawn by the day.

Mr. Hayhoe's thoughts were hopeful; he looked forward to the morrow, but he was content that the evening should stay longer. By harvest time, at least, if not before, he intended to convert his friend, John. That thought gave him pleasure, and Daisy Huddy was no more a sinner, which pleased him too.

But Priscilla was sad; she looked longingly towards the churchyard, and prayed that one day she might meet Death there, and compel him to give her back her child.

XXI

Strange Music

As THE years move onward, sounds change. Sounds that used to be listened to in older times are not heard now.

Climb up Madder Hill on any still, frosty morning, you will hear no horse trotting on the turnpike road; the gentleman who once owned a smart gig and a high-stepping hackney has changed his gear.

Neither will you be likely to hear the cry of a wild bird; ravens are scarce now. Only a pair of them live upon the cliff near to Mockery Gap; if they fly inland, they are thought to be rooks. The cry of a curlew is not often heard; only a few snipe can be noticed, drumming, over Tadnol moor in the springtime.

Sounds that have once been common, when they are heard again, are sure to attract attention. They carry back the minds of those that hear them to forgotten times. They awaken feelings that have slept long. Without knowing why, and scarcely knowing what it is that one listens to, one's thoughts travel backwards into the past.

One may have heard steady, resounding thuds—mere sounds only, the beating of carpets perhaps, but enough to awaken the remembrance of older times. One shuts one's eyes and enters a barn. The dust flies, there is a smell of dry straw.

Two men are at work with flails. One of them—John Sherwood, who wears side-whiskers—wields dexterously a strange weapon, steadily beating a heap of beans—dry and black—that are stacked in the barn. Presently the black stalks are taken up and the beans sifted and placed in sacks. John Sherwood drinks from a stone jar.

Lost days have been found again; sounds move one backwards. What was now heard through the open window of the Dodder Inn caused the older men who were there to awake as from a deep sleep. Dillar, old Huddy, and Dady recollected freer, gayer times, when a man—if he had the money to spend—could drink at any hour of the day as much as he wished, days when no one tampered with the sun or turned the lock in a tavern door.

Dady bethought him that no one minded then what a man did. You could kill what you chose—so long as you let the Squire's game alone—and kill how you liked.

James Dawe remembered the time when one could hoard to some purpose, when poor people were really poor, and all wanted bread.

Farmer Mere had his thoughts too, that came from the sound that was heard. A country girl was an easy prey then; no one interfered with those who had money. The law knew its betters. One could do as one chose then. Children's ages were not inquired into. You could pick up a wench where you wished, and bastards had to keep themselves in those merry days.

Time changes sin, fashion in vice alters. What is cruelty to one generation, to another is only a compliment. Mr. Mere wished for the old times.

Those who sit idly themselves and hear some one at work, wonder what the worker is doing. There is jealousy in labour, as well as in love. When a workingman is idle he thinks that all others should be idle too. The mob distrusts anything that all do not share. If another works while they drink, he may be getting something more than they.

But what was the sound that set all thoughts wandering into the days gone by? The whetting of a scythe.

A scythe is still used in country places for cutting a path for the corn reaper. But harvest was not yet, and a scythe that has been recently ground can be sharpened in a few minutes. Even this is not done as it used to be, when fourteen mowers might be seen at work in one field, for now no one troubles whether a scythe cuts as it used. The art of scythe-play is lost.

No one spoke at the Dodder Inn. All listened as if strangely fascinated. The sound continued. Dady, old Huddy and the rest wondered. Each man wished to know who the artist was who sharpened so keenly, taking no rest. Whoever it was knew his weapon.

Though a countryman hardly ever knows himself, he always knows his own village. When a soft gust of summer wind brings the sound of a laugh to his ears, as he is setting out a few plants, he knows well enough who the merry one is, and names him, as he disentangles the roots of the little cabbages. If the voice of a scolding woman is heard, he will smile and know that it must be Mrs. Briggs—for no one else can use words so plentifully.

"Damn 'ee for a little toad!" It's Mr. Huddy who thus reminds Winnie that he is her father—a reality that she sometimes forgets. Old Mrs. Dillar coughs; she spits, too. Her ways are human. All that is heard is known.

The sound of sharpening came from Card's cottage.

"But, surely," thought Mr. Dady, "John Death's scythe must be sharp now, sharp enough to cut any meadow grass in Dodder village!" Did the man wish to make the scythe's edge like a razor? Did he mean to mow Mr. Hayhoe's lawn?

Evidently Card's new tenant had been all his life a mower;

the song of the whetstone that he used was truly Catholic. Mr. Titball laid his hand upon his picture-book.

The sound continued. There was no waiting, no respite, no rest. "The man must needs have a wrist of iron," thought Mr. Dillar, "to continue so long."

But the Bullman Arms was not the only place either where the sharpening could be heard.

Mr. Hayhoe heard the sound too. He had taken up *The Watsons* for a few moments after Mrs. Hayhoe had gone to bed, intending to read for a little by the study window. Mr. Hayhoe closed his book and listened. The sound made a strange music; it became loud, then soft. It grew angry. Stone upon steel, one could almost see the sparks fly; wild fierce rage was in the quick clash—utter destruction. Then, though the sharpening continued, the sound was softened, while around it, in some green meadow, the larks were singing.

Again there came a steady rhythm, a continuous note, and in this sound Mr. Hayhoe recognized the quick passing of time, and the certainty of man's end.

Mr. Hayhoe sighed. His own going would not matter— though he hoped he would not have to lie a-bed too long before making his last journey—but some others had gone too early. There was his favourite—Jane. 'Twas enough to make any man sigh to think of her. Oh! why had she not been permitted to write a few more books! What good titles she could have found, what charming characters! . . .

Priscilla had not undressed; the summer airs crept in at the window, and she looked out of it.

Can a woman ever forget the sweet ways of her child? If only she could see him once more, only to remind her that he had once lived! Death, who had taken him, could he show him again? She would give all—her soul even, her promise of Heaven—to see him once more. Could she but meet Death, how she would court him! She would not mind what she did for his pleasure, so long as she obtained her wish.

The sound went on.

Sarah Bridle heard it in bed. A slight cramp in her leg made her think that the limb was broken. She was lying, not in Dodder, but midway between Darfur and Khartoum. She had been left behind in the desert. She was unable to move, the caravan had left her to die, and passed on. They were nearly out of sight. The night was come, the clear, white stars were her only companions. Her master had sold her to a new merchant, who had loaded her with his wares—rich silks of Damascus, the velvet of Tyre. They had loaded her too heavily. Others had drunk before her at the last pool; she could not bear so great a load; she staggered and fell.

The sound of the sharpening of the scythe became a laugh to her—the laughter of a hyena. The beast drew near to her, its laughter that at first was far away, came closer. Her gangrened limb began to rot. She knew the stench. She struggled to rise, but fell again upon the hard sand. More than one beast approached; she saw dark forms creep near. Each of them smelt corruption.

Sarah screamed in terror. . . .

At the Inn, the sound of the sharpening—that at first had merely interested—now began to excite anger.

Mr. Mere was angry that a man should work so long without yielding some profit to his employer. So much energy was being wasted, and all that the man was doing did not put one penny into the pocket of his master.

Would the sound never stop? Had the scythe that needed so much whetting been in use, more than half of Bridle's field had been mown. And then, at the last, "after all the sharpening," thought Mere, "should a wrong stroke come, the edge must be dulled, and all the labour wasted."

Dillar and Tom Huddy were angry too. Who paid this man? Some master—who perhaps was richer than Farmer Mere? Did Squire Lord employ him, whose workmen every one envied, and who, in harvest-time, used to put seven reapers into one field? Mr. Lord might have bid John come to him on the morrow, and he was getting ready his gear.

"Some folks be luckier than I," said Mr. Dillar. A simple fly flew into the room and settled upon the bar-table. Dady went softly to the fly, and killed it with his thumb.

Mr. Solly shuddered. A sound that went on so long was not likely to mean much good to him. Was all this whetting only the proper preparation for cutting down his nut-trees? Perhaps it was a good axe that was being sharpened, and no scythe. Some one might come in the night and destroy all his grove. Love has many servants. Who is not willing to obey his commands? But perhaps it was the god, himself, whom he heard. The naughty mischief-maker might, as likely as not, be sharpening his own arrows.

Mr. Solly, who was fond of stories, recollected the battle of Hastings. Because Love could not come to him nor shoot through his thick grove, would he aim his bow upwards into the sky? Solly had always heard that Love was a good shot. He might easily send up an arrow that would descend the chimney and transfix a poor man, even in bed. Solly thought he had better move his bed a little further from the fire-place.

Then the sound stopped.

Mr. Titball moved slowly to the side-table. The time had come to close the Inn. When the Inn was shut, it was not proper that the grand homes of the English gentry should be left open. Mr. Titball nursed the book lovingly. Again he placed it upon the table and covered it with a clean duster. Then he took down from a shelf a bottle of strong cordial waters, and filled a small glass. He held the glass respectfully above the great book, and drank to the homes of England and to their honoured possessors.

The proper ritual had been used; the Inn was closed.

Old Huddy and Mr. Dady were the first to leave. Dady looked about him in the lane; he wished to kill something. He expressed this desire to Tom Huddy, saying that, were he a bluebottle, he would know what to do. Tom Huddy moved a little to one side.

Dillar started to go to his cottage, then he changed his mind and walked in another direction. He had a wish to see an old woman named Bessy Hockey, who lived a little way out of Dodder upon the Shelton road. She had promised him a cabbage, he said.

Solly was startled when he heard that; he walked hurriedly in the opposite direction, to Madder. When he reached his nut-bushes, he believed he espied a little hole between two trees, through which a turnip might have scrambled. Mr. Solly unlocked his garden gate, went into his house in a hurry, and put a chair against the door.

Upon the chair he placed a Bible—to keep Love out.

XXII

The Old Fox Trapped

WHEN James Dawe set his hand to a plough, if he looked behind, 'twas to help himself forward. He was never one to allow an uncertain bargain to be made. If he caught a prey, he always bound it so that it could not escape.

He was not yet sure of Mr. Mere. Even with the evening already passed and the summer's night—a rather sombre one—closing in, Dawe had yet more to do. He must work, he must gain, for the time was short.

To him the sound of the sharpening of the scythe had said that there was no time to lose. The sound told him that he who gathered gold, and he who cast away gold, would soon be the same. There was one place to which all, the spendthrift and the hoarder, the cruel and the kind, were being hurried—the grave.

James Dawe's hearing was remarkably quick. He could hear a bat fly, he could hear a dog breathe, he could hear a hare scamper. He knew what every sound meant. Though life is a trackless forest, Dawes believed there was one sure path—the path of gain. The ants told him so, and the moles. The sound of the sharpening had said something more— that all gains have an end.

The end is sure: now is the time to trap and to take— now. The sharpener is at work, the stroke is being prepared. Before going to the bank near to the Inn, James Dawe had baited the trap—the bait was Susie.

If the treasures that he believed to be buried in Joe Bridle's field were to get safely into his hands, he must make haste to secure the field as his own. He had done much at the Inn, but not all. Mere's lusts were raised—Dawe had helped in that—but the sound of the sharpening had done more than he. The merry happenings of his youth were brought back to Mere's mind, but in a day or two he might grow cold again.

Once out in the lane, where the soft evening air moved slow—as though it prayed to the night to heal all sorrow—James Dawe touched Mere's shoulder. Mere turned to him.

Dawe, with a humble gesture, as if to acknowledge the hoped-for honour, invited Mere to sup at his cottage.

Before he had left to go out, he had told Susie what she must do. Susie prepared herself; she expected the company. She wore a summer frock, decorated with red poppies. Her father had commanded her to put all the food that there was in the house upon the table.

James Dawe brought Mr. Mere in. As soon as they were seated, the miser unlocked a cupboard and brought out a bottle of spirits. Mere looked at the bottle: he also looked at Susie. Both pleased him; he had a wish to taste each in turn. The old fox saw the bait, and it was good.

When supper was finished and the plates cleared away, Susie asked her father whether she might go to bed. James Dawe said "No." He wished to inflame Mr. Mere, and then he intended him to see the girl undress. Old men have their fancies. If Susie went upstairs too soon, Mere might not be ready for the treat.

Dawe filled the farmer's glass.

He wished Mr. Mere to think of only one thing. Beauty, he knew, can weaken a man. Beauty can be terrible as well as pleasing, for who does not know that the most lovely flowers cling ever to the edge of the deepest pool? If Mere saw Susie in that way, he might love her and be kind to her. Dawe meant to prevent the danger of that.

He smiled to himself, seeing in what manner Mere looked at Susie. Beauty, he knew, fades in your arms, it vanishes like a coloured cloud; it leaves nothing behind, it goes down alive into the pit.

Dawe had other matters than beauty to show his guest—the body of a woman. He wished to be sure of his prey. He had not expected the success that he had so easily obtained at the Inn. It had always been one of the marvels of the world to him that any man could give any kind of property—either money or land—for the purchase of a woman. His own mind—earthy and subtle—had ever thought of that kind of payment as an almost impossible matter to understand. Who, indeed, would give money to perform a mere carnal act that brought no gain—or give gold for a slave that could be had for nothing! Though astonished, he had seen in the world that which compelled him to believe that much money was bestowed in this way. Once let a wise man become a fool, he knew, and a certain kind of goods could be cried up to any price. Though the actual value of the thing enjoyed might be little, yet much could be added to the price by other considerations.

His own wife had refused; he had cursed and beat her. She had been a heavy weight to him—a mere consumer, no gain. He had never understood why she had ever objected to being sold. Such pastimes, he had been told, pleased the women. That she should hold back from such an advantageous proceeding made James Dawe doubt his wife's sanity. Who could refuse such a simple way of bringing money into the home? The men he brought to her laughed about her. She made a fine fuss about nothing, and so he used his strap to her, and she died in childbed. . . .

James Dawe was not the one to forget a lesson. Seeing how his daughter grew, he intended to make sure work with her. This time there would be no mistake. To make one's wife a whore is a pretty wish—'tis a change to the dullness of one's home. Though he had failed to do that, he had done something else—he had killed her. A woman who will not do what she is told must be punished. He would not kill Susie himself; he would marry her and leave the killing to her husband. James Dawe liked revenge.

He once again filled Mr. Mere's glass. Where the farmer's eyes went to he could see plainly. Susie moved uneasily; she went here and there in the room like a mouse upon whom a snake has fastened its small eyes.

She began to tidy the room, hoping that when he saw her thus busy, Mr. Mere would go. Mere only drank and looked.

After sitting beside the table for a while, Susie asked her father again whether she might go to bed. James Dawe nodded. He told her that he was going upstairs too, because he had the title-deeds of a certain farm in his bedroom that he wished to show Mr. Mere. Susie knew that her father never left a guest alone in the parlour. He had taken others to his bedroom. Susie hurried away; she was glad to escape the rich farmer's eyes.

James Dawe bid Mr. Mere empty his glass. Then both the men rose, mounted the seven stairs, and entered the miser's room. Although Susie had lit a candle for them, they did not take it.

Once in the bedroom, Dawe showed the spyhole to his companion.

Mr. Mere was interested in this procedure. James Dawe evidently intended to deal fairly. Mere always liked to see what it was he was buying. When the farmer bought a cow in the market, he took pleasure in viewing her, until he was sure what the beast's value was. This girl that he intended to purchase had a higher value than a cow. A good beast but added to his profit. Susie had another attraction. He recalled his old pranks to mind. He had been young in cruelty; he was now old in guile. He might reverse the process. He put his eye to the hole in the wall. . . .

Susie, glad to escape, had begun to undress herself in a leisurely fashion. She had only that very afternoon finished making for herself a new linen nightgown. The front of this garment she had embroidered with forget-me-nots.

When she was partly undressed, she took up the nightgown and examined it. She hoped it would fit. She had made it by guesswork, without a pattern. She completely unclothed herself. Then she held up the gown to put it on.

But she did not do so at once. She had finished her sewing in a hurry, and had forgotten to take out the tacking. She began diligently to take out the threads; this took longer than she expected. Presently the last thread was out: Susie slipped on the gown, sighed happily, and crept into bed, blowing out her candle.

While the light had burned, Mr. Mere had not kept his eyes off her; he now wished to have to do with her at once. He had no mind to wait till the wedding. James Dawe had expected this, and as soon as Mere withdrew his eye from the wall, he caught hold of him.

"Wait," he whispered, "till thee be married. 'Tis then thee mid bite and maul she's little toes. If thee attempt her now, 'twill all come to nothing; she'll jump out of window —Susie Dawe bain't no Daisy."

But Mere persisted; he must go to her. He pushed Dawe aside. The miser still clung to him; he showed a strength that surprised Mere. His arms were like iron bands. They struggled together in the darkness.

Soon Mere would have got the better of his adversary, thrown him aside, and rushed into Susie's room to cast himself upon her. Only outside in the lane some one laughed.

Mere went to the window. Being a rich man, he had always been a careful one too. He did not like to be made fun of. Whoever had laughed, had laughed at him. But who in Dodder would have dared to do that? The laugh in the lane had an odd quality about it; it was the laughter of one who in an argument knew that he would have the last word. There was no respect shown to Mr. Mere in that laugh.

For one moment Mr. Mere was afraid. Then he began to reason with himself, and decided that Susie could wait. If he persisted in this deed, perhaps Mr. Pix might hear the story, and Mr. Mere liked to be thought well of by the stewards of the Great.

But who was it that laughed? Mere believed himself to be the man to silence any impertinent watcher.

He opened the window and looked out into the lane. Some one was walking up and down in the still beauty of the summer's night. This man walked a little way, turned, and came back again. He stood and nodded at Mere. He was John Death.

XXIII

Winnie Huddy Runs a Race

WHAT we expect does not always happen. Sometimes a holiday, instead of pleasing a man, makes him restless.

The pleasure-seeker hopes to be happy, amusing himself, but finds that he cannot sleep at night. This, or something else, will happen to him to make him discontented. In a little while he will wish himself back at his work. If he be a writer, he will stare gloomily into a bookshop, and curse all authorship. If he is an engineer, he will peep into the dingy gates of a foundry and envy the doorkeeper—a large black spider. If he is a Member of Parliament, he will read Gladstone's speeches.

John Death was a mower, and so—feeling a little out of sorts—he had spent the evening whetting his scythe. When he had finished doing that he did not wish to go to bed. The thought of Susie Dawe kept him from sleeping. Though the hour was late, he went to her cottage and overheard what was going on there. That others, as well as himself, should wish for Susie amused John, and so he laughed.

When Mere left James Dawe's cottage, Death saw him go, but even then John did not return home, for he thought he would like to walk over Madder Hill.

A man upon a holiday is a pryer. When he goes to any part of the country that is new to him, he will pry about and see all he can. He will even peep sometimes where he has no business to look. John had now given his parchment up for lost, and he had already begun to look for other matters of interest. Love was one of them, but he wondered why he thought so much of Susie.

In the way of his trade, he had seen a large number of young women, though—being taken up with other doings than lovemaking—he had not regarded them. Now, having nothing to do, he felt differently. Idleness breeds love. John had to make the best of it, and the best to be made was Susie. Ever since he had seen her name written in Bridle's field he had loved her. At first—for a mere jest, perhaps—he had set the image of her in his heart, but now he longed wholly to possess her.

He laughed at himself for being so serious, and Love laughed at him too.

"Perhaps," he thought, "if I went for a night-walk, I should not feel so foolish." He might forget Susie if he looked at the stars.

John Death slowly climbed Madder Hill, from the summit of which he looked down upon Madder village. The village was utterly quiet and deserted, and upon the low meadows near there lay a white mist.

Death descended the hill and entered Madder. He went to the green and stood upon a stone that was there. And there he felt himself to be a lonely thing. Who had cared for him? Who had ever loved him? Many had called him, many had made a sudden use of his terrible power, but who had loved him?

Could he ever be really loved? He stood there alone. All Madder was silent. No one likes to be sad, and John Death least of all. The weight of his loneliness troubled him; he must rid himself of the burden. He must amuse himself somehow. He must walk off and seek some entertainment.

A summer's night is never really dark, and John was able to look about him quite easily. Near to the village church there was a little cottage surrounded by a thick grove of nut-bushes. This grove attracted John's attention. What did it hide?

With many another prying gentleman, Death was extremely inquisitive. If he came upon any mystery, he wished to probe it to see what it contained. He liked to see to the bottom. From the look of the grove he concluded that the nut-trees had been planted to keep some one out. Death smiled to himself, and looked around him for some place in which to hide.

Near to the cottage there was a low wall, made of the rough, local stone, and easy to climb. Death, who does not always wish to be seen, hid behind the wall, peeped through a crevice, and examined the grove of nut-bushes. Such a protection, he assured himself, must have been grown there for some important purpose. Evidently the grove was planted to keep the owner safe. Safe from whom? Death was vain. Like many another important person, he considered that he was the one that everybody ought to think about. And when he saw how thick the nut-bushes were, he believed that they had been planted on purpose to keep him away. He believed that he, alone, was the one who should be feared by all mortal men, and why not, then, by Mr. Solly?

But Death soon saw that he was wrong. The night wind brought the sound of the Shelton church clock. The clock struck twelve.

Some one came by from Dodder, a slight figure, a nymph of the night—a child.

Earlier in the evening the sound that John had made when he whetted his scythe awakened Winnie Huddy. The sound made Winnie restless; she tried to go to sleep, but she could not. She took up the rag doll who always slept with her, and pinched its nose.

"I be going out," she said, "and thee must mind house time I be gone. I be going to see how wold Solly's nuts do grow."

Winnie slipped on her clothes and her shoes, and ran out. As she went downstairs she heard Daisy sigh and old Huddy snore. Besides seeing how the nuts were forming, Winnie had something else in her mind that she meant to do.

She had been told by Susie Dawe that Mr. Solly had grown the nut-bushes to keep out Love. Winnie did not know who Love was, but she thought it would be amusing to pretend to be Love, to creep into the grove and frighten Mr. Solly. Besides she regarded her doll as a baby, who ought to have a father. And a fine father, she knew, Mr. Solly would be, with all his nuts to give away. There was nothing Winnie liked to do better than to frighten a man.

On Madder Hill she had a little fright herself, that she did not expect. As she went by a lonely thorn-bush, she thought that some one stood in its shadow—for the summer moon, though low down, threw a shadow. Winnie thought that a man stood there—Mr. Jar, the tinker.

The sight of him made Winnie run the faster; she skipped down the hill like a rabbit, and soon came to Solly's house. She waited a little, resting on one foot and then upon the other, wondering what to do. She was astonished at the size and thickness of Mr. Solly's nut-bushes. They were as well grown as her father's beard. Behind all those trees Mr. Solly was probably fast asleep. She wondered what Mr. Solly had eaten for his supper. If he was going to be the father of her doll, she supposed that he must also become her own husband. Perhaps he had supped on bread and milk. Such a diet, Winnie believed, was proper for husbands. She would have one basin and Mr. Solly another.

Winnie stood on one leg and took off a shoe. She took

out a little stone from the shoe. She shivered and looked at the wall, then she turned to Mr. Solly's grove and prowled around the place, seeking for an entrance. She crept silently like a young panther. Coming to the gate, she tried to open it; the gate was fast locked. She shook it sturdily, but it would not open. She could neither get through the gate nor yet climb over it.

She walked round the grove again, peeping everywhere, and stepping cautiously upon the grass, that was soaked in dew. Going round the third time, she saw a little hole between two nut-trees, through which she thought she might creep. Her wish was to crawl in there, find a way through a window into Mr. Solly's house, run up to his bedroom, and shout "Camel" into his ear. That was what Winnie wished to do to Mr. Solly, because she had always known his politeness to Miss Bridle.

Winnie looked again at the small hole in the nut hedge. She had heard it said that where your head can go your body can follow; she thought she could easily creep through the hole.

She was about to make the attempt when Death leaped over the wall, dislodging a stone, that fell with a clatter. No sooner was he safe over than he rushed upon Winnie.

He was very angry because his pride was hurt. He had thought that the wall of nuts had been grown to keep him out, and, behold, it was only Love that Mr. Solly feared. Death had never been so slighted. He knew himself to be the one who ought to be feared, but now he saw that it was some one else who was dreaded. John felt the insult most keenly. Unfortunately it was not possible for him to revenge himself at once upon Mr. Solly. There was only one way for Death to do that—to Unclay this man—but no order had come.

To be merely slighted was not the worst of it. Death had a private fear of his own. He always felt ashamed when any one spoke kindly of him, or said they liked him. If Solly feared Love so much, he might feel that Death was his friend. And when any man felt like that, Death was ashamed.

To calm his anger, John wanted Winnie. He would be the cat and she the mouse. He would pounce upon her and amuse himself for a little. He would soon cure her of her wanton fancies. But the fall of the stone had alarmed Winnie, and when Death grabbed at her, she jumped aside. Then she ran away. Winnie was a light child and could run like a fawn. John Death was hampered by his shoes; they had always pinched him a little.

A dead man's shoes do not always fit. The feet that hung from the tree in Merly Wood, from whence the Sunday shoes had been taken, were smaller than John's. And, run as fast as he could, he did not overtake Winnie as soon as he expected. She was even able to get a little ahead of him, and began to climb Madder Hill, her strong little legs shining in the moonlight.

Had Winnie shown any fear at all, or relaxed her pace for a moment, John would have caught her. But Winnie only thought of the whole matter as a fine game. She had recognized John when he leaped over the wall, and thought that he had come to Madder to court Nancy Trim, and was only running after her for fun because the other young lady had gone to bed.

But Death meant business; just then he was in no mood to be played with. Had Winnie knelt to him and begged him to let her alone, he might have done so, but to run off so fast provoked his wrath. He would catch her for his sport, and ill-use her on the cold Madder Hill. After that he would cut her throat with a sharp flint.

There is always a mischief ready for an idle hand. The loss of his proper employment had made John restless and ill at ease. He had never been tormented by any one as he had been by Miss Winnie. She never tired of making game of him. When he walked down the Dodder lane, she mimicked his manners. And when he looked for his lost parchment, she told him it was hid under Mrs. Moggs's skirts, and ran away laughing.

As they went over Madder Hill, Death gained upon Winnie; the steep climb took her breath away. She panted and could hardly run, and even forgot to go a little out of her way to avoid Tinker Jar. Jar was still there, standing in the shadow of the bush. And, as Winnie passed by, she thought that Jar touched her.

She ran now as well as ever; she even leaped and skipped, and in a few moments reached her home.

Upon the summit of Madder Hill, near to the thorn-bush, Death's steps were stayed.

XXIV

Mr. Hayhoe Receives a Command

A QUEEN of England once said, when she signed an important document, that then she learned for the first time that the laws of men were very different from the laws of God. . . .

The spring had become summer, and Mr. Hayhoe had not lived in Dodder for many weeks before he learned that the will of Lord Bullman towards his dependants and the will of God Almighty to his human family were not very closely connected. Nor was the conduct of these two noble ones— though Mr. Titball considered the one as good as the other —always similar in purpose.

Upon some points, however, their united outlook may be observed to be the same, for it is said of the Almighty that to Him all the nations of the earth, except that which is His chosen, are as nothing, and Lord Bullman regarded himself as being just as superior to all others of the Children of Adam.

God enjoys goodness, Lord Bullman liked his own way, and Mr. Hayhoe was always fond of dripping.

Ever since Mr. Hayhoe had been a little boy he had liked dripping, preferring it, with pepper and salt, to the best butter. But he never troubled himself to learn what dripping was or where it came from. Had any one asked him this question, he would have replied innocently that he believed dripping was a kind of soft paste made of boiled beans.

Had he been laughed at for saying so, Mr. Hayhoe would

not have been in the least surprised. He had always regarded himself as a very stupid man. To him the greatest wonder of his life had been that he had managed to pass his final examination at a Theological College; and, indeed, it was only a huge love of the Gospels that could ever have made him get a little Greek—enough to satisfy the examiners that he could pray with a sinner. But, though no one could have been more astonished than Mr. Hayhoe was when he got through, yet had he but known how the Bishop of Sarum revered him when he read his papers, and indeed no truly pious examiner could have done otherwise, he would have been more astonished than ever.

Mr. Hayhoe had ridden an Ass, then a Mule, then an Ass again. He had been a curate, then a vicar, then a curate again. When he was the vicar of Maids Madder, he bought golden ware for the Holy Altar. This purchase ruined him. He had given all to God, and his creditors—having such a good example to follow—took all from him. Becoming a bankrupt, he was forced to leave his living, for he was troubled at what people said about him, and became a curate again, doing casual duty—and so came to be employed at Dodder.

He lodged at Shelton, where his son died. One day, looking out of his window, he saw Farmer Lord's great bull—tied by ropes—being led by to market. The huge beast, that every one said was extremely fierce and terrible, looked as docile as a lamb.

This sight gave Mr. Hayhoe courage; he decided to go the next day and ask Lord Bullman for the living of Dodder. He went bravely and, finding my lord busy about a gate, he opened it for him, and was promised the living as a reward.

Though hardly a moment passed without Mr. Hayhoe thinking happily that Dodder was his own, yet Lord Bullman—as soon as he had given him the living—forgot all about his promise. He had his wife and the gout, and they were enough for him to think of.

These two often troubled him, and there were other things that troubled him too. His first disappointment came when he married. Before that day, he had always been given the rightful honour that he knew he deserved. But his wife, alas, gave him no honour at all; she thought him a great fool. She had promised to obey him and she never did so. She taught her children to laugh at him when he told fine tales at breakfast.

He had to submit to such treatment, but he did not enjoy it. Whenever he went to bed, he told himself that the laws of the country were sadly out of order. He was deprived of his rights; he could not even run into his own kitchen and cry "privilege!"

But for all that, Lord Bullman had much to boast of, while Mr. Hayhoe had not anything. Christ, perhaps—but what coat of arms had ever Jesus to wear? When was He seen, oddly dressed, upon a first of September, striding, with a couple of spaniels at his heels, after the partridges? Did He ever lord it finely over His brother magistrates at the Quarter Sessions, or cough and guffaw as He stept out of a great car at the hustings?

Mr. Hayhoe was peculiar. Besides honouring Jesus and eating dripping for breakfast, he loved his wife. And Priscilla loved him too.

At breakfast a good man is generally hungry; when he sees the table laid, he is glad. When there is toast, he knows that his wife is a kind woman. If the tea tastes pleasantly, he knows that God loves him. The last supper upon the earth is always a sad meal; the first breakfast in Heaven will be happier.

At breakfast a good man is pleased, but a son of Belial is plagued and tormented. Because he does not know where true joy is to be found, he has no proper appetite. He cannot eat even little trout patiently. He is afraid of the bones; he is troubled by God. He moves his legs uneasily, and exclaims that the coffee is burnt. He smells the bread and finds it musty. He looks for a cigarette, but God has hidden the packet. He sits down again, catches his coat in the chair, and bursts a button. His mind is troubled by his sins: there is a dead bee in the honeycomb.

Within Mr. Hayhoe all was well; it was only from without that he was sometimes a little tormented. The Manor Farm was near the church, and the church was near the Vicarage. Sometimes at breakfast Mr. Hayhoe would hear the ugly growl of Mr. Mere's fierce dog, coming from the farmer's yard. That sound proved only too surely that there was evil in the world—cruelty. The dog had a nasty bark. One day, Mr. Hayhoe thought, it would do some one a mischief.

If the farmer saw a trespasser in his fields, he would send the dog after him. Once Mr. Hayhoe heard the farmer shout at his dog and send him after John Death, who had walked into Grange Mead, looking for his parchment.

Mr. Hayhoe, who feared for his friend, hastily put on his boots, without tying the laces, and hurried off to the field to prevent John being bitten. He never thought for one moment that the dog might bite him instead of John. He climbed the gate into the field—and stopped suddenly. The dog was near to Death, but did not touch him; it only raised its nose in the air and howled dismally. Then the beast cowered down, turned, and ran off. . . .

Priscilla Hayhoe liked strong tea, but she knew that she

ought never to make the tea strong, because of the extravagance. If she ever put an extra spoonful into the pot, something unlucky always happened. After such an act a sure retribution would follow.

But, even with this knowledge, Mrs. Hayhoe would sometimes pop in an extra spoonful. When she did so, she blushed and tried to hide from her sin. In order that the black look of her tea might not accuse her, she put more milk into her cup. Or else she tried to pretend that by long standing the tea had become a very dark colour. She would wonder if Mr. Hayhoe had seen. She believed that he knew all her funny ways, and yet in reality he knew none of them.

One morning Mr. Hayhoe was eating his bread and dripping with a good appetite, and Priscilla had put in one more spoonful of tea than usual, when the postman came.

Priscilla went to open the door to him. He was an old postman; his name was Mr. Potter, and he was a loyal churchman. He looked at Priscilla with concern, as though he knew the contents of the letter that he handed to her. Priscilla gave the letter to her husband, who read it at once.

Though the letter only came from the agent's office, there was printed upon the envelope the Bullman arms. The letter was from Mr. Pix, who demanded that old Huddy, together with his two daughters, should be turned into the road. The cottage belonged to the glebe, and Mr. Huddy, who had once been gardener, rented it off the incumbent. Mr. Hayhoe had never received any rent, and he had never asked for any.

Certain persons in Dodder had hinted that there might be a reason for this leniency. But the truth of the matter was that Mr. Hayhoe had often paid rent himself, and knew how unpleasant it was to part with his money to a landlord. There was another reason, too, that prevented him from accepting what was due to him; he feared that some of the money might be the wages of sin.

According to law, the Huddys need not go, but a law, made in London, does not always reach country places. A new-made law is a bad traveller; it stays a while to drink with the Mayor of Maidenbridge, and forgets the villages. In country places the powers that rule have older manners.

Lord Bullman expected his orders to be obeyed. And this time he gave a reason. "Daisy Huddy," wrote Mr. Pix, "is known to be a whore"—Mr. Pix underlined the word in red ink—"and she even hangs a scarlet thread out of her window as a sign of her trade."

Mr. Hayhoe sighed deeply and finished his bread and dripping. Priscilla sighed too, and, looked at the teapot. She wished that God wasn't quite so quick to notice little faults. She knew she had done wrong; she ought never to have smelt the tea in the caddy, for it was the scent of the tea that had tempted her to put in more. She knew it was all her fault that the letter had come.

"Alas!" cried Mr. Hayhoe, rising and looking out through the open window into the garden, "what good do these sweet summer airs do to unforgiving men? The hearts of men are exactly the same in these kind, warm days as they are in the coldest winter ones. To see before him a field of buttercups cannot melt the heart of a Lord Bullman."

"But it may soften him," suggested Priscilla.

"Alas!" exclaimed Mr. Hayhoe, "what has Daisy done, what has Winnie done, to be turned into the road? In order to earn a little money Daisy has sinned deeply, though every one says that it is only a very little money that Mr. Mere gives her. Daisy once served at Lord Bullman's mansion. What did she learn there? But all this trouble has come because I read to her the book of Joshua. So it is I that am to blame."

"Mrs. Moggs did hint to me yesterday that you had something to do with it," observed Priscilla innocently.

"Ought I to obey Lord Bullman?" cried Mr. Hayhoe. "Wouldn't it do better service for God, to allow Daisy to stay where she is, to forget the Bible, and to learn a new and more chaste manner of earning her living?

"My dear," said Mr. Hayhoe, who was very much troubled, "surely I cannot obey my lord in this matter. I am aware that, as the lay rector here, he is in authority over me."

"Ask God what you had better do," said Priscilla.

Mr. Hayhoe knelt, with his head near to the unlucky tea-pot, and closed his eyes. He remained thus for ten minutes. Then he arose and looked for a sign.

Beside the dripping-pot, there lay a dainty, white flower. What God had placed near to him, it was not for Lord Bullman to send away.

"Though Mr. Titball may not think so," cried Mr. Hayhoe, "there is One above Who is greater than a baron."

"There is, indeed," said Mrs. Hayhoe, softly putting the tea-caddy away, "and I am sure you are right in keeping the Huddys near to you. As Daisy is a sinner, she is in the greater need of our care and assistance. Were she sent out of her home, she might find a worse; and there is no village in the world as good as Dodder for hemming a nightgown."

"And none better," cried Mr. Hayhoe, "for reading *Pride and Prejudice* aloud. I will begin this evening."

"And I," said Priscilla, gladly, "will find a sheet for Daisy to darn."

XXV

This Time Mr. Hayhoe Looks

To RECEIVE word that an evil attempt is being made to hamper God's mercy, though it may make a good man sad for a moment, does not depress him for long.

Mr. Hayhoe attended to his duties during that day in a happy manner. He had only to do what God told him—and he knew what that was—and all would be well. Who would not wish—as soon as Mrs. Bennet was mentioned—to hear more of her? In every good book a light shines, that compels the reader to be joyful.

When Mr. Hayhoe thought of changing Daisy from a troubled, into a merry girl, he was glad. In sin there is much dolour, in fair virtue there is happiness. To consider what he might do for Daisy pleased Mr. Hayhoe, but when he thought of his own affairs at Dodder, he became sad again.

Whenever he had gone to labour in any new cure, he had always had the misfortune to fall out with the great. No one who had great riches—either invested money or landed property—had ever liked him. He was always at a loss to know why. It was not that he ever expected to be liked for what he was himself. He thought of himself only as a poor clergyman—a conservative, as all churchlovers are. Perhaps it was that which did not please the gentry. They may not have liked so timid a man agreeing with them that old ways of peaceful meditation are better than modern noise and clamour. Perhaps they thought that a poor clergyman should be a watchdog in a kennel—a follower of Mr. Wilkes, a barking Whig.

Sometimes Mr. Hayhoe thought that it might be his sermons that offended. When he preached about a Bible virgin, the Squire always frowned, and if he said much about Jesus, Farmer Mere spat in his pew.

Mr. Hayhoe always tried to behave correctly; he endeavoured to dress as well as he could afford. He spoke respectfully to the well-to-do, and tried always to speak to them so that they might understand what he said. He would talk about bullocks to a farmer, and sometimes he would mention dung or land-tax. To a landlord he would talk about the poor laws, the beauty of gorse blooms, and the different ways of making a field gate.

And what harm could there be in such subjects of conversation, and yet no man in possession of a decent income had ever liked Mr. Hayhoe! . . .

Tea-time came. In her little parlour, Mrs. Moggs's kettle was singing, a sound that she liked far better than a thrush's song. The work of that day was over, and Mr. Hayhoe set out to visit Daisy. When last he had visited her, he had only read the Bible, and never looked at her. That was before he knew what Daisy did, and when he had finished reading she was gone upstairs, and he went away too.

The best of men—be he a great saint, or the chief of sinners—must have, if he be a man, a little trepidation in his heart when he ventures to pay a visit to a harlot. Even a prime minister who goes to see—for the good and welfare of the nation—a poor wanton, goes to her with a certain trembling of the heart and a feeling of compassion, that he never carries with him into the Houses of Parliament.

Mr. Hayhoe hoped to do Daisy good. He could trust himself, of course. But so innocent was he that, though he had met a number of ladies in one way or another—and more than one who held high positions in Society—yet he had never, as far as he knew, met a whore. And now he could not but wonder how such a sad creature would look.

Would her frock be dusty, and her hair tumbled? Would she stare at him like a piccaninny? What would she say?

Though he was not aware of it, the time that Mr. Hayhoe had chosen for his visit was most unfortunate. Had he taken the trouble to inquire in the village, he would have been told that the hour chosen by him to see Daisy coincided with the time that Mr. Mere used to go to her.

All unknowing as to this, Mr. Hayhoe stepped gladly along the street, with a book in his pocket. In front of Daisy's door, in the middle of the lane, he found Mr. Mere. Mr. Hayhoe hesitated, walked on a little, hesitated again, and stood still.

Farmer Mere approached Daisy's door, and kicked at it with his iron-shod boot. He spat in the lane and swore terribly. Then he turned to Mr. Hayhoe.

"Ha! ha!" he shouted, "here he comes, the old dog-fox, that vixen do wait for. But door be locked as well for thee as for me, and 'tis best thee go and find another doe to clip and cuddle. Here be a fine treatment of the people's warden, that another man, behind locked door, should be milking me bought heifer. And bain't I come to have a taste of she too?"

The farmer's words set Mr. Hayhoe a-wondering. What was Mr. Mere? He looked at him earnestly. He appeared to be human, but appearances—Mr. Hayhoe knew—are sometimes deceptive.

"Perhaps," thought Mr. Hayhoe, "he may not be a man at all, but only a shape like one." Mr. Hayhoe had once taken brown boot-polish to be lemon cheese. Was Mr. Mere no man at all, but an odd kind of hyena? There was already a camel in the village, and so there might be a hyena too! Perhaps, in this country, they would walk about in the daytime and wear boots. Strange things are often seen. Mr. Mere was born of a woman, but so are many other monsters.

"But until he bites my head off," thought Mr. Hayhoe, "I must still consider him as a man."

Mr. Mere cursed obscenely and spat.

"I had hoped," said Mr. Hayhoe, addressing the farmer, in quiet tones, though forgetting for the moment to mention a bullock, "that you, Mr. Mere, had intended to marry Daisy Huddy. I promise you that she can count very well all small monies, she can be polite and kind too, and though she sits in church where I cannot see her, I went once to her home. I never looked at her, but I believe she is not uncomely. I am not sure, I think that once I saw her going towards Mrs. Moggs's shop to post a letter. She was a long way off, but she seemed to walk like a Christian woman who deserves a husband. And you, Mr. Mere, should not think yourself—though you possess so much land and so many pigs —a superior being to poor Daisy, who is, I fear, a creature of sorrow."

"Let me get at she," shouted Mere. "I'll soon know what creature she be."

"She is a poor injured maid," sighed Mr. Hayhoe.

Mr. Mere laughed loudly.

"I believe I know what she be as well as thee do," he replied. "But who be in there wi' she, tell me that, Mr. Hayhoe?"

"Her father, or it may be little Winnie," answered Mr. Hayhoe, "though I believe at this time in the evening Mr. Huddy usually goes to the Inn, but I will knock at the door and inquire if I may enter."

Mr. Hayhoe went by the farmer and knocked softly at

Daisy's door. The door was opened to him at once, but as soon as he was inside the cottage, it was closed and locked again.

Every pious and God-loving man is secretly afraid of a girl, and would, if it were possible, avoid being left alone in a young woman's company. For what man can tell—and certainly no clergyman—what will happen, when one is forced to be alone with a maid? The youthful lady may be quiet enough at first, and intent on filling a pincushion with bran. She will talk graciously of the places she has seen, of the fine people she knows, and of how many times in her life she has been a bridesmaid. She may even sit decently for a while, as well as talk modestly. But presently she will spill some of the bran and then her demeanour will change. She will throw down the pincushion and then— A kind and wise man will pick it up.

It is sometimes awkward to be God's servant, but, as such, Mr. Hayhoe had sought to do his duty. When he found himself in the low cottage room, he knew that this time he must look at Daisy. He could not avoid her now. He carried no Bible today, but another book in his pocket. Yes, there she was, standing before him in the dim light; she even curtseyed.

Mr. Hayhoe was extremely surprised. He certainly expected to see something quite different—a sort of soiled harsh thing, a wild-eyed strumpet. Or a Madam Bubble, scented and odious. But what he saw was a young girl, pretty and demure, with yielding frightened eyes, and with hair only a little darker than her sister Winnie's, that was almost straw-coloured. Mr. Hayhoe looked at her for a moment, and then quickly looked away.

He thrust his hand into his pocket and found *Pride and Prejudice*. When he read to Daisy he knew that he would

have to keep his eyes fixed upon the book, as he had with the
Bible. "Will Jane protect me," asked Mr. Hayhoe of his
heart, "if God is absent? I must sit near the window when I
read."

Mr. Hayhoe gazed nervously about the room, and saw
John Death. Never had he been better pleased at the sight
of another man. Death was pleased, too, and shook Mr.
Hayhoe's hand warmly.

"I am still looking for my lost property," said John
amiably, "and I am still upon a holiday. You know what
women are?"

"I only know Priscilla," replied Mr. Hayhoe.

Death smiled.

"A woman does not always know what she is herself," he
said. "Miss Bridle is very much mistaken when she thinks
herself a camel, and our pretty Daisy is quite in the wrong
when she calls herself a wicked sinner."

"She should never think that," said Mr. Hayhoe, looking
at Daisy.

"Since I have lived in Dodder," observed Death, "I have
become an antiquarian."

Daisy blushed; all long words had but one meaning for
her.

She shook her head slyly at Death.

"Oh, just you fancy," said Daisy to Mr. Hayhoe, "John
isn't in the least afraid of Mr. Mere—and look what he has
given me!"

She showed Mr. Hayhoe a golden bangle, of very old and
curious workmanship. Mr. Hayhoe looked at Death mournfully.

"Of course she would not take it for nothing," said John,
gaily.

"Oh, but that was nothing," laughed Daisy. "And I never

knew I could get so much given to me—I mean so pretty a thing—for doing so little, and I pleased John so well, that he said my body was like a dove's breast."

Mr. Hayhoe looked out of the window.

"It was only kind to show Daisy," observed Death, "that there are happier usages in love's doings than that damned farmer Mere has ever shown to her."

"How do you know that Farmer Mere is damned?" inquired Mr. Hayhoe.

"I met some one walking on Madder Hill who told me so," replied Death.

"Perhaps you mean Tinker Jar," said Mr. Hayhoe.

Death nodded.

"I have come to make Daisy happy, too," cried Mr. Hayhoe. Death bowed. He went to the stairway door, that he opened widely. Mr. Hayhoe turned very red.

"Oh!" he cried, "you mistake my meaning, John. I only meant that I would make Daisy happy by reading a book to her."

"Ah!" said Death. "If that is so, then I will certainly stay and listen, for I believe that you have Keats' Odes in your pocket. He's a fine poet and knows whom to praise when he listens in a darkening evening to the song of a nightingale. And now, after Daisy and I have been so happy in one another's company, to hear a good poem read will give us both pleasure."

Mr. Hayhoe shook his head doubtfully. He was uncertain what to say. He ought, he supposed, to reprove John for having had to do with the girl. He was extremely surprised at the behaviour of his friend; he had never expected him to act so naughtily. But as Mr. Hayhoe was a rural clergyman and knew country habits, he thought that Death might only have been questioning Daisy—as timid lovers do sometimes

—about nature's mysteries. Perhaps they would marry. If the idea of a wedding was in John's mind, an ill-timed rebuke would be very much out of place, and Daisy was certainly not hated by John as Tamar had been by Ammon— and so a marriage might come of it.

That was Mr. Hayhoe's hope. He had always been so happy with Priscilla, and even the death of their little son had brought them nearer to one another. If Mr. Mere would not take Daisy, why should not John have her?

A baby to be baptized rejoiced the heart of Mr. Hayhoe. He knew that there could not be too many Christians in the world. He enjoyed saying "Bo!" to an infant in the vestry after a service, and when the tiny thing was a girl, she always winked at him. Then he would let her hold his little finger.

"Perhaps," thought Mr. Hayhoe, "Daisy may be the means of keeping Death in Dodder."

John had pleased Mr. Hayhoe so well that he did not wish to part with him. If Death stayed in Dodder, and was always near, Mr. Hayhoe believed that his own life would be very happy. Mr. Hayhoe had never been in the least nervous with John. Often when he had talked with him he discovered that John thought much as he did upon most subjects. He did not believe that so kind a man as John could hurt the heart of any girl, unless he bound it up with marriage lines. John could sharpen a scythe, and no doubt he could mow a field. And who, indeed, was most to blame for Death's being guided to Daisy's bedroom by the scarlet thread? Why, he himself. Who had read the Bible to her? Mr. Hayhoe. His conscience smote him very sore. It was he who had been unkind to Daisy, and John only kind.

"But it is certainly queer," considered Mr. Hayhoe, "how I can never, even in circumstances that look a little unholy, think anything but good of John. I do not believe that he could act very ill. Though his conduct has shocked me, yet I cannot help thinking as well of him as I have always thought."

Mr. Hayhoe sat beside Death upon the sofa. He forgot that he had come to the cottage to read to Daisy. He might have been alone with Death, for he thought only of him. They talked happily together. And moments went by.

XXVI

A Dead Rat

"Is it not strange," observed Mr. Hayhoe, "that our dissolution, which is approved and predestined by God—Who must know what is good for us—is so rarely agreed to by mortal man?"

"It is most curious," observed Death.

"Though it is hard," said Mr. Hayhoe, "to find a modern poet who is not in love with destruction."

"Their verses certainly should be," answered Death dryly, "for I only know one of them who writes prettily, and that's a woman."

Mr. Hayhoe was about to reply, when a horse galloped down the lane, followed by another, and both stopped at the cottage door. Voices were heard outside, a command was given by one man to another to take care of his beast. Then there came a great knocking at the door. Daisy Huddy peeped timidly out of the window to see who was there. She turned fearfully to Mr. Hayhoe.

"It's Lord Bullman," she cried out, "and he's pulling at the scarlet thread."

"He only thinks it's the bell-rope," said Death.

"Ah, what ever can I do?" sobbed Daisy. "He looks so angry."

"Why," said Mr. Hayhoe, "I should open the door to him, or else he will break it down, for evidently he does not wish to be noticed standing in the street."

"Every one is looking at him," observed John, who stood near to the window.

"He won't want to go upstairs, will he?" sighed Daisy, "if I let him in?" Then, drying her eyes, she said: "Is a lord like the others?"

"Exactly," replied John, "only a little more serious in a bedroom."

Daisy, who was reassured, opened the door. Lord Bullman strode in; he had the appearance of a very fine game-cock, if one may imagine such a fowl dressed in suitable clothes for riding, and ready to cry "Halloo!" instead of to crow, and ready enough, too, to swagger and lord it upon a fair dunghill—and so we have the man.

Lord Bullman looked at Daisy, and she regarded him in return a little wonderingly. Her visitor appeared to be almost as surprised at her simple and childlike appearance as Mr. Hayhoe had been, for she looked too young a thing to be as hardened in sin as Mr. Pix had affirmed.

But Lord Bullman was only shamed for a very little while by Daisy's looks; he was no hedge-priest, as Mr. Hayhoe was, to be abashed by a mere girl, who seemed so innocent. He had seen that kind of thing before; he was a magistrate, whose duties made him stern.

He coughed, and began to chide her. He accused her of naughtiness, of all idle wickedness. He said that, as the lord of the manor and lay rector, it was his bounden duty to clear the village of such drabs as she, who pollute the body politic.

"And why don't you have," he shouted, "a bell that rings?"

"The men in the story knew what it meant," sobbed Daisy.

He told her to pack, and go. But having once said that, he began to observe her more kindly.

"Do tell me," he inquired in a milder tone, "the meaning

of the scarlet thread that you hang out of the window? I pulled it, but nothing happened."

"Don't you read the Bible?" asked Daisy in astonishment, having gained a little confidence now that Lord Bullman seemed kinder.

Lord Bullman looked down.

"Only when I can't find a fox," he said. "Then I read a verse or two and hope to have better luck next day—but what is the thread tied to, my dear?"

"To my bed," replied Daisy.

Lord Bullman stepped towards the stairway door.

The evening was dull, and the cottage parlour was duller still. Lord Bullman had not so far seen either John Death or Mr. Hayhoe, who sat silent upon the sofa in a dark corner. But no sooner did Lord Bullman go to the stairway door than Death laughed. Mr. Hayhoe rose hurriedly.

"My lord," he said, "I assure you that this young woman is upon the highroad to repentance. She has already begun to make amends for her sins by her willingness to darn my socks. And when I suggested reading to her aloud, her only stipulation was that the book I read should be a novel, and contain more than one wedding. And surely that desire alone shows a fine wish to lead a new life."

Lord Bullman stared from Death to Mr. Hayhoe.

"I am sorry to see you here, sir," he said, addressing the clergyman, "you, to whom I thought of giving the living of Dodder, I find in the house of a prostitute."

"I only came to read to her," answered Mr. Hayhoe simply.

"Out of a common book, I fear," said my lord, with a wink.

Mr. Hayhoe bowed to the company, wished Daisy good night, opened the street door, and withdrew.

Lord Bullman glared fiercely at Death.

"Why don't you go too?" he asked him angrily.

"Because," answered Death, "I prefer to stay here."

Daisy fled upstairs; she did not like to see men quarrel. Lord Bullman laid hold of Death by the shoulder, intending to force him into the street. But he had hardly touched him before he loosed him again. Lord Bullman shuddered.

A curious scent filled the room—a scent not altogether unknown to humankind—the smell of corruption. The odour had risen slowly, as the mist used to rise from Joe Bridle's pond.

At first it was but a faint, sweet smell, that is often dreamed of, and resembled slightly the scent of dead flowers that have remained long in water that has not been changed. At first the scent might have been but the mere stuffiness of a cottage room in summer, where the windows are shut and the thatch rests heavily upon the roof. But soon the smell became more noticeable. The atmosphere of the parlour became horrible; a stench rose up.

Lord Bullman moved away from Death.

"Who is dead here?" he asked angrily. "Why did you not tell me there is a corpse upstairs? Is old Huddy dead?"

"Step up and see for yourself," replied Death.

The dread smell increased.

Lord Bullman opened the street door and hurried out. He mounted the horse his servant held, and galloped away.

"It's only a dead rat," Death called after him.

XXVII

Susie Dawe

SUSIE DAWE had always been obedient to her father. Ever since she could remember, a word from him had been a law to her. Whatever a man may be outside, he is always the moving power in a country cottage; though he is but a poor sort of god, worship, of a kind, is always given to him.

Susie would never have dared to contradict or to dispute the will of her father. In a girl's way, she even loved him. He had made her life; he had digged into a pit, and had drawn out this girl child. The reason for all that she did came from him, in every way he controlled her doings, and the least rebuke from him made her feel ashamed.

He had queer ways, but they only showed the difference between him and other fathers. Susie liked to see him as different. She had certainly nothing to blame herself for with regard to her conduct to him. Ever since she had been a little child she had done nothing else but work for him. Even while at school she had always risen early to do the housework, and hurried home to get his meals.

Mrs. Moggs could remember how Susie used to go to her shop to buy the groceries, when she was too tiny to see over the counter, and before that, Susie herself could just recollect a woman—a Mrs. Sheet—coming to clean the house and look to her, when she was a baby. But, as soon as Susie could toddle, the woman was sent away.

Susie was only a very little thing when her father sent her off into the fields and hedgerows to gather what might be had without money and without price. No maid had quicker hands than Susie; no one in all Dodder could pick blackberries as quickly. She gathered with both hands, and stripped the hedges into great baskets, as if she milked them.

As to James Dawe himself, he appeared to do nothing for a living. He only crept about like an old wolf, seeing, hearing, and watching. If it were possible, he never liked to use what was his own. The very water that he had in his own well he did not like to dip out, and he would send Susie to fetch water from Mr. Bridle's pond rather than diminish his own supply. Had he been able to, he would have hoarded the very air that he breathed, and he had often sent Susie to a neighbour's dung-heap to bring back as much as she could carry in pails, to his garden.

James Dawe wore cord trousers and a leathern coat, and Susie had never seen him in any other garments. Neither did she ever see any of the wealth that people said he possessed. She was never allowed to enter the room where he slept, and no man ever came into the house unless Dawe invited him— which was very seldom. James Dawe ate the cheapest food —soaked bread, powdered with salt and pepper, and for dinner, boiled vegetables and sometimes a little green bacon. He drank only tea.

Leading such a hard and meagre life, it is a surprise to learn that Susie was happy. But if a young life be but a natural one, joy will somehow or other find a way to creep into it. Even though the environment may be dreary, a child's heart can yet dance and sing. She will skip, however muddy the road is, and laugh at the sad rain that beats upon the gravestones in the churchyard.

Perhaps it is in a child's soul that God plays, allowing Himself for the moment to be unmindful of His troubles and of the sad sorrows that He has created for Man. Perhaps

He sometimes leaves Himself and becomes Winnie Huddy.

Though Susie had been kept so close, yet her father was not always in the way to keep her continually engaged. She found time now and again to run down to the shop and talk to Mrs. Moggs. And often, too—for Miss Susie planted no nut-trees around herself—she would be found at the gate when Joe Bridle was passing, and would sometimes even say a merry word to Mr. Solly, that always caused him to stare hard at the ground, when he came by upon a Sunday.

She was glad that Joe Bridle talked to her. He was the kind of man that any young girl might look up to and wish to marry. And yet he did not altogether please her, though she hardly knew herself why he did not. Perhaps it was a certain slowness in Joe, an unusual harmony, that was hard to disturb, she did not like.

Susie was doubtful whether he could ever lose his reserve and become enraged or lustful. She had never once seen him strike his horse, or storm and curse because the cows would not hurry home. He was not the sort of man to do those things. He had never, so far as she knew, been engaged in a tavern row, offering to fight a Dady or Dillar, neither had he been found drunk in a ditch, nor seen cracking home-bred fleas in the road. Nor had he ever been known to visit Daisy Huddy.

But who is it that can tell where a girl's fancy can run to? It is as hard to follow as the flight of a swallow in the air. What is it that she seeks, what does she want in a man? Beauty it certainly is not, nor staidness, nor honesty, nor yet a loving heart. Neither can it be baseness that she prefers. Nor foolish pride. It is never goodness that she wishes to wed.

She wishes to possess something that she only can call her own—all other things matter not. She is a thief; she wishes to steal from a man something that she wants to be hers, and that she can hand to her offspring as hers alone. She wants to pretend that what she has stolen from the man is her own in the child. She wishes her husband to be neither superior, grander, nor cleverer than another, but only different.

She wishes to rob a man of something that she sees he has, yet he knows not that he has it. And she will make him believe that she weds him for every reason except the true one alone.

In the choice of a husband, a girl is guided by a sure instinct—she chooses for the future, her choice is towards a new development. She notices some trait or other about a man that may become an heirloom for her descendants. Though she steals this from a man, she will say that it is hers. What she robs a man of, she never gives back to him. A woman is a bad sharer. She wants something for herself that no other woman can ever have. She would have every child of hers marked with her mark, so that she should be pointed out as the mother. She will hunt out a man only because she believes that something can come from her womb, by the use of him, that will be hers only. A woman longs to live wholly in her child, as herself alone.

Or else, is a young girl guided by the stars in the choice of a husband? Do they lead her, those magic signs in the sky? Do they make signs to her? Do their far lights point out the man who may please her the most, open her womb, and cause life to dance to a new measure?

She, and not the man, breaks the new ground. To produce a fairy is her wish—a kind of immortal. Or she may wish to bear a toad, and so she marries a wealthy banker. What, indeed, has the power of love in a girl's heart to do with the matter? A wise girl distrusts all fine, high-lifting thoughts; she would rather dig like a mole than fly like an eagle.

Joseph Bridle was a good, easy, merry fellow, straightlimbed and well to look at, with a faithful eye that a girl could find comfort in, as well as pleasure. And, by the look of him, he could be wanton too, if the occasion were proper. Though his feelings were amorous, his thoughts were chaste —the right man for a merry girl to marry.

To live under Madder Hill, and to feel its influence, had made Bridle more kind than many. Children would run to him, and he would give them what pennies he had in his pocket. And, though Susie could see what a fine father he would make, yet she had her eyes elsewhere. . . .

James Dawe had seen his daughter grow, and he waited his time. The time was nearly come.

When a man waits, expecting to gain, he sometimes grows impatient. Dawe grew more silent to his girl, but, in the evening, when she went to bed, he would go to his bedroom, too.

Dawe scarcely seemed human. Had he beaten Susie a little and loved her a little, matters might have been different. A father's manners are very odd to watch. But still Dawe looked. He did no more than that. He was not a likely man to lose money by any folly of his own. And besides, he hated his daughter.

There were a number of simple truths that James Dawe was aware of. He knew that if you leave butter in the sun it will melt; he also knew that all women—both young and old—are sly cats. God has many wants—so a poet once said—but James Dawe had but one now. He wanted Joseph Bridle's field.

He liked to think, too, of how he would get the field. He would have pleasure both ways, in the giving and in the receiving. To give a sweet body of flesh—all those timid corners and delights, all the fair beauty of a girl—and to receive in exchange a field of cold sods. He liked that.

If ever a religious thought came into James Dawe's mind, it came to him now. To every man, sooner or later, a chance comes of Salvation. A chance to gain all by one deal. Once the offer is made, and once only. To pass by the opportunity is to lose all. A man is suddenly aware that something must be laid hold of—now or never. Let the one moment go, and heavy darkness closes over our heads, the waves cover us. In the midst of the great storm, a silence comes. Some one speaks. Our chance has come. Amid all the rush and clamour of desire, all that we wish for, we may then take. A Divine revelation is shown—a momentous bliss.

Mr. Dawe's chance had come—a treasure might be his. But God does not appear to every one in the same manner. Dawe knew Him as the treasure in Bridle's field; Winnie Huddy believed He was Mr. Solly's nuts.

And to him who loiters late upon a summer's down—because then a little gale moves and scents the air with thyme—if he be ready to breathe deep, a blessed wonder will pass over him and promise a perfect joy and utter forgetfulness.

To another that walks upon the mountains comes a young doe of excellent shape and with the fairest limbs, who bids the man rejoice for ever in her loveliness. But, peradventure, he turns aside from her. A shady tavern beside the highway invites the weary traveller to rest a little. He has silver money to pay for the red wine, and yet he does not enter, but goes sadly on his way to destruction. He has missed his chance. When he passes that way again, the tavern will not be there. The shady trees will be cut down, the arbour levelled, the Inn sign cast to the ground. . . .

Mr. Dawe was sure of himself, he would have the field, he would dig up the treasure, and what a fine rich son-in-law Farmer Mere would be! He had two large manors, he had certain other odd fancy possessions, and a dog—Tom.

A father's kindness can sometimes be too kind. Often, because he does not lust after his daughter, he hates her instead. Sometimes he does both. And he may also be, as well, a little jealous of her—and headstrong, too, when his own will is opposed.

Susie had never wilfully opposed her father, but once or twice she had pretended to, and for that he had never forgiven her.

Once when he was out, a creditor had brought him money in a letter. For some reason or other Dawe took up the letter, looked at the envelope, but did not carry it into his room. Then he went out again. . . .

Susie thought that money was a silly thing because her father made so much of it. That was but natural. For every child thinks that what a father makes much of must be foolish. Even Judah thought his father's concubine was stupid, and so he crept into his father's bed. Judah did not do so because he liked the woman, but merely because his father's bed was the most comfortable in the house. It was the woman who complained, because Judah was tired and went at once to sleep.

Susie smiled to herself when her father went out, and slipped the letter into her workbasket. When Dawe returned and looked for the letter he could not find it. Susie said that she was sure it must be somewhere in the house, though perhaps it might have slipped through a hole in the floor. The miser's soft hairy face became purple with rage, but he did not beat Susie. He sat down upon the floor and howled like Mr. Mere's dog. Susie, who only intended to hide the letter as a little joke, was terrified at her father's behaviour.

But often a little joke can have a terrible ending. A boy points a gun at a sister and shoots her dead. A miner lights a match to frighten a comrade and the mine blows up.

Susie did not know what to do. She could only look at her father, who howled and beat his head against the floor. Then he rose up, went into the woodshed, and fetched an ax and crowbar. With these tools, he began to pull the house to pieces, to find the letter. All that came in his way he began to tear up. Had he supposed the letter to be hid in the Dodder churchyard, he would have rooted out, one by one, every coffined corpse, until he found what he had lost.

Dawe meant to find the letter. He pushed the furniture to one side, and began to wrench up the boards with the crowbar. Soon he would have laid the whole cottage flat.

After tearing up some of the boards, he looked at his girl, who stood trembling. He ordered her to undress—but the letter was not hidden under her clothes. He took up the ax again, but with his next blow he overturned the table where the workbasket was, and out fell the letter.

He never spoke to Susie; he only returned the boards to their places, and went out of the house. But his thoughts were not kind. Though the Son of God could be crucified, yet a human father is not allowed to crucify his daughter, even though he may wish to do so.

But there are lawful institutions besides a cross and great rusty nails that can be nearly as useful for a nice revenge. Marriage is one of them. Sometimes a young girl may not fancy—however much it may be praised by the poets—the carnal act of copulation. It is then that the fun begins. To keep a modest innocence in every young woman is highly desirable, but the well of cruelty is deep, and natural longings are not always fed by kindness alone.

Because Susie had hidden the letter, James Dawe intended to destroy her, and what better weapon could he use than Mr. Mere's cruelty? He wished Mere to be hanged too, but one thing, he knew, leads to another. He would trap them both—the old fox and the lamb—in the same snare.

One evening he gave Mere a hint. They had met near to the churchyard wall, and Dawe began to speak of the many ways in which a simple creature could be given pain. He said that pain makes a woman long. They arranged a day when Susie should be left alone in the house.

Dawe looked at Mere cunningly; they nodded to one another.

XXVIII

Mr. Mere Makes a Beginning

A SIMPLE creature is very easy to catch; she never expects anything unpleasant to happen, and so is never ready to defend herself. Amongst a litter of crumbs a small mouse might easily feed in safety, and yet she will run further, climb up to a shelf, and nibble a musty piece of cheese—the bait.

God is the great hunter. In order to fill His larder, He scatters mouldy cheese about—carnal desire. The sun is above, and all the fair flowers of the valley glisten with dew. The trap looks pleasant.

Then there is the bait—woman. Her wiles are inconceivable, her arts manifold, her desires everlasting. My friend, you are caught. An infant cries. He is bound in the eternal bonds; he has become a living soul. A laugh is heard in the sky, and for a while the child plays happily, all unconscious that he is trapped.

But he soon learns that the fair earth is but a mortuary. He is enclosed fast in a prison. He beats his head against the walls, he looks this way and that, but there is no escape. He must die in the prison. The trap, that at first seemed so wide, he now knows to be very small. The distant stars close in upon him, he is suffocated; the tomb opens, the trapped rat squeals. . . .

No month can be more lovely than June. All the country ways are then at their best. A wonderful beauty moves in the sods, and at the opening of every new flower a bird sings a happy song. A June evening has no rival in loveliness, for the heavy languor of the full summer has not yet come.

In Dodder village the white and red roses bloomed in the hedges, as Mr. Mere walked down the street. Though the roses had not been noticed by the dwellers in Dodder, yet Mr. Mere was seen. Dillar was at his window, shaving. Half his face was covered by soap. He looked into the road and smiled.

"There's wold b—— Mere," he called to his wife, who was skinning a rabbit in the back kitchen. "'E be going down to talk to Susie; she be the one to entertain the old men."

Mrs. Dillar laughed loudly. Her hands were bloody. Close behind Mr. Mere there walked Tom, his dog.

Tom was in fine fettle that evening; he had dined off buried lamb. He stank like a fox. He appeared aware, too, by the way that he looked up at his master, that they were out for a frolic. Perhaps he was going to be given something else to bite—sweet flesh, maybe—not filthy, buried carrion, but firm, living meat.

Before they started out, Mr. Mere had even patted Tom. He had looked at him thoughtfully too, as if he envied him a little. Indeed he did envy him, for what he wished to do often himself, the dog did. Mr. Mere had long teeth too— he could bite like Tom. He could growl and rend a carcass to pieces as easily, and attack a living being as fiercely.

In the street, before he reached Susie, Mr. Mere met James Dawe. The two men spoke no word to one another; they passed by as though they were strangers. Dawe had just come out of his cottage, and Mere was going towards it. After they were gone by one another, Dawe turned. He looked at Tom; he also noticed that Mere carried in his hand a knotty holly stick.

The summer evening grew ominous; there was evil in

the air. Sometimes at dawn the awful will of the Almighty rises to do good, and sets—when the evening comes—to do evil. There is no holding back His terrible purpose. In His right hand He holds evil, in His left good; He deals out as He chooses. Man can do nothing. God is no tamed beast.

Susie was in the parlour dusting when Mere called. Her father had set her doing one task after another all that day. She had filled up a great barrel with water from Mr. Bridle's pond. She had made a chicken coop for a new brood, and had been early out in the meadows to gather mushrooms. The day had been very hot, and Susie, when she ran down to the shop, told Mrs. Moggs that she only wore three garments.

Mrs. Moggs laughed. What young girls wore always interested her.

"Why, you be nearly all skin," she said, leaning over the counter, and trying to touch her. "And thee best take care of they men." Mrs. Moggs handed Susie the loaf, with a wink. . . .

Susie put the duster aside and opened the door. She thought that Mr. Johnson, of the Maidenbridge Drapery Stores, might have called, knowing that her father had gone out, and wishing to sell her a few pretty ribbons. When she opened the door, Mr. Mere stepped in.

Susie blushed; she was surprised to see him. The summer evening, though so soft and pleasing, had frightened her. As soon as her father had gone out, a curious fear had entered the house. A young and frightened girl can look like a dove, or like an old woman. Susie looked like a dove, and a dove can be timid. She was not altogether sorry to see Mr. Mere, for she felt lonely.

Her thin summer frock had shown her off so finely, and she was so tempting a young woman that a wood wasp—

who had lost his way, and happened to be in the room—flew out of the door when Susie opened it for Mr. Mere, because he feared that to look at Susie might endanger his soul. Even a little she-mouse, who had peeped out of her hole while Susie was dusting, retired hastily to her nest and informed her spouse, in a hushed whisper—for fear the children should hear—that it would be better for him to stay safe at home rather than to peep out at such beauties. Also a chair that Susie moved, so that she might dust a small shelf where Mr. Dawe kept a few books, creaked mournfully, hoping that Susie felt tired and would like to rest a little. But Susie had not rested, and the chair looked jealously at the sofa, thinking that she would lie down there. . . .

There was no girl in Dodder who would not have been proud to open the door to rich Mr. Mere, and Susie could not but be glad that he had fancied her, instead of searching amongst the well-to-do farmers' daughters for a wife to marry. But she pouted a little and regarded the farmer inquisitively, wondering how such a rich man would behave in his own home. He certainly had rather an odd look, had Mr. Mere, and he eyed her fiercely. But what a fine thing it would be to marry so rich a man!

Susie turned to place a chair for her guest, and she hardly noticed that Mere shut and made fast the door.

Although some hours would yet have to go by before the summer evening became night, yet, as a heavy cloud hid the sun, the parlour grew very dim.

Mr. Mere did not take the chair that had been offered to him, but instead he went near to Susie, and, as he stept to her, he bid his dog, with an angry gesture, lie down by the door. Susie expected no harm.

At first he looked into her eyes, until she turned away. Then he felt her body with his hands, sometimes pinching her flesh, as if to test her plumpness. As he had evidently by his manners come to court her, Susie showed no objection to what he did. His wife had died many years before, and Susie supposed that those were but Mr. Mere's ways when he chose a girl to marry. Perhaps he only touched her to see how her frock was made. For even a wealthy man likes a wife who can sew.

Without any warning, his manners changed. He served her like a sheep and cast her upon the floor.

Susie, who was quite unprepared for such a sudden assault, fell heavily. Mere took up his stick and shouted to his dog. He urged the dog to leap upon her, to tear and to worry her.

Mr. Mere knew Tom's ways; the dog liked to bite and gnaw. But, for this one time in his life, Farmer Mere was mistaken in Tom. It is said, and not untruly, that the fiercest animal can sometimes be cowed by beauty. Beauty has a strong power. It can destroy like a lion, and yet it can save like a mouse. Perhaps the dog suspected a trap; some one else might leap upon him. He looked inquiringly at his master.

Susie, half stunned by her sudden fall, lay still upon the floor. But Tom would not stir, he only sniffed the air, looked up at his master, and uttered an ugly snarl.

Mere was enraged. Susie sobbed uneasily; she hardly knew what had happened, and yet she cried because her frock was torn.

Mr. Mere cursed his dog; he set him at the prey. And what he said should have made God blush. But still the dog would not move.

Mr. Mere began to beat the dog with his stick; he dragged it to Susie.

Susie shut her eyes. Heavy blows fell upon Tom, but the

dog did not move. He was covered in blood, and yet he would not leap upon the girl.

Mere's lust grew terrible. He now began to strike his dog, meaning to kill. But Tom saw a chance of escape. He turned suddenly, leaped through the closed window, shattering the glass, and escaped. Though he had received his death-blow, yet he had not touched Susie.

She heard the crash, her eyes were shut and she did not know what had happened. Then she felt the fangs of an animal sink deep into her shoulder. She screamed and opened her eyes. Mere was kneeling over her, but the dog was gone.

XXIX

Signs and Wonders

A GIRL-CHILD wishes to see signs and wonders. She waits impatiently, hoping that as each new day comes a sign will be shown to her. When she sees the sign, she believes that it will not be long before the wonder comes. But, being young, she does not yet know the world.

She has crept into the world crying, through a portal where suffering and desire jostle for pre-eminence, and one day she will go out by another gate, with a sad groan. Between the infant's cry and the woman's last gasp there may be many days for her to live, and in the earlier portion of those days the girl-child will have to run a race. Whether she likes it or not, she will have to run. Nature—that cruel slave-mistress—will be behind her, with a knotted cord in her hand.

The young girl may seem a pretty thing; she may use many gay pastimes for her delight. She may stay, for a while, in a rose garden, or lean over a rock pool and play with the little fish—but she must on. Every girl wears those red shoes that compel her to dance for ever. There is no stopping those red shoes. They may be a misfit, but wear them she must, and dance in them she shall. They will never allow her to rest, a furious demon drives her on.

A fine paper-chase it is, too, that she has to run in. Her young body wonders at first what it lacks, and why she must follow a piper who leads on so strangely. The merry piper who leads on so gaily is but a man. He pipes and the women follow.

A fine hunt ensues. The young women are a pack of hounds; they follow the bucks, that wear large horns. The hounds will win the chase; they will catch those merry stags unawares—an easy prey. The hounds pursue gladly, and without knowing how it has happened, they themselves are the ones that are caught. And the nearest green bank is used for a bridal bed. There, a pretty pastime may be practised with sweet usage, or perhaps, instead of loving manners, a furious frolic may come of it, cruel and hostile to love.

From such doings lust may emanate, or love and gentle content.

But perhaps hideous cruelty alone is there, and its claws bloody. This wonder may come quick and sudden; at other times it is very slow—a ponderous bulk that moves to destroy. Or else it shows its victim for her own face in the glass. 'Tis her own sweetness that brought in the terror. She called for the music, 'twas the piper who played. Her outcries, her screams are forgotten, and she returns again and again to kiss the rod.

Her young eyes, moist and clinging, gaze at the terrible sign. Her knees bend tremblingly; she has entered the pagan grove where the pole is set up. She knows herself to be a sacrifice to the god. The god demands her; his prey must be given to him.

But over all that happens, a watcher stands and looks. This watcher is Madder Hill. Above life—that grand and woeful calamity—Madder Hill looks and yields a kind of consolation to those who bend to it. It may be but the sweet odour of white clover, or the winter's sun setting in the sea, that tells other tales than the fury of constant becoming and continuous ending. Madder Hill is the same yesterday, today, and for ever. Our eyes have seen it, and not another's. . . .

Mere knelt over Susie. He wished her to become conscious, so that she might be fully aware of what he meant to do to her now.

But Susie was still dazed, and to do what he had a mind to do with her, in that state, was not what he wished.

Even a madman, such as Mere seemed to be, does not like to be watched. And the eyes that were now fixed upon Mr. Mere soon drew his attention to them. Mr. Mere turned and saw John Death at the window. John was smiling.

Mere rose, with a curse; he left Susie, unlocked the door, and went out of the house.

Susie had not seen Death, and as soon as Mere was gone, she began to recover her scattered senses. She had supposed that she was going to be killed, and was surprised to find that she was still alive. She had expected, from her fears, to be far more hurt than she was. She was surprised when she found how easily she could get up. The blood from the bite in her shoulder had ceased to flow, and though the wound pained her, she forgave the poor dog who, she supposed, had bitten her. Feeling better, she went into the back-kitchen, and washed the bite; she then went upstairs to change the torn clothes. She cried over them, as if they alone had been hurt. Then she looked into a cracked glass and saw that she was still the same girl.

As well as forgiving the dog, she even thought better of Mr. Mere, now he had gone from her. Mrs. Moggs had told her to beware of the men in her thin clothes. Perhaps it was the pink frock that had done the mischief. Men, she knew, sometimes became quite wild—like bulls. A girl ought to be careful what she wore; Susie even smiled. She supposed that Mr. Mere must have grown tired of visiting Daisy Huddy so often. She was glad of that.

Of course, as a Dodder girl, with so little to spend herself,

Susie had always been envious of Daisy. Had a poor man—such as Joseph Bridle was—only visited Daisy, she would not have cared, because Joseph never had anything to give away.

But Mr. Mere was a very different matter to Joe. Many called him the Squire of Dodder, and the highest pew in the church was his to sit in, if he chose. He never entered Daisy's cottage without carrying, in the inner pocket of his coat, a well-filled wallet. And, though his purse was hardly depleted at all when he came out, yet to be near such wealth must have been very pleasing to a girl. And Daisy would often boast of what he used to show her.

Susie bared her shoulder before the glass, and looked at the wound.

The dog had not hurt her much, and where the bite was no one could notice it. But the dog—she was aware that the man had beaten it horribly. Had it leaped through the window to die?

As Susie felt better, she began to trouble less about what had happened to herself. Perhaps Mr. Mere was shy, and shyness, Susie knew, sometimes makes a man cross. Perhaps Mr. Mere had beaten his dog in order to gain confidence himself.

Mrs. Moggs had often told Susie how a strong man will throw a girl down, a little roughly sometimes, and marry her very gently a month later. Many strange pranks, Susie knew, were often played in a country place before the wedding bells rang. And a man of Mr. Mere's wealth was not likely to be too kind to a poor girl.

"Perhaps," thought Susie, "I ought to have been kinder to him."

Mrs. Moggs had told her, more than once, how a man expects a girl to behave. She now almost wished that Mr.

Mere would come back to her again. She even ran out into the lane to see if he still loitered near. In the lane she found John Death waiting for her.

Susie was glad to see him; what she had gone through had made her restless, and she stept happily to John. She knew him as a pleasant man to talk to, with a merry, roguish look, and, even with a beard, he did not look uncomely. Susie had always liked the look of John. She liked the way he played with the children upon the green. He allowed the little boys and girls to play with him at all hours, unless he was sharpening his scythe or searching for his lost parchment.

He had always spoken politely to Susie, as if she were a fine lady and he a gentleman, and he spoke to her, too, in a way that no other man had ever done. When Susie mocked and teased Joe he always became gloomy and sad, but John Death never cared what a girl said. He would answer as saucily and give as good as he got.

Something, Susie felt, had to be done with herself that evening. She was a flower that a storm had blown down, and now she longed to be culled.

But John, when he saw her, appeared a little quieter than usual. He looked at her more seriously than she liked to be looked at—though not as Joe Bridle was wont to look at her. John's eyes spoke of different doings than his.

He asked her about the dog; that was why, he said, he had come to the window. He had been playing ball with the children upon the green, and had heard the crash and wondered what it meant. In the lane he had seen the dog, all bloody. He saw it roll over, then it got up and staggered into Joe Bridle's field.

Susie begged John to go with her there, and to kill the dog. She could not bear, she said, to think of its being in such agony. "Mr. Mere," she cried, "never finishes anything off; he likes to leave an animal in pain."

On the way to Joseph's field, Susie was conscious of a strange fascination that drew her to Death. He seemed a man who could do more for a girl than many another. There was a power in his step and a purpose, too, and the nearer he was to her, the more she was aware of his comeliness. He was different from any other man that she knew. As they walked to Joseph's field, John talked to her pleasantly; he evidently wished to put her quite at her ease.

He began to talk of many little things that every country girl likes to hear of. He spoke of the tradesmen who came from the town shops, and of their cunning ways with their customers. One afternoon a certain Mr. Dicks—who travelled for a draper—had called upon him. Mr. Dicks sold both men's and women's clothes. He looked a little curiously at John's trousers, and asked him whether he would not like to buy a new pair. John replied, with a smile, that he wished to purchase a girl's frock. Mr. Dicks was quite prepared for such an order. He hurried out to his van and returned with a pretty red dress that he knew would exactly fit Daisy Huddy.

Susie laughed. She liked to think that even Mr. Dicks knew all about Daisy's bad ways. She liked to think, too, that Mr. Mere had quite finished with Daisy, for on the same day that Mr. Dicks had called upon John, he had also carried a bill for another frock to Daisy, that evidently Mr. Mere had refused to pay.

But as to John, Susie did not seem, curiously enough, to be jealous of him. He was the kind of man whose merry temper permitted him to do exactly what he chose. No man who had ever lived in Dodder was quite like John.

He was the sort of man, Susie supposed, to take a girl

into a field of soft grass, please her there, and then go off himself and leave her to admire the yellow buttercups.

Susie looked at Death longingly; he had started her thoughts dancing. They bounded like tennis balls, then they flew like the winged seeds of the sycamore and fell upon Death as upon a good ground. He alone could fully satisfy her; he alone could give her himself wholly and utterly. She knew not how it was, but she became aware then that he loved her too, and she, being a girl, wished that he might soon make her his own.

As soon as she thought so, she knew that he was all-powerful over her, and had he changed himself into a thorn-bush, she would have clung to him as lovingly. She longed to run merrily down the lane of love, at the end of which is Death.

They loitered along without need to hurry. And, even though the task that they had to do—to find the stricken dog and to kill it—was not a pleasant one, yet Susie, now that John was her companion, did not mind the adventure.

There was nothing that he did not know, there was no village girl that he was not aware of. He even went so far as to make fun of Priscilla Hayhoe's hat, that she wore in church. He had something new to tell her, too—that Mr. Hayhoe read to Daisy Huddy each evening of the week. "And once," said John, "when Farmer Crawford, who always considered himself a fine fellow—though he was but a small man—came to see her and heard the following passage read, he retired hurriedly without knocking at the door.

" 'Handsome! Nobody can call such an undersized man handsome. He is not five foot nine. I should not wonder if he was not more than five foot eight. I think he is an ill-looking fellow. In my opinion, these Crawfords are no addition at all. We did very well without them.' "

Susie laughed, and John held her nearer to him. All the power of a thinking creature went from her; she appeared to be swallowed up in him, and he in her. This feeling was one of the most exquisite joy. She lost herself in her desire to find him alone. All that she had been went out of her, and only joy was left.

No such wonderful feeling had ever come to her as she talked to Joe Bridle. Though John only thought of pleasure, that pleasure went very deep; his carnal merriment was monstrous; he could, she knew, drink all of her and leave nothing but a mere husk.

Bridle was different. He wanted her as a helpmate, to be but his property, her sweet flesh to bear children to him, to live, to suckle, and to rear them, and to be always to him his loving spouse. Joe Bridle wanted her for himself, his jealousy was Godlike. He was all hope and gloom, and he often troubled her.

As Death had told a story or two, Susie thought she would begin too. She began to invent tales from what Mrs. Moggs had told her. She pretended that she had been out with the boys and told John what they had done to her. She told these tales to prevent John being shy. They were all lies.

Then she said that she believed that she would soon be married to Mr. Mere. When she said his name she spoke proudly. But Death only smiled; he did not take his arm from her or turn away, as Joseph would have done.

"Ah!" he said, smiling upon her, "I rather like Mr. Mere." He grew thoughtful for a moment, and then observed gaily, "I believe, one of these days, Mr. Mere and I may become better acquainted."

"It's nice to be happy," said Susie.

"Why, even the dead think so," cried Death, "and

though Mr. Hayhoe does say that all will rise at the Last Judgment, yet old Barker and Nancy Prim wish to rise no farther than the charnel grass, and to rise there only for naughtiness."

John mocked at every one. He observed that Lord Bull- man never went to bed without lamenting that young girls and religion were far too much neglected in these modern days, and that both the one and the other ought to be more easy to obtain.

"And, as to my lord's own fancies," cried John, "why, he owns himself that all his children were only begotten to please Mr. Titball. Those two," observed John, "would often talk together like brothers when they visited the cellars. Mr. Titball would guide his lord by the light of a large lantern, and would show him the vast bin where Sir Thomas Bullman—my lord's great-grandfather—used to keep his wine. 'Every day he drank three bottles,' Lord Bullman once observed, 'but the bin was never empty.'

" 'Miracle!' cried Mr. Titball. 'And his family? He had more than one son, I trust?'

" 'He had many children,' replied Lord Bullman, sadly, taking up a bottle to examine the cork.

" 'I knew it,' replied Mr. Titball, and led his master to the cellar door. . . ."

XXX

The Large Quiet

WE HAVE not wrought an outrage upon Nature. Merriment does often follow in the wake of despair. After every mortal sin that is committed runs Puck a-laughing. The gay rogue skips merrily, trundling a hoop. The ugly sin hobbles on, the hoop gets between its legs, and the sin falls flat. Then the little jester performs a mock burial. He names the sin Despair, lays it in the grave, and dances on its body.

Puck calls himself Wanton Dalliance.

He dances for a while upon the grave and then he turns his back and runs off. Despair, seeing that his enemy is gone, leaps out of the ground, and takes the nearest path to the tavern; then he mingles wine and pours it into a cup. He gives this cup to man.

"Listen," he cries, "and drink. There is Death in the cup; there is also complete forgetfulness. Drink ye all of it. The drink is good. The wine warms the man, and he does not know that, by means of this cup, he is going to be destroyed."

The man leaves the tavern in a happy manner. The summer sun warms every green bank, the large trees bless the man with their soft shadows. He is gay and frolicsome and climbs a smooth hill. He gives chase to a little butterfly, a chalk-hill blue.

That butterfly is his own life. He wishes to catch and to keep it; he grows tired with the chase and lies down upon a bank of yellow flowers. The flowers are his days—a few yet live, but many are already dead, faded and gone.

He lies amongst them and watches those that yet live wither and die. Then he leaves them, and it is night. . . .

John Death led Susie into Joe Bridle's field. As he opened the gate for her, Susie, who was laughing at a merry word of his, began to tremble. Sounds that were not happy came from the middle of the field where the pond was. They were the groans, yelps, and horrid snarls of a beast in awful agony.

Susie put her hands to her ears, and begged Death to hurry. John merely stroked his beard and continued the same pace. They walked through the field, and came near to the pond. The grass was soft and green, the summer wind blew, a holy sigh came from the great elm.

The wounded dog yelped pitifully; it bit the grass in its agony. The knotted stick had cut its skin into ribands, one eye was beaten out of its head, and yet it lived.

John came to where the dog lay.

"Kill him quickly," cried Susie. She went a little apart, threw herself upon the grass, and buried her face. She waited trembling, expecting something awful to happen—the same fearful outcries that she had often heard when her father killed his neighbour's cat with a club, so that he might have the skin to sell.

But though Susie had not covered her ears, she heard no sound. Soon she knew nothing, for the breath of life that so troubles the children of men was for a few moments withdrawn from Joseph Bridle's field.

The pond lay dim, as if it were again become a part of those burning waters that were the earth before life came. All the summer grass withered in one moment; the sweet flowers were gone. A lark, that had only just risen from its nest to sing its evening song, fell headlong and lay as though dead. The tall elm tree, heavy with green leaves, became like dead and blasted wood, the leaves shrunk to naught.

But life went not all alone, when it left Joseph's field. Pain and terror, joy and torment vanished too. Another state ruled and had its being instead of these—Death. The Large Quiet was come—the great inaction, the uttermost release, eternal peace.

Nothing moved; all things partook of the holy stillness of Madder Hill. The hill brooded silently, and bowed low to Death.

But even during those moments of silence, a murmur deeper than silence could be heard—the murmur of all those that are at rest. A joy, unknown to any living thing, was in the field—not life, but a joy unspeakable, the joy of everlasting sleep. . . .

Susie lay still. The peace of Death had been with her, and after that was gone the field and she lived again. She had lain there for an hour.

Susie sat up and rubbed her eyes; Death was nowhere to be seen. Only Joseph Bridle was there. Joe had taken off his coat, and was busy filling in a grave where Tom had been buried. He told Susie that Death had called him, and that when he came into the field he found Mr. Mere's dog Tom lying dead, and fetching his spade, he had dug a grave for him. He supposed that Susie, who was lying on the grass with her head turned away, would not wish to look round until all was over.

The dog's death hardly appeared to be of any moment to Joseph Bridle. He would have gladly buried all the dogs in the world if, after doing so, he might be with Susie alone in his field.

As soon as he had patted down the grass upon the grave, he went quickly to Susie. He looked upon her with the greatest delight. She rested there like the fair bloom of a splendid flower, that for the first time had opened to receive the glorious beams of the sun.

Her beauty, too, was even more wonderful than he had ever beheld it before; she appeared to have awakened out of a deep sleep. Her eyes looked upon Joe with a strange sweetness and love, and her body trembled with hope and joy.

She could not please Joe enough. She kissed him joyfully, and between her kisses she looked lovingly into his eyes. Then a laugh was heard beside the field gate, and Susie was changed. She leaped from the grass lightly and remembered Death.

She began to tease Joe. She told him that he had nothing to say for himself, she called him a stupid fellow, a mere doorpost.

He had certainly been very silent with her of late, for love made him dumb and had blinded him to all things except love. Such a state of mind is made to be tormented, and is only sent into the world for one good purpose alone—to fall easily into the arms of Death.

"Oh, Joseph," cried Susie, "do you know what is going to happen in Dodder in a month's time? There is going to be a fine wedding. Who do you think is going to be married?"

Bridle made no reply. In the gathering darkness Susie thought that he looked strangely at her, and she noticed, too, that he touched something that was hidden in his bosom with his hand. Would he beat her with his strap, or would he lay hands upon her in another manner?

But Joseph Bridle did nothing.

XXXI

Susie Lights the Lamp

Susie had gone to Joe Bridle's field, as a girl likes to go—in company with a man who pleased her. She had gone there in the evening sunlight that was then warm and pleasant, but now that she was returning, all was dimness.

She shivered uneasily. What had happened to her in the field she hardly knew, though she remembered, with pleasure, that Death had been with her. She believed that, in some way or other—she really could not tell how it was—this man had made her completely happy. But now she knew that she lacked something. Perhaps Bridle had taken her happiness from her, coming into his field when he was least required there. It was like Joe to disturb a girl's pleasure. The love that he had for her was so persistent—as dark and heavy as the night.

While she had been with John, Susie had not even thought of the evil treatment that she had received from Mr. Mere. And had she thought of it, she would only have found excuses for the farmer. But, now that she walked home with Joe, the wound in her shoulder began to pain her, and she wondered what Mere had meant in setting his dog at her. He had certainly acted very wickedly. And why, when she had seen him in the parlour, had the dog's eyes a look so full of pity for her? She had noticed that look before in an animal, a look that expressed a profound pity. Perhaps the dog knew that Mr. Mere was a bad man, who really wished to hurt her.

"But with all his money," thought Susie, "Mr. Mere must be good." And if she did not marry Mr. Mere now, all Dodder would laugh at her. Of course she might take Joseph. But he could do nothing for her; he had not enough to keep her alive. He had always been an unlucky man with that field of his.

Susie had run out excitedly from her gate; she now returned dolefully, and felt as though she could cry. Her father was not there to see her, and so she could cry by herself, and her tears did her good.

Feeling better, she lit the lamp. The light gave the parlour a more cheerful look, and Susie was happier. Some one walked past the cottage singing a country song. A child laughed—Winnie Huddy! Why was she out so late?

Susie began to tidy the room.

She was happy doing so. She put the sofa straight, arranged the chairs, and laid the mats flat. Soon all was as she liked it to be. Her shoulder did not pain her now. The room was tidied, and what difference had the odd behaviour of one man made to her or to the room?

The plates and cups that she now set out upon the table for supper were the same as heretofore. If such things as these ran wild, clattered together, raped one another and broke of themselves, a girl might indeed have cause to trouble. But whenever did a pan or a clout—when kept clean and tidy—refuse to do its duty, or rebel against its lady? When did ever table turn sulky and refuse to be loaded with good fare at Christmas, or a mat say that it must not be shaken, or a kettle scowl instead of boil?

With such things remaining faithful, those humble watchers at man's parlour games and pretty feats—though a lamp may, as Lucian tells, be called as a witness—a woman's heart is sure to be eased. For these sticks, pots, and china

cups are rightfully a woman's true gods. A steady and stead-
fast purpose pervades them. A bed has a friendly and benign
look: it wishes to be kind.

Cunningly to devise mischief, to bite the life out of her
heart, to drive a poor creature into madness, to cast down a
girl and to pour upon her the issue of many a foul desire,
that's the way of a common man. To plume himself, to strut
like a barncock, to tease and torment his prey, that's the way
of a fine gentleman.

A sad lot indeed must a woman have with only a man in
the house and no furniture. All movables are her allies, her
faithful friends in the long battle. Let her but begin to dust
the bookcase, and the man will go. Perhaps he will go off
for ever, walking past her when she is watering the flowers.
There would be no harm in that, as long as the furniture remains. Even if all men departed from Dodder, no girl need
trouble, provided that the window-plants remained. . . .

Susie ate a little and, as her father did not come home,
she left some bread and cheese upon the table, and went to
her bedroom. She was well pleased with herself—at least
three men desired her. She looked in the cracked glass.
Seeing her own loveliness, she felt a little sorry for Joseph
Bridle. He was too good a man for her; she wished him well,
and decided to speak more kindly to him when next they
met.

Susie began to undress. She took off her stockings and
her frock, and stood before the glass to examine her wound.

She heard some one enter the house. She supposed her father had come home. The steps came upstairs, passed her
door, and entered her father's room. Perhaps it was not her
father.

Susie lay down upon the bed, without getting into it. Her
body trembled exceedingly; she tingled everywhere. She

ached with longing. Her heart beat so loudly that whoever was in the next room could almost have heard it. She moved eagerly upon the bed, as though she clasped a lover in her arms. She wished that Death watched her. What merry things he would have to say about a girl's lively body?

Presently she heard the cottage door close. Some one had either gone out, or else some one had come in. She listened. She heard her father eating his supper below-stairs; he made the usual ugly sounds.

Her father came slowly upstairs. Outside her door she heard him sniff. He coughed too; evidently there was an odour in the air that he did not like.

He began to mutter to himself. Then he went into his room. Soon all was silent. Susie slipped into bed, and fell asleep.

XXXII

Susie Hides in a Lane

LOVE is heavy to carry. Though at first it settles upon its victim like a butterfly, it quickly changes into lead.

When love came to Joseph Bridle, he soon learned the weight of the god. He might have been Christian, but Joseph's progress was very different from the Pilgrim's. Instead of being born in the City of Destruction, Joseph lived near to a Delectable Mountain. This mountain was Madder Hill. There a man walked sometimes who resembled a homely shepherd—this was Tinker Jar. As soon as Love fastened the burden upon Joe, the peace of Madder Hill left him. He was forced to quit that peace, and go quickly; he must escape.

But whither could he go? To the City of Destruction, where one lived who could alone ease him of his burden—by taking his life away. And there was no casting away his burden before that day came. The thought of Susie filled him utterly; she was the universe, she was a terrible monster, and yet the sweetest thing that ever man saw. . . .

When Susie awoke, she found that she was no happier than Joe. Although her peace had never been quite like his, yet she journeyed the same road.

Susie rose from her bed, knowing that she loved John Death. If John did not content her soon, and fill her whole body with his love, she knew that she would die. In a kind of way, he had already entered her body, for his eyes had fastened upon her and she could not shake them off.

She heard the village sounds, but she could not listen to

them. She wondered how it was that ever a poor girl could feel so strangely. 'Twas a terrible jest to play upon her—this woeful desire.

God is merciful, His trade is to forgive, but Love's trade is to hurt and destroy.

Susie awoke, tormented by fierce jealousy. She, as well as every one else in Dodder, knew that John Death, attracted by the scarlet thread, had often visited Daisy Huddy.

Nothing escapes the one eye of the old woman who is Dodder. She can look, she can also speak, for every one in Dodder has been given a little piece of her tongue. Nothing is ever missed that happens in a village. Even the winter's night, or the summer's day, when a child is conceived, is spoken of; the compact is known and the hour talked of. Nothing that lives under Madder Hill can ever be hid; all insects, and all lights and shadows are the whisperers. The old woman points before one knows oneself, to where one is going.

Perform all with the greatest secrecy, get the church key from old Huddy, and dance to a country tune in the Squire's pew—the very hassock and psalter will tell. Go down like the beast into the valley and enter the hollow tree, the worms will see you—your merry doings will be extolled by the rabbits.

The old woman sees all that is ill done—it is that she rejoices in. But do good, and you will never be noticed. Nothing is ever seen in that kind of fancy. All eyes are shut, and all ears closed to a good deed. And rightly so, for it is destroyed, if spoken of. . . .

Susie gazed into the glass as she dressed.

"Surely," she thought, looking at herself, "John must find me a sweeter morsel than ever Daisy Huddy has been to him. Every one knows that one has only to touch Daisy

and she begins to cry. When Mr. Mere goes to her she can
be heard crying from the road." She would not be fearful
like Daisy, and she longed to receive any pain that John
could give to her.

Susie came downstairs and prepared the breakfast for herself and her father. Her father ate in silence, and then he
went out to measure Joseph's field. Did he but find a square
yard of earth less than what Mr. Mere said that the field
contained, he would cancel his bargain.

The day passed slowly with Susie; she tried to work, but
nothing went right. She laid things in their wrong places,
she slipped and broke the handle of the teapot, she allowed the
kettle to boil over into the grate.

In all her movements in the house, she only had one
thought—to meet John Death and to yield herself to him.
In her wish there was no pleasure, only intense longing.
When the evening came, Susie could bear to wait no longer;
she laid her father's tea, and went out.

She stood in the lane and her heart beat fast. She looked
down at her feet; they were certainly a girl's shoes that she
wore. John must be near to her, he could never have travelled
off again, to leave her desolate.

She listened. Of course she could find out where John
was. She would only have to wait a little time in the lane to
know that. Some one would be sure to laugh presently in
the village, and the laugh would tell her where John was,
for every one used to laugh at the funny things that he said to
them.

Susie pouted and stamped her feet. Perhaps John might
have gone that evening to visit Daisy. How could she get to
know if he were there? She could not pull Daisy out of her
own bed and place herself there instead. But, anyhow, she
meant to walk along the street and listen beside Mr. Huddy's

door. If her love shamed her, she could not help it. She did not wish to spy and yet she was compelled to follow Death. She must find out where he was.

He might, she thought more happily, be all alone in his cottage preparing his supper. If that were so, he would accept her help. His cottage would be sure to need dusting, and perhaps his bed might need making. Susie listened for a laugh. She only heard the sound of a haycutter, far away in one of Mr. Mere's fields. Where was Death? Could no one tell her?

Susie began to walk down the lane towards the Dodder green. The evening air was scented with sweet clover. Two swifts flashed past her, a cuckoo called—its note was changed, summer was come.

Near to the green, Susie met Winnie Huddy. Winnie had a scarlet thread in her hand that she was rolling into a ball.

"You mustn't quiz me about it," she said slyly to Susie, "and I don't envy you your Mr. Rushworth."

"What are you talking of?" asked Susie. "I don't know any Mr. Rushworth, and I only stopped you to inquire where John Death might be."

"Oh," cried Winnie, carelessly, "I don't pay no attention to him, 'e do only talk to girls who no one else don't want."

Winnie laughed and ran off.

Susie turned down a narrow lane. Why she took that way she hardly knew. Perhaps she thought that Winnie might call after her again, and so she got out of her sight as quickly as she could.

The tiny lane that she had chosen to go down was near to the Dodder Vicarage. It was but a place to toss odd rubbish into. People who had any refuse to get rid of would carry it into this lane and leave it there. From such manure as old tins and rags, nettles, docks, and burrs grew finely.

The lane began deceitfully. It looked pleasant enough at first, the beginning was grassy. One went along for a little, admiring the may-blossoms, and then all at once fell into nettles, old boots, dock leaves, and broken bottles. If one struggled on, nothing better would come of it. There was no pleasure in going on there. The lane soon narrowed; it became only brambles, long trailing brambles with sharp thorns.

To struggle through these brought one into no fairyland, for, at the end of the lane was but a slough made of cow-dung.

About half-way down this lane there was a gate, through which Mr. Mere would often go when he went to the Inn. From this hidden gate everything that went on in the village —cries, laughter, jeers, and the wagging of the old women's tongues could be easily heard.

Susie waited beside this gate. She waited, knowing that Death would come. So sure was she that he must soon come to her, that she even persuaded herself that he had told her to meet him there. She waited expectantly, yielding herself to pleasing thoughts of love.

The evening was very fair; no sound disturbed the summer peace—unless the rooks did so. For these dark birds seemed unduly excited for such an evening. During such lovely weather the birds ought to have been teaching their young to fly, or else seeking for worms in the water-meadows. And yet they whirled wildly in the sky.

Susie wished so much for Death that she knew he must come to her; he could not deny her fierce longing. Happiness, a long life, sweet children, a loving husband, might never come, but he would come. Of course Winnie knew where he was, and she would be sure—if only to tease her sister—to tell John who had asked for him.

Time moves sullenly while a girl wishes and waits. Each moment that might be so precious to her—were he but come—mocks her and passes by. Duration—that many-headed beast—gives her no comfort. She hears a step. That moment smiles, the others pass on, unthinkingly.

But no moments, to a waiting girl, are silent moments. They come by like an army, and they pass with the tramp of many feet, treading down hope and trampling the wished-for joy into the mud. They all pass by, and all the girl knows of them is that they are gone.

Presently Susie heard voices in the lane. She climbed the gate and, creeping a little way into Mr. Mere's field, she crouched down under a gorse-bush, whence she could see into the lane without being seen herself.

The speakers came near to her; she knew them. They stopped beside the gate. Susie was astonished; she had not expected John Death and Priscilla Hayhoe to come there together.

There was no one in Dodder who did not know the goodness of Priscilla—the Queen of Heaven Herself could not be more pious. And only the worst, only the really abandoned women, ever went down that lane. Only the naughty ones who, though they might themselves be well-favoured, were said to meet very ill-favoured ones there.

If any girl allowed herself to be taken by a man where those docks and nettles grew so finely amongst broken crocks, her modesty and her happiness would run from her in a hurry, and no doings in that lane ever led to a joyful wedding.

Susie listened breathlessly; she could hardly believe her own ears. John was talking to Priscilla exactly as he had talked to her. His jests were the same, his inquiries were as strange. He asked Priscilla, in his most happy manner, the oddest questions: In what manner did her husband sport and play? and was it after saying his prayers, or before, that he was the most merry with her? Susie expected, when she heard this, that Priscilla would fly from such idle words, but she did not appear to be in the least offended by what he said.

Susie knew that Priscilla remained very near to Death. He seemed to fascinate her in an extraordinary manner. She listened to all he said, and never rebuked him once for the merry freedoms he took with her. She let him say what he liked, and nothing that he said could prevent her from wishing to know more about him.

"How comes it"—Priscilla spoke in a low tone—"that you are able to please and content all the people in Dodder—all the poor people, I mean, and the children? Every cottager praises you, and you make us all forget our troubles when you are near. Even my husband forgets Lord Bullman when he talks to you."

"I daresay," replied John gaily, "that Lord Bullman would be very glad if I forgot him too."

Priscilla gave a little scream of delight. What had John done?

"You have a strange power," said Priscilla. "What are you?"

"Your lover," answered Death.

"You never knew my little boy, did you?" asked Priscilla, in a very low voice that Susie could only just hear.

John Death did not reply. He only guided Priscilla through the nettles to a mossy bank under the hedge. Susie crept nearer. She wished to see what was happening. She was so eager for John Death that she would even share him with any woman. She crept as cunningly as any vixen chased by

XXXIII

Love Defeats Mr. Solly

No ONE heeds a child. Winnie Huddy, who was only nine years old, could run off anywhere, even at night, without being missed.

Her father, Mr. Huddy, though not really an old man, looked like one. He was wizened, his beard was hoary, and he stooped. He rose early, worked all day in the fields for Mr. Mere; the evenings he spent at the Inn, and the nights in sleep.

He listened to all the talk that came near to him, just as he listened to the winds blowing in the fields, and always ate what was given to him by his daughter Daisy without a murmur. All that he required of his home was food and shelter. What otherwise went on there was no concern of his. A girl spoke, 'twas but a noise; another sobbed or laughed, 'twas only sounds. Women moved here and there in the house: he believed each woman had her use. He knew what it was. At the Inn a gale would often blow: women caused it. The talk was about them. Their ways must be mentioned there—their likes and dislikes, their considerate doings—so that the cheapest beer might taste like the best.

Though all sounds seemed alike to Mr. Huddy, yet he was aware of one slight difference. Certain words were the March squalls, others were like summer showers.

If no carnal fancies made a breeze at the Inn, Mr. Huddy might have fancied himself in church and have cried out "Amen." Sounds, at least, ought to tell you what place you are in. Some kind of difference ought to be made between the grave and a bed.

The money that Mr. Huddy received from Farmer Mere he gave to Daisy, and she, in return, presented him with a shilling each evening to spend at the tavern.

Mr. Huddy supposed that John Death was only the sound of a September storm at a funeral. Others were different— variable breezes. The people of Dodder knew that John Death was a merry wag. At times his merriment took an odd turn; he would frighten some of them.

Once he gave Mrs. Moggs a shock. A mouse ran out of a bag of oatmeal, and she asked Death to kill it. What happened then Mrs. Moggs would never tell.

Only Winnie Huddy knew all about John. She was not in the least afraid of him; she had proved her own strength in the race with him over Madder Hill, and even if Tinker Jar had not been there, she was sure that she could have reached home safely.

When any sudden impulse came to Winnie, she would obey it at once. She would never wait to think. To think made her miserable; she preferred action. For some while after her attempt to visit Mr. Solly, Winnie forgot all about him. Mr. Solly had gone out of her little head as easily as he had got into it.

But one evening, without any warning and without any thought, she sat up in bed, shook her hair out of her eyes, and cried out: "I am going to marry Mr. Solly."

Then she laughed. She laughed because she meant to get the better of her sister Daisy, and be married before her. This meant a complete change in Miss Winnie's ideas for her future welfare. Earlier in the evening she had decided upon a different course of conduct. She had left the scarlet thread, that her sister had given her to play with, in Mr.

Bridle's field, but she had a pair of red woollen socks that would do as well. She had hung these socks out of her window —that looked into the back-garden—but only a cat had noticed them. She had expected that at least Tinker Jar would come to her when she put them out.

Winnie had said rude things to her sister and so had been sent to bed early, but she had only taken off her frock. Now she put it on again, ran into Daisy's bedroom, looked out of the window, and made faces at those who passed by below.

She was quite alone in the house. Daisy had gone to the Vicarage to mend the drawing-room carpet, while Mr. Hayhoe read to her, and Mr. Huddy—as was his wont—was at the Inn.

Seeing Mr. Mere pass by, Winnie threw an old boot at him, and retired to her room. There was a tiny looking-glass in her room, and she looked into it. She smiled at herself, winked naughtily, and made this observation: "I shall certainly marry Mr. Solly and live in his nut-garden."

"I have never yet," cried Winnie, speaking to her doll, after giving it a good shake and putting its clothes to rights, "I have never yet been able to eat as many nuts as I want. And, besides that, the time has come for me to show Mr. Solly that he is not always right in his opinions about people. Mr. Solly believes that all women and girls are roots and cabbages, and I am the one to show him that he is mistaken."

Winnie became serious. Evidently Mr. Solly, through no fault of his own, had misunderstood Nature. She, herself, had mistaken one thing for another and had later discovered her error. Miss Bridle had once given her a kitten that Winnie had supposed to be a Tom, until it bore her a family in the drawer where she kept her dolls' clothes.

That mistake showed her ignorance, and she supposed Mr.

Solly to be ignorant too. It was most probable that he really thought all women were roots. And it was clearly her duty to show him where he was wrong. To put him right in so important a matter would deserve a large reward. In the fullness of time, when she grew bigger, Mr. Solly would marry her.

Winnie undressed her doll and placed it in her bed, and beside the doll she laid her hairbrush.

"Now listen to me, Gertie," she cried. "Mr. Solly has planted those nut-trees to keep out Love, but I shall creep in and eat the nuts."

Winnie's mind had not to be made up; she never wasted her time over such a slow process; when she wished to do anything, she did it. She put on her shoes and ran out into the lane.

The Dodder street was empty: Winnie escaped in a hurry. But she did not go the quickest way to Madder; she circled the hill, running along under the green hedges. . . .

In any change that comes to a man in middle life, there is danger.

When Mr. Solly was a young man he had been a great reader of history, but as he grew older he began to read poetry. He had not read very many verses before he conceived the idea in his heart that love was a dragon. Once he believed that, the one object of his life was to keep love out, and so he grew a plantation of nuts and locked the garden gate.

But however much a poor man may be upon his guard to keep out an enemy, a day will surely come when—through a chance forgetfulness—the foe is admitted. Troy fell, and Jericho. Love's chance came when Mr. Solly left the key in the garden gate.

About the time when Winnie Huddy told her doll that

she intended to marry, Mr. Solly went out for an evening walk. He let himself out of his nut-garden, and was about to lock the gate again and to put the key in his pocket, when a large snake—that had been hid in the grass nearby—raised its head, shot out a forked tongue, and hissed at him. Solly was alarmed; he hurried off without waiting to take the key from the lock.

Either the snake was, he thought, a very large viper, or else—and this was the more likely—the reptile was the very dragon that he feared so much. He began to run without turning to see which way the snake went.

Whenever he was at all troubled or disquieted, Solly always went in one direction—towards Madder Hill. Madder Hill was the safest place that he could go to when the bull was tied up. He had never met a spring cabbage there, and the ground was too hard for spinach. Only in the autumn, there were blackberries, but he did not fear them.

Mr. Solly hurried to the hill, but he did not leave his fears behind; he carried them with him. What was it that had raised its head so angrily and hissed at him beside the gate? Something worse than a snake. He looked anxiously at a gorse-bush, wondering whether a Jerusalem artichoke might not be hidden behind it.

He continued his way sadly. Suppose the dragon had flown through his bedroom window, what should he do? If Love had entered into his house by the casement, his peace would go out by the door. What havoc would then be made of his life, what turmoil! Instead of being a sober unity of gentle manners, he might have to become two people—or even three or four—and some of the family would be sure to quarrel and to make a noise.

Up till that day he had felt safe. As long as he had been

able to keep Love out, he had seen women only as field crops. But if the dragon had got into his house his virtue would leave him—when he next saw a cucumber, he might be lost. It would be a girl. Nothing could save him then.

He recollected once having asked Mr. Tucker, the clergyman of Madder, what he thought of his nut-garden, and whether it was really thick enough to keep out Love. Mr. Tucker had shaken his head over the nut-trees; he feared that they might hide an idol.

"I am not sure, either," he observed, "whether or no—Love being a pagan god—he might not like nuts. Your only chance, poor Solly," he said, with a deep sigh, "is to seek sanctuary. Love is always careful never to enter a church, and if you desire to be really secure you have my permission to sleep in the Squire's pew—no love ever enters there."

Mr. Solly bowed, and withdrew.

"Alas!" murmured Mr. Tucker, when Solly left him, "I trust that this unhappy man has not changed his religion. Before he began to plant those heathen nut-trees, he used often to come to church. I cannot believe that he gave up the practice because it seemed to him, from the company gathered there, that every Sunday service was a harvest thanksgiving—though I know that the lesson from Deuteronomy was not to his taste. I fear, alas that too many nuts have driven him mad. . . ."

Half-way up Madder Hill, Mr. Solly stopped to listen. He thought he heard some one running beside the hedge that was below the hill. He felt nervous, every sound alarmed him, and he hid himself behind a bush. Resting there, he wondered what he had better do.

What if that dreadful dragon really occupied his dwelling? He was not St. George, nor was he Death, whose way with Love—that old serpent—every one knows of. Was it safe to go in? Or would it not be wiser to remain all that night upon Madder Hill, and then to venture home the next morning to see who was there?

Mr. Solly began to tremble; had he lost the key? He turned out all his pockets; the key was nowhere to be found. He believed that he had left the key in the lock. He was not surprised. When a nervous man sees a horrible dragon near to his gate, he is likely to hurry away and forget the key. And, besides, he had always expected that one day he would forget to take the key from the lock.

Mr. Solly, sitting under the bush, looked down at his house. He could see the roof and the chimneys. What did they hide? How would Love behave? There was the basin of bread and milk that he had prepared for his supper before he went out. Love would know from that basin that some one lived there. Had Love only found a book of verses, he might have run away—but bread and milk would be sure to tempt the god to stay.

Mr. Solly shivered. A sea-mist crept up and surrounded him. Upon a spider's web near to him some little pearls of water were collected. He rose, shook himself, and decided to go home.

No lonely man ever enters the door of his house—if the hour be late—without expecting to see either the Devil, or God, hiding behind the parlour door.

The gate of his garden he found to be wide open, and neither did he trouble to shut or to lock it, for he knew that the enemy was in his fortress. He opened the front door, expecting the worst. The house was quite dark, and Mr. Solly lit a candle. He then sat down at the table, intending to eat the bread and milk that he had prepared beforehand.

The basin was empty.

Mr. Solly looked sadly at the empty basin, and listened.

He heard the regular breathing of a child who was fast asleep. He did not turn at once to look where the sound came from. He put his elbows upon the table, rested his chin in his hands, and regarded sadly the empty dish. The god had come —or else had sent one of his servants—to destroy a good man. There was evidently a girl-child asleep upon the sofa.

Mr. Solly gave himself up for lost. But, being a brave man—though in the power of the foe—he did not despair. To submit when one is fairly conquered is the behaviour of a hero. Only a foolish bird will struggle in the net—a wise man knows when he is beaten.

Looking at the couch from which the breathing came, Mr. Solly saw Winnie Huddy fast asleep. One of her bare legs hung down, with her foot just touching the floor—the other leg was upon the sofa. Her yellow hair she had stolen from Love. She smiled in her sleep.

What could Mr. Solly do?

After looking at her for a few moments in deep thought, Mr. Solly went out from the room and quickly returned with a warm rug. Gently raising Winnie, he wrapped her in the rug, so that she might lie more comfortably. Winnie only sighed contentedly; she did not awake.

Mr. Solly knelt beside her and raised her hand to his lips. He worshipped Love. Then he went to bed.

XXXIV

A Trade for John

For a whole month Mr. Solly kept himself shut up in his nut-garden. No one knew why. The Madder people believed that he was bewitched. He might have been so. He was exactly the kind of man that a witch would pick out to cast a spell upon. He was one of those who see the gravest danger where most only see a merry pastime. He believed that everything that a man does is of terrible importance. Though all things usually were so quiet in Madder, Mr. Solly believed that raging devils were about.

The simplest sights only did not make him shudder; he could admire the lambstails upon his nut-bushes, and the ferns under his bank, but wondered even that he could enjoy these without fear.

Though Mr. Solly remained at home, Winnie Huddy went out each evening. She would climb Madder Hill and visit Mr. Solly. Once there, she employed herself industriously, sweeping and cleaning for Mr. Solly and doing his errands. She would remain for a while and then returned home, in a very gay mood, over Madder Hill. No one noticed Winnie's doings except Mrs. Moggs, and she called her into the shop one day and asked her where she went each evening.

"You go to see your friends, I suppose?" said Mrs. Moggs, with a wink.

"I visit my new home," replied Winnie, "that I have to keep tidy at Madder."

"I did not know, Winnie, that you had a relation there," inquired Mrs. Moggs.

"I have Mr. Solly," replied Winnie, "whom I am going to marry, because of his nuts."

"Why," cried Mrs. Moggs, "I thought he planted those bushes on purpose to keep young women away. He would have been much wiser had he filled his garden with thorny brambles."

"I am fond of blackberries, as well as of nuts," answered Winnie, "and so I would have gone just the same."

"And when will the wedding take place?" inquired Mrs. Moggs.

"Punctually at twelve o'clock upon my eighteenth birthday," answered Winnie. . . .

It is curious to contemplate how labour, when it becomes a use and habit, dominates a man.

John Death had hoped—when he found it convenient to his affairs to take a little holiday—that his time would be so well filled with frolic and naughtiness—that however long it might suit him to remain in Dodder, he would all the time be happy there. But alas! he was sadly deceived.

It was not in his power to remain idle. Almost as soon as he settled into his cottage, he discovered that he could not leave his scythe alone and must needs be for ever whetting it, and longed, as he made music with stone upon steel, to be again at his proper employment. And although no one would have thought so—seeing him at play with the children—he was, when alone, fretful and depressed.

Even the summer sun that rose so early in the morning troubled his fancy, for the sun shone so busily and was so importunate that even at night time, his mighty glow could be seen—and John preferred darkness to light.

And besides, he was growing tired of looking for the parchment that he had lost. For though he liked the earth well enough, it was not always pleasant to have to keep his eyes upon the ground. He had looked everywhere, and, as the paper was nowhere to be found, he was more sure than ever that some one had stolen it.

He first thought of one person and then of another who might have taken it, and at length he decided that his paper might have been discovered and kept by Priscilla Hayhoe.

Her behaviour was certainly a little curious. Did she guess who he was? She had permitted John to take her into the hidden lane, and to talk to her in the happy manner that he used with women. Indeed, when he led her through the nettles to the mossy bank, he had wished to be as playful with her as he had been with Miss Bridle and with Daisy Huddy, only, after laying her down upon the soft bank, he happened —though he knew not why—to look up at Madder Hill.

Upon the summit of the hill there stood a man who beckoned to him, as though he bid him let the woman alone. This man, John thought, was Tinker Jar.

Curiously enough, John, who certainly appeared to be no respecter of persons—and cared no more for Lord Bullman or Squire Mere than for labourer Dillar, obeyed this man and withdrew so silently that he seemed to vanish.

But even his deserting her so hastily in the lane did not make any difference to Priscilla's view of him. She would often meet him in the village, and would ask him the strangest questions about his past life, and about the master that he served. She inquired of him once whether his master had ever come to Dodder, and, if so, what clothes was he dressed in.

"His only garment is a thunder-cloud," John replied— "but he sometimes mends kettles. . . ."

So far, since he had resided at Dodder, John Death had only once entered the churchyard, but he had often seen

Priscilla praying there—kneeling near to the grave of her little son—when he went by. Once she had noticed him in the lane and, rising from her knees, she had beckoned him to come to her, even begging him with a look to rest beside her upon the grass.

Death had always admired Priscilla; she was a kind lady and a comely. She could behave coyly, too, it seemed, though John was not sure whether it was something that she wished to find out in respect to himself that made her behave so. But he desired her the more for that, and certainly, when the sun shone upon her, she looked extremely lovely. A sad flower perhaps, but one that could be culled joyously.

She had not, of course, the power over him that Susie Dawe possessed, but being so gentle and pleasing a woman, he considered that she was only made and created for him to enjoy. Whenever he thought of Priscilla Hayhoe or her husband, John smiled.

In order to meet Priscilla more often—for she spent a great deal of her time in the churchyard—John Death decided upon a plan. Why should he not become the sexton? Mr. Huddy had given up digging the graves since his wife died, being afraid, so he said, that he might hear her talking, did he break any ground there.

John Death decided to apply for the post. Evidently he was not the sort of gentleman that a too long holiday agreed with. To have nothing to do but to be merry did not appear to accord with a nature that was—as long as any living thing existed in the universe—created to be extremely busy.

And here we must note, I think, a curious trait in John's character. He had no ambition. He had no wish to order and command, other than in his ordinary everyday doings. He desired neither riches nor glory, and he considered that if he became a gravedigger, he would have ample opportunity to repeat to himself—as he rested near to the yew-tree, with his spade upon his knees—that wistful Elegy, written by Mr. Gray in a country churchyard.

With a little work, a grave or two to dig now and again—and perhaps an occasional field of grass to mow, so that his scythe might not lose its sharpness nor his hand its cunning—John believed that he might yet be contented in Dodder. He hoped, by these means, to keep up the old agility and sprightliness of which he had always been so proud. For, during all his life, he had never felt so tired and weary of himself as he had at Dodder.

He considered, too, that the Dodder churchyard would be an excellent place—a fine battleground, where a fight would disturb no one—for him to come to grips with a certain old enemy. He had often—being fond of prose as well as poetry—been reminded, as he walked in Dodder, of the Valley of Humiliation, in which Apollyon and Christian fought their fight. And why should not he—a champion too —meet Love and destroy him in the charnel garden?

He had mocked at love in Love's own parvis. He had pleased Daisy Huddy so well that she would have nothing to do with any other man, but only liked to sew and to knit and to listen to Mr. Hayhoe reading stories. He had played bob-cherry with Winnie in the church porch before matins commenced. He had even—for so wanton is a certain oddity, a sworn adversary to all decency and decorum—been free with Miss Bridle. He hoped for Priscilla, and there was one other one—Susie Dawe—that he meant to compass too.

Whenever he thought of Susie a curious feeling came to him that he did not understand. He was utterly ignorant—as so many hard workers are—about the behaviour of his own heart. He did not even know what had made him look so long at the name written in pebbles in Mr. Bridle's field.

To enjoy a girl or two had been easy to him—that was a pastime to which he felt himself naturally drawn. It appeared to have a religious meaning that the grand powers of the Church had never failed to recognize. Martin Luther married a nun.

But what was there, Death wondered, what new feeling moving in his heart, that made him think so curiously of Susie Dawe?

XXXV

Death and the Farmer

THE last day of June was come. John Death stood sadly beside his cottage door. The warm evening pleased him, and the sweet summer breeze brought with it the scent of flowers.

As he had decided to become the Dodder gravedigger, he proposed to himself a little walk that evening, wishing to discover Mr. Hayhoe and to ask for the appointment.

Leaving his own door, he proceeded along the street, and passing Daisy Huddy's cottage, he noticed that the scarlet thread had been taken away. Though he did not know why he should be troubled, the sight of the window with no line hanging from it depressed John.

He was aware that a certain carnal act that commenced, he knew, a very long time ago, had provided him with many years of constant labour. If Daisy's new fancy spread, and all allurements that drew together those who wished to embrace were withdrawn, there might at the last—for all energy runs downhill—be nothing left for him to do. Now that this scarlet thread was gone—that used to hang so temptingly when the sun shone upon it, and could even be noticed during the night—other mischances might follow. Women might learn to think of other things, and then what would come to an honest workman in an allied trade?

Dismissing these thoughts as unprofitable, Death continued his way and, within a few paces of the Vicarage, he met Mr. Hayhoe. They welcomed each other as old friends. Although Death's conduct in Dodder—told to him by Mrs.

Moggs—had not altogether pleased Mr. Hayhoe, yet this worthy man had come to think of John as of one who, although he sometimes appears to act a little curiously, yet is sure to be a true friend at the last. Mr. Hayhoe had never ceased, in his heart, to thank John for having so boldly driven Mr. Mere from the Huddys' door, and also he nursed a rather odd hope—that John would one day get the better of Lord Bullman.

Mr. Hayhoe held up in his hand a torn coat.

"I rent this," cried Mr. Hayhoe, laughing, "in leaping a hedge to escape Mr. Mere, who was after me with a great stick."

"What did you say to the farmer to make him so angry?" inquired John.

"I told him that it was not right to take Susie away from honest Joe," answered Mr. Hayhoe.

"You should have left Mr. Mere to me," said Death, in a low tone. "But you cannot wear such a coat as that again."

"I am going to ask Daisy to put a patch into it, while I read to her," said Mr. Hayhoe, smiling. "I am reading *Emma* now, and Daisy is already extremely fond of Mr. Elton."

"Lord Bullman will soon hear how often you go to the Huddys, and he will deprive you of the living," remarked John.

Mr. Hayhoe snapped his fingers.

"Although Mr. Titball believes that Lord Bullman is greater than God, I am by no means the one to share such an opinion," he said. "Since my lord commanded me to turn the Huddys into the road, I have been unable to give to him that proper honour which St. Peter tells us to render to those in authority above us. But perhaps Lord Bullman may not be aware that God loves Daisy."

John stepped from one foot to another, and changed colour.

"Do you think so?" he asked anxiously. "And does He love Susie Dawe too?"

"He loves them both," replied Mr. Hayhoe with conviction. "He loves all women."

"I am surprised to hear you say so," answered Death meditatively.

Mr. Hayhoe looked at John wonderingly.

"I wish to ask you," inquired Death, "whether I may be the Dodder sexton."

"Yes," replied Mr. Hayhoe readily, "and I am certainly glad that you wish for this employment, for it must surely bring you nearer to the Church."

Mr. Hayhoe bid farewell to his friend and continued his way.

Death watched him go, and remained for a while uncertain which path to take. Looking by chance in the direction of the Inn he recollected that Farmer Mere had sent him a message, earlier in the day, by Mr. Huddy, asking whether he would mow, and for what price, Joseph Bridle's field. Winnie Huddy, who brought the message that Mr. Mere had given to her father while he worked in the fields, informed John Death that the Squire bestowed upon him a great honour by this offer of employment, and she hoped, she observed, that as she had brought the good news to him, Master John would reward her with a halfpenny.

"Mr. Mere," she said, in order to enlarge upon his high condition, "do speak to Lord Bullman, and 'e be, too, a kind of relation to our Daisy."

"What kind of relation is he?" asked Death, with a smile.

"A sort of April husband," replied Winnie, "but thee be only a plain John."

John Death, who, after he had made up his mind to be the sexton, had grown a little happier, now walked along with his usual steady step to the Inn.

He found the farmer already there, waiting for him, and eager enough to drive a keen bargain.

To get the better of any poor man had always been the farmer's pleasure. He could, of course, have sent his own workmen into Joseph's field, but ever since he had set eyes upon Death, he had wished to cheat him. The very first time that he had seen Death in Dodder he had hated his looks, and wished from that day to set him a hard task from which the poor man might only take a small pittance. Death was a stranger, and a stranger was in Mr. Mere's eyes always a proper victim. Besides that, Mere bore a deep grudge against John, because he knew well enough now that it was he who had persuaded Daisy Huddy to lock her door against him. He now hoped to cheat John finely.

He knew that Joseph Bridle's field was very deceptive. It looked smaller than it was. It had a bad reputation. No one had ever been lucky enough to mow that field without striking his scythe against a hidden stone, and once, in cutting round the edge of the pond, a certain Jack Foy had fallen in and been drowned dead.

Some people said that the field was the Devil's because it had three corners; others affirmed that it was God's—for the same reason. But anyhow, from the strange undulations in the field and its three-cornered appearance, it was a difficult matter to estimate its right size in acres, roods, and perches.

Mr. Mere always set to work to overreach a man by the same method. He knew that a drunken fellow often agrees to a deal that is very much to his own disadvantage.

When Mr. Mere wished to impose upon a workman,

he invited him to Mr. Titball's Inn and made him drunk.

At a proper rate of wage Joseph Bridle's field was worth four pounds to cut. Mr. Mere had decided to give only two. In order to make any man drunk enough to agree to anything, Mr. Mere was usually compelled to spend five shillings, but even after that was taken away, he could still defraud Death of a good sum.

As he walked to the Inn Mr. Mere had felt in a merry mood. His wedding day approached, and he was sure that he would then have Susie Dawe utterly in his power to treat as he chose. He was conscious, too, as he walked, of being unusually thirsty. The day had been sultry; strange and ominous clouds had hung over Dodder, and seen through them, the sun looked like blood. And even when the mist that partly hid the sun had drifted away, a black and sombre cloud remained stationary upon Madder Hill.

At the Inn Mr. Mere had found Huddy, Dillar, and Mr. Dady. The men were unusually gloomy. It was a day for drunkenness, and they knew it. The heavy cloud that had pressed upon Madder Hill lay heavy upon them too. The only escape from that cloud was in drunkenness. Unless that great revival of spirits—which comes by deep draughts— came to them, they would be betrayed.

But the money that each possessed was hardly enough to make them even merry, and only wholesale drunkenness would suit their case.

But though they had not the means to drink to excess, a former neighbour of theirs—John Card—was more fortunate. The knowledge of his good luck caused them to be more gloomy than ever. It was said that, since John had let his cottage at Dodder to Death, he had been able every night to get tipsy under the proper guardianship of Mr. Toole, the innkeeper of Tadnol.

Death had paid his rent in certain old valuables. From what he gave to Card, it seemed probable that he had discovered a vast treasure. He paid his rent in bangles, necklets, earrings, and rings of old gold. And the more he gave, the higher rent did Card demand.

When Card was drunk, he boasted of his good fortune, and every one wondered where the hidden treasure was found. Whoever came upon a lonely stone in a field would lift it up to see what was underneath. Mrs. Moggs leaned down so far into the well to try to see what was at the bottom that she nearly overbalanced, and had not Joseph Bridle come by at the time and caught hold of her skirts, she would certainly have fallen in and been drowned. More than one had gone at twilight—when they supposed no one to be about—to search in the churchyard, but nothing had ever been found.

Only one man made a mock of their folly—James Dawe; but he now-a-days was often to be seen beside Bridle's field gate, as if to watch who went in there.

Although this evening some of his customers were a little low in tone, yet Mr. Titball himself was extremely elated. He had received a visit during the morning from Lord Bullman. Mr. Titball was entirely overcome by such an honour. Lord Bullman had even sat down upon a parlour chair. After saying a word or two about the utter shamelessness of a certain red fox who had run off with a peahen from the grand gardens, and then observing that the weather was warm, Lord Bullman softly drew Mr. Titball aside. After seeing that the door was shut, Lord Bullman asked Mr. Titball, in a low tone, about a treasure that had of late, he believed, been discovered at Dodder.

"Folk do say," replied the landlord, in a loud whisper, "that 'tis all found in the churchyard."

Lord Bullman had called for a lemonade. . . .

Mr. Titball took the glass from the mantelpiece and showed it to the company.

"My lord then inquired," said Mr. Titball, speaking proudly, "whether the clergyman here, Mr. Francis Hayhoe, was orthodox."

"And what did thee say to that, landlord?" asked Mr. Dady, looking gloomily around for a fly to kill.

"I did say," answered Mr. Titball, "that Mr. Hayhoe visits Daisy Huddy."

"And what did his Lordship reply?" asked Mr. Dillar.

"He must certainly have been pleased to hear it," observed Mr. Dady, who had found a fly, "for 'tis they orthodox ways that fine gentlemen, who do live in great houses, do fancy the most. 'Tain't no playday with them to visit a woman, for where food be plentiful, 'tis real work that be done."

"I fear that you have not understood my lord," said Mr. Titball, who did not altogether approve of the matter in Mr. Dady's observation. "He merely wished to know whether Mr. Hayhoe revered and respected the constitution of his native country."

"And what did you say to him?" asked John Death, who now joined the conversation.

"I replied that Mr. Hayhoe was married," answered the landlord.

"And Lord Bullman spoke further, did he not?" inquired John.

"He did," replied the landlord, "for he said, or rather swore"—Mr. Titball blushed—"that Mr. Hayhoe could have the living if he assisted him in bringing back again an ancient and kindly law, that had fallen out of use in these degenerate days."

" 'Tain't no hanging law I do hope," asked Mr. Huddy, anxiously.

"No, only a bedding one," answered Mr. Titball, softly. "My lord did say," he continued, "that as the hunting season was over, and he had nothing better to do, he had occupied some of his valuable time in reading English history—that was of course chiefly concerned with the doings of his own ancestors. 'In those far-off feudal times'—these are my lord's own words—'there were many sound and just laws that have never yet been repealed, and one of them—the "droit de seigneur"—should certainly be revived.' "

"And what mid thik be?" inquired Mr. Dillar.

"The right of the lord of the manor," exclaimed Mr. Titball, "to bed each betrothed virgin the night before she is married. And the Church, my lord said, was benefited by fees as well as propagated in perpetuity by such nice doings. And, as soon as my lord obtains the blessing of the Bishop and the assistance of Mr. Hayhoe, he intends to make a beginning when a lawful occasion comes."

"With whom?" enquired Mr. Dady, who wished, for the first time in his life, that he were a lord.

"With the next bride," answered Mr. Titball.

Dillar and Huddy laughed loudly.

"There bain't nothing told," inquired Mr. Dady eagerly, when the laughter that had become general was subsided, "about the rights of a poor dairyman, in that written law? For, though a young bride be the proper cream and butter for a nobleman's bed, yet surely, a clause in the law must direct that no poor working-man should be left out? All women bain't going to be married, but bain't there nothing said about Widow Hockey who do live at Shelton?"

"Nothing at all," answered Mr. Titball, sternly.

"But," asked Mr. Mere, "is there no mention in this law about a proper payment due to the husband, when my lord has been the first to consummate?"

"He is awarded a kingly decoration," answered John Death.

Mr. Mere looked sharply at John, who appeared to know more than he thought he did. The farmer began to fear that he might have to spend more than five shillings in making him tipsy. He began to ply John with rum, and drank himself, too, to keep him company.

Many a man had entered the Inn in Mr. Mere's company, intending not to be robbed of his rights, but as time went on, the cunning farmer would get the better of this intention, and the man would withdraw from the Inn, having agreed to the lowest terms for the work.

But now things were not quite the same. The money in Mr. Mere's purse began to diminish, but Death appeared to be just as sober as when he first entered the tavern. To every two of John's glasses, Farmer Mere had only drunk one, and yet he knew that he had spent near upon fifteen shillings. Had Mr. Mere, then, caught a dragon in the net that he had set for a tomtit?

Mr. Mere moved his chair closer to Death.

"For how much will you mow Joseph Bridle's field?" he asked of him, "for I have bought the grass to carry off to my own barton?"

"For five pounds," answered Death readily. "For that price I will cut the grass as close as a cropped grave."

"Do you think me a fool," cried Mere, in a rage, "to pay a strolling vagabond such a price as that for the cutting of a little field?"

Death touched Mr. Mere with his hand. Mere rose unsteadily, as if he wished to flee, but he soon sat down again and stared at John.

"You agree to my price?" asked John.

Mere nodded.

XXXVI

The Best Liquor

THE gloomy feeling that earlier in the evening had invaded the Bullman Arms now passed away. Those who had little or no money to spend bethought them that once or twice before a rich giver had entered the tavern, who was named Weston, and there was not one man who returned sober after his visit. And now, though they knew not why, Mr. Titball's customers were aware that soon drink would come to them easily, and without payment.

A curious attraction drew the men closer to John Death, as though he were the one from whom a supreme good might at any moment come. John sat on a small stool and a circle was formed around him, for each peasant was aware that from him the peace of eternal intoxication could be had.

Having agreed with Mr. Mere to mow Joseph Bridle's field for a price that old Huddy had whispered to him was a proper one, John Death—as a man will, who knows that he can earn good money—wished to be merry.

Although he was a fine leveller in his own trade—regarding all men in the same manner—yet John had always, as time went on, been able to separate good literature from indifferent work. And it was not only the writings, but the sayings of great men, that he liked to hear of. One of his favourites, who had spoken many shrewd words—and a man that Death had always liked, though the Doctor had not always liked him—was Samuel Johnson. Death now recollected one of the great lexicographer's sayings, "A man is only happy when he is drunk."

The time was now come, considered John, to prove the truth of this observation, and to initiate those present into the holy mystery. John, too, felt in himself the necessity for amusement, so that he might endeavour to forget his love for Susie Dawe, a love that—contrary to the accepted opinion of the Apostle Paul—instead of casting out fear, begot that very feeling in John's heart.

John had never known fear before. But now it began to trouble him, for he feared that something or other might step in between him and Susie, so that he might never enjoy her.

He feared love.

A jest or two with Winnie had been but an innocent merriment, and he had shown Daisy that even lust can solace and be kind. He had cured Miss Bridle. But no joy had he found with Susie, he feared her power over him and wished to forget her. She had led him too far already into a land that he did not know—a land of milk and honey, where the nightsounds were soft, where doves cooed in the darkness, and where Sorrow wandered, weeping.

John Death called loudly for drink, and the order that he gave was so generous that Mr. Titball went to him with the question, that of all questions is the most important: "Who is to pay?"

Death took out of his pocket a handful of Roman money that bore on the one side the head of the goddess Roma, with her winged helmet, and on the other the two Dioscuri on horseback. They consisted of denarii and sestertii.

Mr. Titball took the money in his hand; he did not think it the right colour. Death smiled. He put his hand again into his pocket and filled it with gold coins, aurei, upon which was the head of Marcus Aurelius.

Mr. Titball seized the gold greedily. He knew that he held now the value in money that far exceeded all the drink that he had in the house.

While he looked at the coins the thick black cloud that had rested upon Madder Hill covered the Bullman Arms.

Each man drank heavily; they drank to Death. They had drunk healths before, but never such as this. They knew that they drank to a great king. The only king to whom a proper loyalty and worship should ever be rendered. All must bow low to him. All other lordship is as nothing to his. He alone is the supreme power, and what is the dust of a hundred generations to him? A little heap of ashes, a few bones—that is all.

Within the strange darkness of the black cloud that now filled the tavern parlour, a phosphorescent light emanated from the drinkers, that guided Landlord Titball to them to fill their cups. Every one laughed and drank. And strong liquor was needed to keep up the merriment, for each to each other looked curiously. They saw one another as cadavers.

Those who in life were ugly were worse now. Out of the rotting eye of Mr. Mere, a worm crawled, and yet the farmer drank each cup with renewed relish. Old Huddy raised his mug to his lips that were but blackened gums, and drank to Death, who eases every labourer's task, laying him down in a bed from whence no farm cock can hurry him at dawn. Landlord Titball, moving in a ghastly manner, had the appearance of a ten years' burial, that filled the cups dexterously with mouldy hands. Mr. Dady looked even more horrible. The flies that he had liked so much to kill had become alive again—as all flies will in Hell—and had bred maggots in his body. Mr. Dady was a loathsome corpse, and yet he drank freely to Death. Dillar would have laughed, as, holding back his head, he poured the last drop of Mr. Titball's brandy down his throat, but he could not laugh, for his jaw was fallen and stiff.

John Death drank carelessly. In such company as was about him, Susie might easily be forgotten. What was a mortal girl to him? Her fair body, her woman's breasts, all her sweet presence, did they come now, would get another semblance. The cold look of her, wasting apace in a grave, was indeed likely to cure every one of love—except Death.

Death raised his cup and drank to Susie. . . .

He finished the last cup of liquor in Mr. Titball's cellar. But, raising his hand, by his almighty power the tavern parlour was changed. It became the vault of the Bullman family, that was under the Dodder church. The parlour table was a leaden coffin, and now, instead of Mr. Titball drawing the drink, Death was the tapster. The cups were empty skulls.

One member of the Bullman family had, in very olden times, made excellent verses. It was to his coffin that John Death applied a gimlet. The rich red wine ran free. The cups were filled so fast that John hardly needed a little bone that he had found to check the flow. Death had gone to work knowingly; he had tapped the right corpse. Beauty is eternal; he drew wine that flows for ever.

Death had opened an immortal flagon—a spring of true poesy. . . .

As suddenly as the darkness had come, so the light came again.

And when they awoke out of their drunken sleep, the Dodder peasants found themselves sprawling in odd attitudes upon the parlour floor. They awoke gloomily, for although at the first when they had begun their drinking all had been well with them, the last cups had been sad. While they had drunk from Mr. Titball's cellar, a fine vision had opened to them. They saw what they liked. Women, easy to come at; winter faggots, piled up high; enormous gammons; hogsheads of ale. But the last wine had made them sad and sent them to sleep, for they had followed the flight of a golden bird, whose song they could not understand.

Landlord Titball was the first to rouse himself. He went to the Inn door, and looked out. It was still evening.

Mr. Titball looked in the direction of the churchyard, that was easy to be seen from the Inn. What he saw there sobered him a little, and in order to stand quite steadily, he recited all the children's names of the Bullman family and, in addition to these, a score or two more that he hoped would come.

Finding that with this exercise he could walk without toppling, Mr. Titball called to the other revellers, who staggered to the Inn door to see what was doing. All Dodder looked still and happy. The swallows were safe in their nests, that were most of them under the eaves of Joseph Bridle's cottage, and the soft light from the sun that was already set, covered the fields. Peace was there. Only in one place, where the greatest quiet should have reigned, there was noise and clamour.

Lord Bullman, his chief whip, his huntsmen and hounds were in the churchyard. The dogs were snuffing in every corner, scenting amongst the graves, and pushing aside the flowers to see what was there, while Lord Bullman encouraged them in the proper huntsman's manner. He appeared to be in excellent spirits, and as the grave-mounds were not five-barred gates, he jumped some of them,

One grave-mound he leaped out of pure good-nature. This was the grave of William Jones—a former huntsman at the Hall—and my lord jumped it to please the poor man below.

A simple story had brought my lord there. His mother, the aged Dowager, had told him that a good foxhound can smell out treasure as well as scent vermin. No sooner did he hear this than he brought all his pack into the Dodder church-yard.

As the manor of Dodder was his, he had a right to what was buried. He galloped to a corner of the churchyard where the hounds were busy. They nosed excitedly amongst the dock-leaves, and at last unearthed an infant skull. This skull Mr. Pix examined, and informed the company that, from a mark he saw in its forehead, the skull had once belonged to an unbaptized bastard. The dogs crunched it up.

The next amusement of the hounds was to follow a large rat that ran into its hole under James Barker's grave-mound. But they were soon aware, from the scent, that a rat is no fox, and they wagged their tails to show their displeasure, for they were too well-trained to dig after rodents.

Lord Bullman rode home in deep dudgeon, and Mr. Tit-ball, turning his customers out, closed and locked the Inn door. Mr. Hayhoe, at Daisy Huddy's, read the last sentence of *Emma:*

" 'But, in spite of these deficiencies, the wishes, the hopes, the confidence, the predictions of the small band of true friends who witnessed the ceremony, were fully answered in the perfect happiness of the union.' "

Mr. Hayhoe closed the book with a sigh. John Death was gone to bed. Priscilla Hayhoe was preparing a salad for supper.

The bats came out.

XXXVII

Love Never Pities

SOMETIMES, during the whole of a woman's life, Love may sleep soundly. A woman may even marry and bear children without awakening the god. Neither noise, nor outcry, nor wanton songs, nor lustful fancies will awaken him.

You may play all the dance tunes you like, or listen to the sermon of an Archbishop, and Love will sleep soundly amongst his arrows. Two may lie down together upon the sweetest mat of yellow buttercups, and Love will never stir a feather of his folded wings. But sometimes an accident will awaken him, or else a lamp is lit and he stirs and opens his eyes.

Then beware, 'tis best to let sleeping gods alone. The mortal who arouses a god out of his slumber must be prepared for any conceivable calamity. He had better at once cover his head with ashes and his loins with sackcloth. A god may stir generously, he may open his hand, and stretch out his arm to give a good gift—and what gift, God-a-mercy, will that be? A grave.

As soon as Love crept into Mr. Solly's house, Mr. Solly made his will. He left all his estate, so he wrote in a very small hand, "To my dear wife," with a sigh. After making his will, Solly smiled, for he was sure that in a very little while after he was married, he would have no estate to leave. At the bottom of his will he wrote, "Love is a robber." . . .

When Joseph Bridle found Love asleep in his field, instead of awakening him, he should have cast him into the pond. But he did not do so, and Love changed into a few shining pebbles, with which Bridle wrote Susie Dawe's name.

Susie's case was different. Being a girl, Love slept in her heart, but pain awakened him—it was the bite of a dog. If in all hatred there is fear, in all awakened love there is pain. Susie felt this to be true, and she wished to be wilfully deflowered by the one that she loved.

As soon as ever that wish came into her heart, her girlhood bloomed marvellously. An invisible touch was set to her soul, and her beauty triumphed. Her eyes shone like clear stars, though when she thought of John Death they became moist. She languished for him; nothing that she did now could take the thought of him away from her. Though she had ever been a quiet and a gentle maid, she was now an altered being. Fierce and naked desires set up their altar within her womb, and gave her no rest day or night.

Often in a summer garden one flower will bloom with unusual splendour; she seemingly has sucked into herself all the rich juice from her less fortunate sisters. But the beauty of that flower will be a danger.

From a lamb, Susie was become a tiger. Her fair body was garlanded by Love. Love himself tended her, stroked her breasts, kissed the soft hair of her neck, gave her nectar to drink, and whispered into her ears that one day she would be a splendid sacrifice at his altar.

For this ordeal Susie wished to prepare herself. She even went to Mrs. Moggs and asked her how she could best please a man that she loved.

"They be most of them pleased with an apple dumpling," replied Mrs. Moggs, and winked lewdly.

Susie went home and longed the more for Death. Come to her as he might, in whatever form he came, he would be welcome. Did he come as another Mr. Mere's dog, she would take him to her. If he appeared to her as a dark thunder-cloud, heavy with the hidden lightning of lust, she would open her arms and receive him into them. If he came up out of the sea, as a huge white-crested wave, she would bow to him so that he might fall upon her. If he came as black as an Ethiopian, or as a leper white as snow, she would await him with all the utter abandonment of a maid's first longing. If he flew to her, carried by the wings of an eagle, she would willingly let him tear her flesh with his mighty talons.

Susie had roused the god to some purpose. Love never pities. He mocks all and destroys many. Susie was now fairer than any flower of the field, and yet she was still but a cottage fancy, a skipping Jenny. She enjoyed the pleasure of her proposed marriage to Mr. Mere, she toyed sometimes, too, with the thought of taking Joseph Bridle instead, and meant to give herself to Death.

When in a gayer mood than usual she would joke with Winnie Huddy about John, but sometimes Winnie would give Susie a wise caution.

" 'E bain't always as respectful to a young lady as he should be," Winnie said, " 'e do tell Mrs. Moggs that all women—whether young or old—be his to do what 'e be minded wi'."

"But oh, Winnie," Susie whispered, "you don't know how much I want John."

" 'Twould be better for thee to have Joseph," replied Winnie, and skipped down the lane.

XXXVIII

Susie Wishes to Hurt

THE day after the drunkards' festival at the Inn, Susie went to visit her aunt, Mrs. Manning, who lived at Shelton, all alone with her five cats.

The cats and Mrs. Manning were eating their dinner when Susie arrived, and seemed more sorry than pleased to see her come in, because they feared that she might want to eat some dinner too. But Susie would take nothing, and so the cats and Mrs. Manning finished what was there. Each cat had a plate set upon the floor, in which Mrs. Manning placed its share. And, though her own dish was upon the table, she ate like a cat, putting her head into the platter and crunching the bones.

Susie waited until Mrs. Manning had finished, and then she told the news that had brought her there. She said that in a little while she was going to marry rich Squire Mere.

Had she said that she was to marry poor Joseph, her aunt would have scratched her. Mrs. Manning's ways had grown exactly like her cats'; and she used to sharpen her nails upon the wall.

Mrs. Manning fawned about Susie, she even rubbed against her, and asked in a cringing tone for all the bits that came from the farmer's table. She bid Susie put them aside, wrap them in paper, and order the milkman to deliver them at her cottage.

Susie promised to remember her, stroked all the cats, and said good-bye.

Though Susie had gone to Shelton along the road, she chose now to return home by the way of the downs.

As she walked upon the soft warm grass, the summer wind met her and blew caressingly through her thin frock and breathed upon her skin. The downs were so tempting to wander over that Susie went a little out of her way and sat down to rest near a rabbit warren.

The rabbits, who were out feeding, ran hurriedly into their holes, but soon, as all remained quiet, they peeped out again and began to feed and to be merry. A number of the rabbits were but half grown and knew nothing of snares or gins, and all the stoats in the neighbourhood had been killed by Keeper Dunkin.

As there was nothing to trouble them, the rabbits were gay. They lolloped a little, leaped into the air, and lay upon their backs, so that their white bellies gleamed in the sun. They even began to play in a wanton manner, running after and leaping over one another, and giving no heed to Susie, who watched their frolics.

She liked to see how they jumped and tumbled, and fancied they were entirely happy in their games. No one hindered or rebuked them, no dog barked, no fox was abroad. Near to the warren there was a stunted elder-bush that had withstood many a winter's storm, and was now garmented with scented flowers. The rabbits played about this bush in high glee. There was nothing to disturb their enjoyment; they could leap and be merry. When they wanted to rest, they nibbled the sweet grass.

But suddenly and quite unexpectedly a large black rabbit seized a young doe. The doe screamed. A magpie called out "Murder!" and every rabbit scampered in a hurry to his burrow.

The hillside was now entirely deserted; there was not a

creature to be seen. The warren might have been uninhabited, and the elder-tree might have lived there for ever alone.

Susie returned to the path, and she had not walked many steps before she came upon Joseph Bridle, who was waiting for her behind a small knoll. Joseph had been told by Winnie, who always liked to have a finger in everything, that Susie Dawe had gone to Shelton to visit her aunt, and that she expected her to return by the downs.

Joseph Bridle had hurried off when his work was done, without stopping to eat any dinner. Love whispered a fine story to him, saying that, if he used Susie after a certain country manner, he would compel her to be his. Love had been talking to Susie too, but his story to her was not the same as to Bridle. Love had told two different tales, and when he does that, unity is broken and a battle begins.

Susie, who wished to give herself to Death, had no desire to receive any kindness from Joe, however bold he might now wish to be. She needed more than that—a furious embrace—a burning in agony, with fire—and then, stillness. Though she had often in the past loved Joseph, she now began entirely to hate him. He stood, she knew, between her and Death.

As to Mr. Mere, she hardly thought of him at all; indeed it was only a wedding that she thought of, and her father had managed that. The wedding had already been much talked of, and John Death, as well as Winnie Huddy, had teased her about it. John had even hinted that some fun might come of it, and indeed he expected to be able himself to play a joke upon the farmer upon his wedding-night. A joke of John's.

When Susie heard the doe rabbit cry, she thought that she screamed too. And, because she was tormented, she wished to torment. Her own body rebelled and bit her; let her bite another! Her girlhood was now become something dangerous, something that wished to harm.

She knew what she must do; to pain in a subtle manner is easy to a woman. To lie down where the yellow flowers grow, to show a woman's cunning intimacy nearer and yet a little nearer, guiding the steps of her victim, who sees no farther than her allurements, until straightway he falls into the abyss.

John Death knows a thing or two; he had taught Susie how to dispatch a gloomy lover. Not all at once, either, not with one bite, but in the way that Tib, Mrs. Manning's cat, toyed with a fat mouse—a bite here and there, to show it how to die.

When Susie first saw Joseph Bridle behind the mound, she thought that he might be Death, but she did not show her disappointment and greeted him kindly. Joseph came to her; he saw her as pure glory, a delight—as love. He sprang gladly to her. He showed the fervour of his own passion, the green earth could hardly hold down his feet, he rose mighty in his desire to greet his beloved.

But Susie intended to alter all that fine gait, she would bend and break this large, frolicsome oak. She would make Joe peep and grovel, bow low to ask a boon, and fail to obtain it.

Susie walked quietly with Joe Bridle until they reached a green tumulus. Here a king had been buried, and more than one virgin had erstwhile been despoiled of her birthright. Here, Susie said, she wished to rest a little, and she lay down. Joseph saw her as his own. Her frock, her shoes, and the little puckers in her stockings, could never be, nor she who wore them, any one's but his. She was taken out of his body, bone of his bone, and he must gather her to him again as his wife.

Susie lay as if she wondered a little—as Eve must have

wondered when God made her—what it was that her husband would do to her. Then she smiled. Seeing her smile, Joseph supposed that his happiness was near. But yet he hesitated to consummate.

He was a man who liked all things to be done in order; he would much rather that their coming together should not happen so glaringly in the sight of the sun. And neither might the sun alone be the one to see, for often strangers walked upon those downs in the summer.

Susie moved her body. She invited his embrace. She imagined to herself that it was John Death who stood above her. And she longed for him to use her as a woman who loves wishes to be used by her beloved. She raised herself a little, and by an unmistakable gesture, bid him come to her. . . .

A thing of beauty may be changed in a moment. When suddenly the winter's chill leaves the fields, and a summer's day, with all its blessedness, covers the earth with warmth, instead of accepting the day as a gift for himself, a man will often be only surprised by it, and a little frightened. To be suddenly offered, as a free gift, what one has sought for a great while tremblingly, will often take away a man's breath and leave him cold. Bridle feared for Susie. He looked aside. He needed another god's blessings than the sun's, to be free for this pretty work.

Then Susie's brow clouded; she lured him to her no more. She sat up and began to taunt him, calling him names.

"Thee old moppet," she said. "What do 'ee want wi' I upon this pretty hill? Go down to Shelton and get Auntie to 'ave 'ee; 'tain't no young girl thee do want to marry, but an old wife who do keep cats. Thee be a fine man indeed, who be too pious to touch what 'ee do want. Maybe thee be afeared that Mr. Hayhoe mid see what thee be up to; they little rabbits bain't so cautious!"

Susie sprang up to mock him. She danced before him, uttering odd expressions, and kicked up her legs. Then she walked by his side, chattering like a magpie—very gay and pert. Her face was flushed and angry. Her companion had scorned her worse than ever Dodder girl had been scorned before.

She did not care now what she did. With a laugh she tore off her frock, and running in front of Bridle, waved the garment in his eyes, as though she baited a bull. Then she grew quieter, put her frock on again, and walking very near to Bridle, began to talk to him in a low tone.

Though she walked so quietly, her words astonished Joe. She talked like an abandoned harlot. She spoke of man's matters, as if such things had always been common to her, and she to them. All her kindly girl's ways now became a lecher's story. She told him all about Mr. Mere and his dog. She described, in crude village language, what Mr. Mere had wished to do to her, and how the old man meant to try his fancies upon her when they were married.

She knew, she said, as much now as any girl in Dodder—even Daisy Huddy knew no more than she.

Then, without any "if you please," she lay down and pulled him to her. But no sooner had she held him in her arms for a moment than she pushed him away from her. Coming towards them, along the downs, Susie had seen a man.

XXXIX

Death Wishes to Kill

A CHANGE sometimes comes over a human creature that is noticed by others more than by itself. A man may be lifted, translated, changed, and yet will appear to himself as the same being.

That last, awful, and final alteration of the human body —out of life into death—is a less noticed change to the man affected than to him who has watched the dissolution.

Susie thought she was the same girl, but Joe Bridle was alarmed by her appearance. From the flush of wanton merriment, her face had changed to a deathly pallor. This change Joseph could not understand, but on the whole he was glad that he had not known her when she lay down to him. For all her nonsense had only been perhaps the natural folly of a girl who has a mind to marry. She would be more willing and more eager when the proper night-time came.

She walked slowly by his side; her maid's blood had cooled, her loose, longing desires were stilled. She walked like one in a trance and seemed scarcely to breathe. Her legs, that only a few minutes before she had flung about so carelessly, could now hardly carry her weight; she staggered and nearly fell, and Joseph was forced to put his arm about her to keep her up, and thus they continued their way.

If one walks upon a path—be it but a thyme-scented track over a down, or the tortuous and difficult way of a man's life—when another figure approaches from the opposite direction, the meeting always comes sooner than expected.

Joseph Bridle and Susie Dawe had not proceeded along the down for many paces before Joe was able to recognize the man who was coming to meet them as John Death.

Country manners come from distant times: they are used now as they were of old. They never alter or change; they are the sediment at the bottom of the cup, that is always there. All is watched in a village, all is known. The old woman has not her one eye given to her for nothing. Young girls are her prey, she watches them like a cat.

John Death had not been long in Dodder before he discovered where news might be had. John had begun to smoke cigarettes; he purchased them in sixpenny packets from Mrs. Moggs, and for each packet he gave her in exchange a finger-bone. These bones Mrs. Moggs kept carefully in a drawer, and every day she tied a new one round her neck. John had told her that the bones of an unmarried girl, who had died in childbed, were a certain cure for an old woman's rheumatism. John said the bones came from the Dodder church-yard.

Besides receiving cigarettes in return for his bones, John was told all the news. For nothing went on in Dodder that Mrs. Moggs was not aware of. Death knew that Bridle had gone to meet Susie, and he went too.

No Dodder man notices a girl when another man is with her. Death approached Bridle, without looking at Susie.

Men meet to talk, and a woman who remains near to them—unless another of her sex is there too—is regarded as a listener to affairs that are not hers to hear. Joseph Bridle stepped a little out of the path, and John went with him, while Susie without saying a word—though walking more slowly than before—continued her way alone to Dodder.

When he met Bridle, John Death was surprised at his own feelings towards him. He wondered why he felt so strangely.

Until he had taken his holiday, Death had never known the pains of jealousy. No one before had ever disputed his right to a victim. Even One father who might have done so, had not stood between Death and an Only son. Death had never had, in all his long life, any cause until now to be jealous. He had always thought this particular vice—as he saw it among the children of Adam—hard to understand.

In order to be jealous, he was aware that one first must love. But as men loved so rarely, their petty jealousies seemed as nothing to John.

Death had never before met a living rival. A new experience is not always a pleasant one, and though John had not spoken to Susie, nor yet hardly noticed her, he fancied by her appearance that Joe had plucked a fruit that he himself had wished to gather. He had husbanded many a girl in the way of his trade, but never had he longed for one as he now longed for Susie, nor had he ever before been thwarted in his desire by a plain man.

Jealousy breeds suspicion, and suspicion—rage. Death was angry with Joe; he also mistrusted him. If Joseph Bridle had plucked Susie away from him, why, then, he might have stolen something else of his, too.

John had not, so far—no, not for one moment—thought that Joseph Bridle had found his parchment and kept it from him, but now, having seen him with Susie, he saw him as a thief too. If a fight came of it, John Death knew that he must win. One who has always been a conqueror can never believe it possible that he should be defeated.

Such an unlikely chance never even entered his mind. With every living thing at his mercy—a small flea and the hugest star—Death was not likely to think that a mortal man could do much against him. Though he could not kill even the meanest without a command, yet the most lofty ones he could cut low. One thought of him—even the thought of his near presence—had often made the most mighty to quail. A hand, writing upon a palace wall, could make a great king tremble. And who was this Joseph Bridle to stand in his way?

Though Joe spoke to John in the ordinary manner that one countryman addresses to another, yet he evidently paid hardly any heed to him, only following with his eyes the departing figure of Susie, growing smaller in the distance until it quite vanished.

Joseph Bridle and John Death were now quite alone.

Up to this moment, Death's occupation had been a humane one—if such a word may be used in this connexion—and his nature had always been kindly. He had never wished to pain, and, indeed, in his final embrace, as many suppose, he gives none, only performing what has to be done. And, as a faithful servant would, he fulfils the commands of his Lord, as quickly as the material worked upon allows.

But now an odd and almost human rage seized John. He longed to kill Bridle. He had not expected to see a fellow of his kind step across his path, and no doubt, he thought, had he been a little earlier, he would have seen a pretty pastime enacted. He ought to have hurried faster and have brought his scythe with him, and then he could have killed the two together, as Dady would have killed two clinging flies.

Ah! but the human holiday had made him think foolishly. For even Mr. Dady could not kill a fly with his thumb, unless some one, who walked now and again upon Madder Hill, knew of it. Neither could John Death kill his rival without a command.

Death looked grim. In the history of humankind, he knew that many a battle had occurred over a woman. Achilles cast a stone at Hector, and why should he not throw another at Joe Bridle?

Near to where the pair stood, there was a circle of grey rock. John Death seized one of these stones and cast it at Bridle. The stone struck him in the chest and threw him backwards, and Death followed up the blow with a fierce onslaught.

But, though the first blow took him a little aback, Joe Bridle was not altogether unprepared. A countryman is always ready to fight for the woman he loves, and Bridle had never expected to win so fine a prize as Susie without a battle or two. In one way he was rather glad to be attacked, for the suddenness and fierceness of the onslaught proved that John had not been so successful as he wished with his courting. They closed together in a strong embrace, and Death, though the older and smaller man of the two, gave Bridle a heavy fall.

Upon Madder Hill a man stood. This man watched the fight. The distance between Madder Hill and the lower down was not great, and from Madder Hill the two who were striving for mastery could easily be seen. The man upon Madder Hill was Mr. Jar, the tinker. Though no constant resident in those parts, he would often walk in that place because he liked the sweet air of the hill.

Mr. Jar spoke to Madder Hill—the hill groaned and thunder was heard. A cloud rose from the hill and moved towards the down.

Though Joe had been thrown, he soon rose and grappled his enemy again. They now appeared to be more equal in strength, and Bridle bent Death under him so that his ribs cracked. He would have laid him along in the grass—cast heavily—had not a singular thing occurred. While he was yet in Joseph's grasp, Death fell asleep. But Joe supposed that he had killed him.

He laid him tenderly down. He had not intended to injure him. When Death was getting the better of him, Joe bethought him of the parchment in his bosom, and putting in his hand, he touched the signature. It was then that a groan came out of Madder Hill, and a cloud rose from it.

A shepherd in the Dodder Lane thought that the cloud had a strange aspect. It appeared to be more a presence than a cloud, and moved with arms outstretched. When the cloud covered the down, Death fell asleep.

John's face was as pale now as Susie's had been, and yet, though he lay so still, he merely slept. He was so happy in his sleep that he smiled like a babe, or as one would who, for the first time in his life, enjoys a surprising and delightful sensation. Within a few moments, however, he sat up and rubbed his eyes and looked at Bridle.

"You are not hurt, I hope?" asked Joe, "for I had no wish to use you too roughly."

John Death smiled.

"Certainly," he replied, "you gave me a very curious feeling when you were about to throw me down that last time, a feeling that I had never experienced before, and for a moment I thought that I was lying with my sister, whose name you must have heard of."

"You fell asleep," said Bridle.

"I thought that I did," answered John, "but I never expected that a foolish wish for a mere girl would have led to such a consummation, and perhaps, had we continued the bout, I might have learned to sleep for ever. So complete a silence and so restful a contentment utterly overcame me. In those few moments a thousand years—all equally pleasing —might have passed over my head. All that I have ever been, all that I have ever done, became as nothing to me—I forgot my own name."

"You slept very soundly," said Bridle, "for when I took you up to see if I had hurt you, you breathed as gently as any little child who, falling asleep in its mother's arms, is laid in the cradle."

"You saw no one come near?" asked Death. "No cloud moving in a gentle silence came over us?"

"I thought there was a cloud," replied Bridle, "that came from Madder Hill."

Death sighed, and, rising from the grass, he began to walk with Joe Bridle towards Dodder:

"I think you must have seen," inquired John Death, who was now quite at his ease with Joe, "the notice in Mrs. Moggs's window, that she has put there to tell the people about my lost property? You have not found anything of mine, have you, in your field?"

"The field is mine no more," answered Joseph, gloomily, "though I may for a few days more call it mine, yet it belongs now to Mr. Mere."

"But perhaps you know," asked Death, "where my parchment is?"

"And if I did," replied Joseph, "I am no blabber of news, to tell another's secret."

"I believe I can compel you to tell me all that you know," said Death in a low tone. "You will understand me better when I tell you that Susie Dawe loves me. Her love may be but a maid's whim of a moment, but love me she does. She has already begged me to lie with her, and I am not the one to refuse a girl a wished-for embrace. But, even when I tell you this, you may yet think yourself sure of her, considering the wayward thoughts and the excitement of love. You may think, too, that it's merely village tattle which says that she is soon to marry Mr. Mere, but I know better. She will marry him. And, even if you do prevent that, I have only to lift my little finger and she will come to me. And I can promise you, Joseph," cried Death, laughing, "that I will not stay as near to her as you were this afternoon without an antic or two. But, ha! ha! I will send her off with a whisk, I will but slap her fine buttocks and order her to lie down to you instead of to me, if you do but tell me where my lost parchment is."

"I trust my love," answered Joe Bridle, calmly, "and though I know that Susie will laugh and talk with any one— and why should not a merry word be uttered by a girl?—I know her as mine own. She has but the happy manners of a young maid who feels the power of her beauty—she likes to tease too—but she will only yield herself to me because she knows I love her."

"That's a fine reason indeed for thinking a girl honest," laughed Death, "and as to Miss Susie, she has certainly taken a strange fancy to my person and will also, before many days are gone, wed Mr. Mere and be bedded by him."

"Never," cried Joe Bridle, "that shall never happen."

"And who are you, then?" asked Death with a sneer, "who can turn aside the hand of fate? Only One can do that."

"I know it," replied Bridle. . . .

Mr. Solly was collecting sticks upon Madder Hill. Winnie Huddy had informed him that she wasn't going to do all the work of the house while he remained idle. "They idle ways bain't proper for a man who be taking a wife," she observed, "so thee best fetch in they sticks."

Going round a large gorse-bush in search of dry dead wood, Mr. Solly came upon Tinker Jar. Solly, who had thought himself all alone, was surprised to see this man there. Mr. Jar sat upon the ground, his cloak was over his head, and he wept. Solly, who had always been a friend to sorrow and a companion to those who are acquainted with grief, inquired of Mr. Jar what was the matter.

"I fear, alas!" said Mr. Solly, compassionately, "that Love has found you out, as well as me."

Mr. Jar nodded.

"Though Winnie is engaged, there is Daisy Huddy," said Solly, innocently.

"I have done too much harm already," answered Mr. Jar.

"He is thinking of his kettles," thought Solly, and finding a few sticks, he hurried back to his house to tell Winnie whom he had seen.

XL

Winnie Insulted

VERY early, and long before any one stirred in Dodder, the sound of the swish of a scythe might have been heard—had there been any one abroad to listen—the morning after John Death and Joseph Bridle had wrestled together upon the down.

Before the first cock crowed, and before the hedgehog, who lived under some old faggots in the Vicarage garden, considered the time to be proper to run out and steal an egg for its breakfast, the field was mown.

There, in Bridle's field, lay the grass and flowers, in sweet undulating swaths, yielding up a delicious scent into the air. Cool and pleasant to the touch, and still wet with the morning dew, reposed the mown grass of the field.

The task being completed, John Death lay down to rest himself where the grass was thickest, and could not but envy the lot of a simple countryman, to whom the early lark sings joyfully, and who labours ever where true beauty lives. Death considered how happily such a life can be spent; toilsome, yet free from many troubles that possess other vocations, for he that in the winter carries the dung into the fields does also in the summer-time rest a while from his labours amongst the lilies that grow in the valley.

Leaving the field before any one had seen him, John Death returned to his cottage and lay down upon his bed, enjoying the holy sweets of rest that come after honest toil.

Soon the sun rose hot, and each day that followed was as

fine, so that within a week Mr. Mere carried the hay, and built of it a large stack in his own barton. When the hay was taken up every one noticed how closely Joseph's field had been cut. So that no more fodder was likely to grow there during the time that Joe had yet the field in his possession.

This was certainly a disappointment to Bridle, who had hoped that, even when the grass was cut and carried, there might have been some food left for his beasts, so that they could have grown a little fatter before they too, like the field, had to be sold.

But the interest that was taken in Bridle's hay being carried off by Mr. Mere was not the only matter that week that was spoken of. There was also the fine news to listen to and to communicate to others, that the gardens at West Dodder Hall would be thrown open to the public the next Sunday afternoon, being the day before Susie's wedding with Mr. Mere.

To enable all to go to the Hall who wished—and even the little boy, Tommy Moggs, who blew the Dodder church organ—Mr. Hayhoe had agreed to hold only the morning service on that happy day, and other village duties—perhaps as important as evensong—were put off too.

Every one in Dodder looked forward to this fine treat. Nothing so splendid, and nothing that seemed to promise so happy an afternoon, had happened in recent years. Every one in Dodder knew the outside look of the grand gates of the Hall, upon either post of which a strange beast was carved. To enter these would indeed be perfect bliss, and to scent one's handkerchief for such an occasion would be happiness to every young girl.

Mrs. Moggs had already begun to caution Winnie Huddy about her behaviour in the grounds.

"You mustn't laugh there, you know," said Mrs. Moggs.

" 'Tain't no church," replied Winnie.

"Mr. Titball says it's far holier," replied Mrs. Moggs, impressively, "and a little girl may learn to follow good ways all her life if she does but copy the sparrows who live in those beautiful gardens."

"They birds bain't always good," laughed Winnie, and ran out to play.

Death, who since he had mown Bridle's field had found little to amuse him, heard the news that West Dodder Hall was to be open to the public, with very real pleasure.

Though he had been appointed sexton of Dodder, no one had died. That was one cause of disappointment. Another was that Winnie Huddy would not let him play with her as he used to do. When he asked her now to run races, or to jump the flowering thistles, she would reply in a matron-like manner that such frivolities did not become a young lady who was engaged to be married to Mr. Solly, and possess—for herself alone—all his nut-bushes.

Death, who was become somewhat self-conscious since his stay in Dodder, and not a little proud too, whereas before this visit he had always been very humble, was not at all pleased to be thus flouted by a child whom he had come to regard as his proper playmate. He had always supposed that to live as a human being was as easy as to die as one. Work and play was all he thought human life to be. His own doings in the past, having been strictly limited to his occupation, had led him to think that man was indeed a blessed being when compared with himself, and that when he and his mystery were invoked by a mortal, it was merely to close a scene that had been acted long enough.

Though humble, as we may say, in his vocation, and taking no credit to himself for what he did, yet he had always had a little necessary pride in his personal attractions, and fancied that people often called him to them because they could not but admire his customary and courtly manner.

John Death came forth from his cottage, and Winnie Huddy skipped up to him. Winnie showed him, with the greatest pride, a sixpenny ring that she wore on her engagement finger. Mr. Solly had given it to her.

"Oh, Johnnie," she cried, "you would never believe what fine things Mr. Solly has in his house, and they will all be mine when we are married. There's a cabinet filled with silver and gold, and a drawer full of shells, and a real pearl necklace that he hangs round my neck sometimes, to see how pretty I look when I wear it."

Death did not reply; he caught Winnie up in his arms and carried her along the street and into the churchyard. When she saw where he was taking her to, she asked to be put down. This simple request she expected him—for she thought he had only taken her up as a joke—to obey at once. She had but anticipated a little play. Between play and danger there is no gulf fixed, but even a little child, as simple as Mr. Wordsworth's Lucy, knows well enough when matters grow queer.

Winnie gave a sudden kick. But Death held her firm, and pressing his hand over her mouth so that she should not scream, bore her further into the churchyard.

Though he had covered her mouth he had left her hands free, and as he carried her under the green branches of the great yew, he felt a sharp stab in his leg, like a wasp's sting, and let her drop. Winnie, who had not liked her situation, had detached a pin from her clothes and pricked him dexterously.

No sooner had Death dropped Winnie than she danced rather than ran to a tombstone nearby, and mocked him. Death looked at her gloomily.

"What is it that you did to me?" he asked, "because, for

the first time in my life, I felt a sudden impediment to happiness."

"An' 'twon't be the last time neither," replied Winnie, who was flushed and angry, "if thee do try to take I under they dark trees."

"But many children," answered Death, "even younger than you, Winnie—both boys and girls—have come here with me, and I have used them as my custom is."

" 'Tothers bain't I," replied Winnie, "and 'tain't to no churchyard that I do want to be brought, but only to West Dodder gardens; but for all that, I don't believe they be so fine wi' flowers as Hartfield that Mr. Hayhoe do read of."

John Death, looking happier, replied gallantly that he hoped to take her there.

Winnie plucked a pink from a grave and ran home.

XLI

A Debt Paid

AFTER he had been so easily defeated by Winnie Huddy, when he wished to take her under the spreading branches of the old yew, John Death left the churchyard and walked into the Madder street in no very good humour. Nor was his temper made happier by listening at Daisy Huddy's cottage door, where Winnie was narrating with the wildest merriment how she had given foolish Johnnie a prick to remember. He was not very well pleased, either, to hear Mr. Hayhoe gently chiding Winnie for permitting a man to carry her off in such a manner.

"Johnnie," cried Winnie, "don't know grapes from raisins; 'e do fancy that a maiden be butter to pat and shape; why, I do believe 'e had a mind to serve I same as wold Mere's bull do serve they silly cows."

"Oh! naughty Winnie," Daisy remarked, "don't you remember that Mr. Hayhoe is here?"

"What if he be?" laughed Winnie, "for bain't I the one to know what Mr. Darcy were after thik Lizzie for?"

Death moved away, wishing a little rudely that he might be permitted to crown the clergyman's forehead in an old and fashionable manner. He wandered on in a sulky humour, wondering how it had happened that a child had so easily outwitted him. He supposed that perhaps Mr. Jar, whom Death had more than once seen walking upon Madder Hill amongst the gorse-bushes, might have kept an eye upon Winnie, so that she could not have been harmed.

"But He doesn't look after them all so kindly," observed Death to himself, who, in his walk in life, had seen a thing or two.

Beside the green Death met Farmer Mere, who was returning from the Inn, where he had just cheated a poor drunken drover out of five shillings. Death stopped Mr. Mere and demanded the money that was due to him for the mowing of Joe Bridle's field.

Mr. Mere, with a grin that the Devil might have been proud of, informed John that he would pay him at Maidenbridge upon the next market-day.

"No deferred payment will do for me," replied Death, in a tone that he had not used since he had come to Dodder, "and no debtor of mine has ever gained a moment for himself by trying to put me off with fine promises. I demand to be paid at once."

The two men stood in the road alone. They stood, as countrymen will, with their legs a little apart, as if each leg were established there to prop up the body, preparatory to a lengthy conversation. Then some one came by.

Death was not surprised. He had fancied when Winnie stabbed him in the churchyard that Tinker Jar was not far off. Winnie could never have been so brave unless a protector were near. Mr. Jar passed close to the farmer, but turned his face from him.

John Death bowed. Mr. Mere cursed Jar.

Death asked again for his money. Farmer Mere jeered at him.

"The hay is all safe in my rickyard," he said tauntingly, "and who are you to expect your wage so soon? Do you think that money grows in a farmer's pocket like nettles in a hedgerow? Even though thee be—from the reverence you paid to him as he went by—a friend to that lousy beggar, Jar, who do go about as a thief to steal, yet what are you to ask money of me?"

Death stept aside and allowed Mere, who laughed loudly, to proceed towards the Manor Farm. And John followed him.

But instead of going up the drive to the Manor Farm, Mr. Mere's legs, against his own will, bore him in another direction.

There is one path that even a farmer who has been successful in defrauding a poor man, and is a little tipsy too, does not care to traverse—the path to the grave. Mr. Mere was surprised that his legs compelled him to go in that direction. But not his legs alone showed him whither he was travelling, for he saw with his own eyes that a certain pageant closely connected with himself was being enacted—a spectacle that no man, whether well or ill, can look at altogether calmly, unless he be a pilgrim in the way of holiness, who moveth no whither without a sweet presence that goes with him.

Mr. Mere now saw, all of a sudden, that he must die. This he had not before been able to believe, but now he knew death to be true. The last gasp that casts a man into eternal darkness must soon be given by him.

Coming near to the churchyard gates, he distinctly saw Mr. Hayhoe in his surplice, with a book in his hand, coming to meet him, and reading words out of the book that Mr. Mere did not much like the sound of. It was not John Death now who was the one to be mocked. There is another who can make a mock of even a Squire Mere or the Lord Bullman. While only he who has learned to love, in sorrow of heart and goodness of life, this grand revenger, and is prepared to sign a compact with eternity, is able to accept the final separation from life with a loving resignation.

Mr. Mere moved unwillingly towards the gate.

"Stay, Squire," cried John, "the direction that you are taking will never lead you to pretty Susie's bed. Do not forget how full of sweetness her fair body is; it's like Priscilla Hayhoe's red-currant jelly, all gracious delight. Her breasts are like round globes and her lips like an honeycomb. I know a great deal about women, more than you think I do, Mr. Mere. I have been the first with a number of them. They lie in bed and call to me to come to them. Of course I tantalize them a little. One cannot always be potent in an instant when one is wanted. A man so much in request as I has to hold back sometimes. Ah! you think that you alone can make a young maid cry out, but I can do so too, when I come to them. I give them pains for their pennies. Their tortured bodies cry and groan and drip blood because of my sweet embraces.

"When I approach these fair ones—and I always appear stark naked—their young eyes grow dim and droop in their excess of love. When I come to a girl she does not know her own mother. As soon as I enter the bedroom, the pretty things will often cast off all their clothing and lie naked before me. They lie in agony because of my love."

Mere strove to turn upon Death, but he could not do so. Death's taunts had awakened all the foul fury of his lusts. Behind him was the bridal bed, and all the merry sports that he meant to use upon his bride, proper to his nature—while before him he saw the loathsome pit of corruption. There he would be devoured in an ill manner. His evil tricks upon earth would change the lowly clods. He would never lie there in a sweet silence, as the good do, to whom the worms are as fair angels and the grave a casket of delight. Only the foulest hell would be his shroud.

Mr. Mere was near to the gates when he thought he heard these words spoken: "The Lord gave, and the Lord hath taken away."

He turned to Death and handed him a cheque for five pounds, that he had received that morning from Dealer Keddle to whom he had sold a fat calf.

John Death looked at the cheque a little suspiciously.

"But I wanted two silver shillings," he said, "to pay for Winnie and myself to go into Lord Bullman's garden to-morrow."

Mr. Mere did not reply. He put his hands to his ears so that he might not hear any more words being read by Mr. Hayhoe out of a book, and now that his legs obeyed him, he staggered off to the Manor Farm.

XLII

A Strange Sweetness

AN ENGLISH Sunday has come to be regarded by some as a mere day, and by others as a sad lady in a cap who pulls at the church-bells, with a wish that she was tolling them. Yet, quite unbeknown and unsought by those who have at certain times—as a conceit, whim, or fancy moved them—commanded that a settled ritual should be used to the glory of God, there has come into being a strange sweetness in country places to grace the Sabbath day.

Whatever can in any way stem the horrid waters of rude and hideous violence, has done and will ever do—though the belief may be utter folly—the greatest good to man. Who may not now kneel or rest or loiter, with this excuse to give to the more ardent labourers, that he worships the Lord? Let the High Temple priests still pretend, if such pretence can give to us poor ones a little release from toil.

The pastoral gods still live in mossy corners. Those who know the green places, that have each day a life and being of their own—wearing a new coat as the seasons change—take notice of the Sabbath day as one of the kind ones. It is a day of magic hours, wherein for a moment the pretty sparrow may forget the monstrous hawk.

Even the lonely church-bell, that in Dodder is rung by Daisy Huddy, who has changed her trade through listening to a good storyteller, may be to one who does not mean to attend the call, a pleasant sound to hear. Those who have the will to love this day—and I am a brother to them—

reckon it as somewhat more gentle and friendly to man than an ordinary working-day, and are glad to watch the slow and orderly manner in which Tom Huddy, having received a spirited command from Miss Winnie, goes to the well for water.

And with no need to hurry, he fills the bucket with Sunday care, brushes his coat upon which a little dust may have blown, and bears the bucket to his cottage in the same sacramental manner. As he came out, so he returns—this day his own master.

Mr. Huddy has always supposed the Sunday to be a fair maid, who may be looked at but not touched, but who lends to the day a virgin grace that compels all ugly toil, and even week-day clothes, to hide in covered places until the day ends. The feelings of even his Sunday trousers must be respected; it would not suit them to be seen climbing a hedge; they must be worn decently, or else the fair Maid Mary might complain.

A week is a long time. During a week the pains of labour may come upon a woman, the babe may be born, its name chosen, and the child carried to church to be baptized. A girl may be courted, married, and be sorry for it during the same period of time. Shepherd Brine may buy a new pair of boots, kick one of the soles off upon the dern of his own door, and be as bootless as before, in one week. Within a week a man may be taken ill, may suffer sadly, may die, and be buried.

It is something indeed to live from one Sunday to another. Though we cannot stop time, we can take more heed to its going, and every Sunday should be carefully noted.

Even the wych-elm beside the Dodder church gets a Sabbath look, as well as Mr. Titball. The winds knowingly rustle the leaves of the tree and set them a-praying, while during matins, upon a Christmas morning, the bare boughs droop a little and pretend to be pious.

It is all pretence, for when no one knows what truth is, what else is there to do but to pretend? All life is pretence, but never death.

That state stands as the one stone unturned in the fields of folly. In all other matters the world is as we like to make it, for not Jesus alone can turn water into wine. A tiny pool may seem the whole of the wine-dark deep, and Mr. Hayhoe's back garden can be a wild wilderness—as indeed it is.

Whoever has noticed cows walking upon the Sunday will observe that they are no episcopalians, for, on their way to be milked, they will loiter beside a chapel while a hymn is being sung—especially if it be by Charles Wesley—but pass the church with a flick of their tails to scatter the flies.

Sunday is a day of surprises.

Mr. Hayhoe puts on his surplice inside out. Daisy Huddy, who attends him in the vestry—to the scandal of some—readjusts the garment. Priscilla Hayhoe, with the hat that all admire, sits in the Vicarage pew and finds the correct place for evensong in her prayer-book. She turns the pages with caution, as though she thinks that something odd may creep out of them—a spider, perhaps, or an earwig—for no one knows what one will find in a church, any more than a woman knows what she will find in her own mind. A strange fancy—that she will not wish to tell to any one —will sometimes come into her thoughts as she follows the service in the book. It will but be a wish to follow after a little mouse that she has seen scamper from the altar table and hurry into its hole under the pulpit.

Then Priscilla looks at her book again; she is thinking of green lawns and fair flowers, a shadow cast by a sundial, a fair fountain in a rose garden.

XLIII

Mr. Balliboy and the Beast

MR. BALLIBOY was the Norbury carrier. But the people of that proud village were offended by him; he had insulted their vanity.

He had committed a sad sin. Mr. Balliboy had once permitted a beggar-woman named Mary—who expected, about Christmas-time, her bastard to be born—to ride in his van from Maidenbridge to where she lived, though none knew exactly where that place was. And so Mr. Balliboy's ordinary customers left him in a rage, and ever after that day they had travelled in Mr. Hawking's car.

But a tale told in one village with intent to injure a harmless man is not always heeded in another, and Mr. Balliboy would often call at Dodder for a load, and there his kindness to Mary, though it might have been heard of, was not believed.

Upon the Sunday that we have reached in our story, Mr. Balliboy arose from his bed with a liveliness in his heart that betokened a prosperous day. He hoped, too, as he put on his boots that the wish of his heart would soon be fulfilled. He wanted to marry.

But it was no woman that Mr. Balliboy desired to wed; he wished to marry an animal. He had ever respected and admired the brute creation, and especially those that bear burdens willingly. He had once, too, overheard a sermon preached by a young man of Folly Down to a bull, and he agreed with Luke Bird, the preacher, that the beasts of the field were more friendly than men. Having often seen, in the way of his trade, how the best women even behave to their husbands, Mr. Balliboy could never understand why the lawgiver Moses made so strict a rule against a man mating with a beast. The gift of speech had certainly done women very little good, no animal had ever learned to speak so unkindly. Mr. Balliboy had dreamed that very night that he had found a creature who would marry him.

"Such a wedding," thought Mr. Balliboy, "is common to all fairy stories, so why should it not come to pass in real life?"

Mr. Balliboy intended to take a party from Dodder to Lord Bullman's gardens. There was nothing he liked better, in the way of revenge for their treatment of him, than to give the Norbury people cause to wonder where he was going and what business he had to do. He rose early, and, in the presence of all who wished to view him, he brushed out and washed his car. And then, after retiring indoors and dressing himself as finely as a bridegroom, with a white flower in his coat, he rattled out of Norbury in a grand manner.

The gardens at West Dodder Hall were to be opened at one o'clock, and Mr. Balliboy waited beside the Dodder Inn, informing all who came near to look at him, that his charge for taking passengers to the great gates was only one shilling, to go and return.

Winnie Huddy was one of the first to come to him, and after informing her of his price, he drew her near to him and inquired in a whisper whether Winnie knew of any creature in Dodder, any friendly beast of burden, that was in need of a good husband.

" 'Tain't no woman I do want to marry, 'tis an animal," he said.

Such a subject as matrimony, Winnie, who had listened to Mr. Solly's conversations and to Mr. Hayhoe's readings, looked upon with extreme seriousness, and she showed the utmost respect for Mr. Balliboy's inquiry. She did not even smile. Indeed the request seemed to her to be extremely sensible, and she replied readily, "Maybe thee'd fancy a good camel, for I do know of one that do bide in Dodder."

Mr. Balliboy looked very glad.

"She don't kick, do she?" he asked timidly.

"No," answered Winnie, "she do only work."

"Then 'twill be a wedding," cried Mr. Balliboy joyfully.

As may easily be expected, there were many who preferred to ride two miles upon a very hot day than to walk. Mr. Hayhoe, always an early man when he went anywhere, was the first to step in. He asked Mr. Balliboy whether he would mind waiting a few moments for Priscilla.

Mr. Hayhoe looked a little troubled, for, no sooner had he come forth from the church after matins than a note was put into his hand by Mr. Pix himself, demanding that he should visit Lord Bullman at once, or else the living of Dodder would go to another.

We are all of us packed into this world—though there ought certainly to be plenty of room—nearly as close together as the occupants of Mr. Balliboy's car, and we are quite as odd a mixture. The car was soon full, but as the custom is with such a carriage, it could always hold another.

At their first coming together, a company setting out upon a holiday is a silent creature: the women look at one another and the men sit gloomily and feel in their trouser pockets. Mr. Titball sat next to Mr. Dady, and Dillar regarded with a fixed stare old James Dawe and Susie, who were going together to see the flowers.

But quite unexpectedly a match was struck that made

all merry. This was done by Winnie, who burst in with the news that Mr. Solly, as well as Mr. and Miss Bridle, were going too, and that they were already in sight. Winnie, who sat next to Mr. Balliboy, touched his arm and whispered into his ear.

" 'Tis thik camel who be coming."

Mr. Balliboy wondered.

"Be she going to ride in car?" he asked anxiously.

"Certainly," answered Winnie, "for though 'tis a camel, she be grown up like a woman."

Winnie was in high glee, and no sooner had John Death climbed into the car and sat himself in front of her, than she told all the company how John had attempted to carry her into the churchyard.

"Sister Daisy do say," cried Winnie, noticing that Death hung his head a little, for no one likes all that he does to be told, "that a man be like a new broom that do want to sweep in all the corners. But a churchyard be only good for the dead to lie in."

"And what are you?" asked John Death, looking at Winnie angrily.

"One of the living," answered Winnie boldly.

Once Winnie had started talking it was hard to stop her.

" 'Tis Johnnie who be paying for I to go today," she remarked, "but when I am married to Mr. Solly, I shall be forced to take him wherever I go, for 'tain't safe to leave a husband alone with the cats."

Solly blushed. He had walked over from Madder on purpose to go to the gardens with the Bridles.

"But we must not leave our nut-garden, Winnie," he said.

"Not when the nuts be ripe," answered Winnie.

Miss Bridle smiled at Mr. Balliboy, who, because the

car was not started, regarded her with much curiosity. Miss Bridle liked him to look at her and smiled the more coyly.

Mr. Mere had not come, for a man of his situation in life never travels in such a mean manner, and, besides, he had many preparations to make for his wedding upon the next day.

And now all was ready, and yet Mr. Balliboy did not start his van. No one knew why, but presently the mystery was explained. Mr. Balliboy shook his head, nodded, shrugged his shoulders, and turned suddenly to face Sarah Bridle.

"Thee be a camel, bain't 'ee?" he asked her.

Miss Bridle blushed and observed that she had always supposed so, though since she had known Mr. Death she had not been quite so sure of herself. Mr. Balliboy looked at her with large admiration.

"Thee be a camel," he cried, "a camel who be going to be married."

"To whom?" asked Mrs. Moggs excitedly.

"To me ownself," replied Mr. Balliboy, and started the car in a hurry.

Now that the car was started, Death became more at his ease, and he ventured to explain to Mrs. Moggs that he had never known any one before who had dared to mock him as Winnie Huddy had done.

"In my habitation, to which I take the young girls that I fancy," observed Death, "none ever dare to prick me with sharp pins."

"You wait till I visit you!" cried Winnie, who had heard what he said.

Death changed the subject, and, realizing that Winnie had the best of him, he began to boast, like another Mr. Card.

"There is no corner of the world," he cried, "no, nor of the firmament either, where I am not feared and honoured. The first principle in every religion is the fear of me. Kings, princes, and popes all bow before me. A mouse is afraid of me, and so is Lord Bullman. I possess a fine weapon with which, as every generation comes, I conquer the world."

" 'Tis only thik wold scythe 'e do boast of," whispered Winnie, in a tone of supreme contempt, to Mrs. Moggs.

They were now beside the great gates, and Mr. Hayhoe, with a pleasing formality, gave Priscilla into the care of Mr. Solly, who promised to show the lady all that there was to be seen, and to conduct her safely back to the Dodder Vicarage, in case Mr. Hayhoe returned home by another road.

Mr. Hayhoe was the first to hurry away. The remainder of Mr. Balliboy's load alighted more slowly. For a while no one was brave enough to approach the gatekeeper, who, dressed for the occasion, showed by her grand manner that she was the head-gardener's wife, to whom the shilling fee was to be given, and from whom permission must be asked to enter the garden.

Mr. Balliboy, still seated in his car, regarded the waiting group with compassion, and in all kindliness informed them of the time when he would return to Dodder. But they still lingered by the car—their ark of safety—wishing perhaps to return home at once rather than to advance into those spacious lawns where noble feet were wont to tread.

But Mr. Balliboy was obdurate; he turned his car, and the company were compelled to separate. Then seeing that Miss Bridle still lingered, he told her, with many winks that showed his happiness, that he meant to marry her in a month.

"And mind thee be still a camel," he shouted.

Sarah bowed.

Seeing the car depart, the visitors to the gardens were forced to be more bold. Mr. Huddy and his daughter Daisy were the first to enter, Daisy paying the fee for admission with two shillings that Mr. Titball had just given to her as a proper payment for washing six pairs of sheets. The Bridles came next, followed by Susie Dawe and her father. And, after them, the rest—with the exception of John Death and Winnie—all came to the gate at once, and received a proper rebuke for their crowding from the lady-keeper, who bid them one and all learn better manners when they visited society.

John Death and Winnie Huddy came last of all, and John gave a coin to the woman that she looked at suspiciously, though she allowed them to pass.

John Death frowned. He walked silently for a few moments, and then, turning more gaily to Winnie, he promised to show her, before the day was out, a tame bear, that he assured her he would make dance a little to amuse them both.

"And now," he said, "I mean to walk for a while in the gardens—alone."

"Don't 'ee go getting off wi' no young woman," said Winnie, "for 'tis I thee be come with."

"I have only to speak a word or two to Susie Dawe," replied Death, "so run after Daisy; we shall soon meet again."

All who came now began to behold the wonders of these enchanted grounds, gazing silently, holily, as if they moved in the nave of a great cathedral, under the very eyes of the Dean. To see the great house so nearly, and even to take a peep through the drawing-room window, where the grand lady might be sitting, with her hands—that could hardly be seen because of her gold and jewelled rings—

lying still in her lap. A sight to make any village-dweller gape with awe and wonder.

" 'Twas hardly possible, indeed," considered Mr. Titball, who looked upon his old home with the greatest reverence, "that any mortal man could possess such a palace, or keep so many dogs and fine servants. Who indeed—save a God—could be sheltered by so many box-hedges when he walks in his grounds, and possess so many great trees to shade him, and so many peacocks for his family to admire?" Mr. Titball almost knelt down to worship his lord.

Mrs. Moggs, too, held up her hands in wonder at all she saw there, and even gazed with awe at a crow who happened, being in no immediate hurry to go anywhere else, to rest a while upon a telephone post. Mrs. Moggs supposed Jim Crow to be a Phœnix.

The others, too, wandered here and there with wide-open eyes, and tongues prepared at any moment to cry "miracle!" The glasshouses amazed every one, except Winnie Huddy, who was chid by Mrs. Dady for unseemly chatter.

"You ought not to talk here," said Mrs. Dady. "These wonderful plants, that be only plucked by lords and ladies, do not like to hear you."

"Oh!" cried Miss Winnie, "they flowers bain't nothing to what Mr. Hayhoe do tell of that be at Pemberton Manor. And there," observed Winnie, with a toss of her head, "a pretty young maiden mid go in free."

And, laughing louder than ever, Winnie snipped off, when no one was looking, a bloom of hydrangea.

XLIV

The Assignation

JOHN DEATH had not far to go to find Susie Dawe. He had begun to be heartily ashamed of himself. For, in order to be thought anything of, he had been forced to boast of his greatness in Mr. Balliboy's car, and had, in response, only been nodded to by Mrs. Moggs, and mocked by a girl-child—surely the deepest degradation! To have fallen so low was indeed gall and wormwood to his soul. The state of his mind can be imagined, when, as the most mighty potentate in the whole world, he had cried up his own wares, only to be laughed at for his pains.

But he now meant to do more than boast. Under a tree he found James Dawe and Joseph Bridle, who were talking earnestly together. Joe was begging Dawe to delay, for only a few days, his daughter's wedding. He had a reason for this request, he said, but James Dawe only replied coldly that the matter was settled: that he had promised his girl to Farmer Mere, and to Mere she must go.

Death left them together and continued his way. In a secluded walk nearby he found Susie. She was expecting him, and he came just in time. Had he not come to her, she would have sought a lonely pond—she knew that there was one in those grounds—and slipped in under the water-lilies. But now she met Death with a cry of joy. She was very pale, but her eyes shone with desire, and she greeted Death lovingly.

They were alone in the path. Death led her to a mossy bank that was nearby, and they lay down.

Susie then began to use all the wanton toying ways of a girl who has abandoned herself wholly to love. She showed herself sighingly, and begged for his embrace.

Death leaned over her, but instead of doing what she wished him to do, he whispered words to her. Susie trembled with terror, and her body grew very cold. She tried to scream, but she could not. She struggled for a moment, trying to rise, and then she lay very still, with her eyes shut.

Death watched her, burning with the fierce passion of love. He let her lie. His love was not the whim of a moment, to be satisfied and eased by a merely fleshly mating. He must have more than that. The consummation that he longed for must be a lasting one. He and Susie must share together one grave for all eternity. No matter whether his dread work were continued or not, no matter for that, so long as he and Susie lay together. But now that she knew the truth about her kingly lover, would she wish to listen to his vows?

Susie opened her eyes and looked at him, but with no fear.

"I assure you," said Death, looking upon her very lovingly, "that though a certain book called Wisdom states that I am not created by God but am only here because of man's sin, yet I may tell you, Susie, that no untruth ever written has been so untrue as that lie. I am born of the sorrows of God; I am the second child, made, as all things are made, of His spirit, of His love. Look upon me. Am I not the most true consolation; am I not the most blessed angel of abiding love? You will find no mortal husband as faithful as me. Even Joe Bridle, whom you love, and who certainly loves you too, will, if you wed him, let you go down into the pit alone, leave you there, and return to his own house. Come to me, and I will be with you for ever."

Susie drew Death to her and kissed him lovingly upon the mouth.

Death whispered to her.

"Yes," she said, in answer to him, "I will come to you in the Dodder churchyard tonight when the first star—the holy evening star—is in the sky. You will be sure to dig the grave—our bed, in which we shall sleep together—and you will give me your love?"

Death looked anxiously around.

"You must tell no one," he whispered, "or we may be yet defeated, for if you say a word to a living soul, our nuptial pleasure will be taken from us.—Perhaps already some one has overheard us!" Death looked in the direction of Madder Hill. "Though what will come of this love of ours I do not know. It is possible that, when our marriage is consummated, the whole earth may pass away and be no more, for I have a wish to strike myself with my own weapon when you are dead. And if that is done, a great cry of sorrow will rise up from all flesh, and the cry will reach the stars that Death is dead, and all things will mourn, for the sleep of God will be taken away. If my law is broken—and I care not if it is, so long as you are mine for ever—the whole firmament will mourn, because the horror, worse than extinction, has come upon it—the horror of everlasting life. The great weeping seas of sadness will sweep over the coasts of light, and men will blind themselves with their own hands and grope in darkness, because of their eternal misery."

"I will come to you," cried Susie, clinging to Death. "I will tell no one. Do but dig the grave deep, only"—and she trembled—"it won't have to be a cut, will it? Can't you press me to death with your body? You won't have to cut me, will you, darling?"

Death looked troubled.

"It must be so," he said; "but my scythe is very sharp. There will only be one gush of warm blood, and then your sweet body will be mine."

Susie held up her face to him so that he might kiss her, but he turned away.

"Tell me first," said Death, "do you know where my lost parchment is—the command to Unclay?"

"Truly," answered Susie, "I do not know where it is."

Death looked at her uncertainly.

"Oh, do not think, I pray, that I could deceive you," she cried. "I could not lie to you whom I love more than my life. I have no idea where your paper can be. Though every one has talked of it, I have heard none give more than a guess as to where it might be hid."

"I believe you," said Death, holding her in his arms and kissing her, "but I only asked you this question for your own sake, as well as for mine. For if the paper is given into my hand, as soon as I have—in a reasonable time—obeyed the order, I must give back the clothes that I have but borrowed, and I will never appear bodily to men again, but only as a presence."

"A very loving one," sighed Susie.

"To the good and to the humble in heart, that know me," replied Death, "I will be always kind."

Susie held him closer to her.

"Must I wait till this evening comes?" she murmured. "I burn in a fierce fire, and long to be cooled. Dig the grave soon, so that no one may find us."

Death laughed lightly, and began to be merry with her.

"Ah, ha!" he cried, "'tis a fine happy end to my holiday,

that a young woman should wish so much that night-time should come, and even longs for a deep grave to be her sweet bridal bed. But come," he said, leaping from the grass, "for your father needs the help of your beautiful eyes to search for a penny that he heard Winnie Huddy say that she had lost in the grass."

Death kissed Susie, and walked away. He had only gone a few steps when he turned and said:

"You will come to me, Susie?"

"Yes," she replied faintly, "I will come."

XLV

Mr. Hayhoe Shakes His Head

AFTER leaving Mr. Balliboy's car and paying his shilling to the guardian of the gate, Mr. Hayhoe stept hurriedly through the lordly grounds and reached the mansion.

He would have preferred to have gone, as Parson Adams would have gone, in another century, to the back door, but as the cloth is supposed to be held in greater honour now than then, Mr. Hayhoe went to the front entrance.

He could not help feeling a little ashamed—for he knew that he was not much to look at—when he pulled the bell-rope, and he was aware that the great door looked contemptuously at him. This door had evidently taken into its oaken heart the spirit of pride, and was become like its owner. Looking at the outer world, as a proud door would look, it seemed to dare with its oaken frown any tramp or poor man—other than my lord's proper servants—to approach within a hundred paces of its power and might. The appearance of this door proclaimed it to be only the splendid portal that led to grander things within.

"Behind my strength and majesty," it said, pompously, "the highest gentility in the land have ever lived, secure and safe. The great lord is even now resting upon a golden chair in the throne room, and quaffing wine from a huge goblet. And, if my lord be absent, my lady will still be there, in her best attire."

The door, having spoken thus, was in no hurry to open.

Mr. Hayhoe had already pulled the bell twice, and there had been no response to his ringing.

"To venture at all," he thought, "into so huge a fastness was bad enough, but to have to pull a great iron bell until your hand hurt, in order to get there, was worse."

Mr. Hayhoe pulled the bell again.

After waiting for a few more moments, the great door was cautiously opened by inches, for the footman supposed that one of the unwelcome visitors into the gardens had wandered by chance that way to ask for a glass of water.

Perceiving a clergyman, he permitted him, in a manner that suggested a very special favour, to follow where he led, and so guided Mr. Hayhoe to a little room in which Lord Bullman received his tenants or gave orders to his steward. Leaving Mr. Hayhoe there, and without inviting him to sit down—a common politeness that one servant should yield to another—the man withdrew, whistling.

To walk upon thick carpets, which he had been forced to do in order to reach that little room, had always alarmed Mr. Hayhoe. Because his feet made no noise, he might well doubt whether his own presence were there at all, and fear that he might be dreaming. But the little room pleased him better when he reached it than the lordly carpeted chambers through which he had passed. To his humble senses this apartment was more real than the greater and more spacious halls.

"It is evidently," thought Mr. Hayhoe, "out of consideration to my feelings that my lord has bid his servant to lead me here. He would have been kinder still had he directed all poor clergy to the kitchen."

Mr. Hayhoe, having nothing else to do—for his presence appeared to be entirely ignored in the great house—began to admire the pictures that were hung in the little room.

In each picture the painter had portrayed the gay doings of the huntsmen and the hounds. In one, the hounds were shown in the final scene of pouncing upon the fox; while, in the next, the grand master of the ceremonies was holding up to the view of all who wished to see the brush of the defeated victim, having just cast the carcass to the dogs. The fine gentleman held a large whip in one hand and the tail in another. A dog looked up at him with holy veneration. In the third picture there was shown a finely attired huntsman, well mounted, whose steed was in the very act and climax of leaping over a five-barred gate.

Mr. Hayhoe shook his head at that picture. All art, he believed, should be inspired by the love of truth, and although he was well aware that the poets lie, he had hoped that painters followed the truth more nearly.

"That fine gentleman in the red coat," murmured Mr. Hayhoe, as he studied the picture, "should have been portrayed, not flying over a gate, but humbly—though perhaps unsuccessfully—trying to open one. For, alas, the monstrous sin of pride is fed by all untrue representation."

After looking at the pictures, Mr. Hayhoe took the liberty—an extreme one, it seemed, in that house—of taking a chair, and sitting himself down, he brought out from his pocket a book that he opened at these words: " 'This must be a most inconvenient sitting-room for the evening in summer: the windows are full west.' "

Mr. Hayhoe looked at the windows, and shook his head. He thought the room rather pleasant. He read on, and forgot where he was.

XLVI

Lord Bullman Walks to the Window

LORD BULLMAN had missed his vocation. He would have made, had he been born in another sphere of life, a very good rural policeman.

He knew a thief by his nose. And if there happened to be any mystery in a case of robbery, he knew himself as the man to unravel it, and to detect the miscreant. Ever since the Sunday suit of clothes had been stolen from the dead man in Merly Wood, Lord Bullman had never grown tired of telling his friends that, though it might not be easy to obtain sufficient evidence to convict, yet he felt sure that the thief resided in Dodder, and that his Christian name was John.

"His nose proclaims his guilt," Lord Bullman observed sternly to his lady after lunch, upon the day when the gardens were open to the public. "Yes, his nose is his ruin," said my lord in a louder tone; "if a man steals one thing he will steal another; this John has discovered old money. I have found out all about it. Card of Tadnol has come before the bench exactly nine times, charged with lying dead drunk in the streets of Maidenbridge. Card is John's landlord, and receives old Roman gold as his rent. John's nose has stolen it."

Lady Bullman sneezed.

Lord Bullman jumped from his chair. He was always unlucky, even in those great rooms. If his wife caught a cold, he always—though he kept as far off her as he could

—managed to catch it too. He thought he felt his throat itch—that was how his colds always began. Lord Bullman walked angrily to the window. Looking out of it, he beheld his lordly grounds filled with strange people. He had thought only a few would come, but the place was overrun by them. Some moved upon the lawns, some in the paths; the public was everywhere.

"What fool was it," shouted Lord Bullman, in anger, "who advised the opening of other people's gardens to the vulgar?"

"I believe it was the King," murmured Lady Bullman.

"Poor misguided innocent," answered her husband, "he knows no better. I think I shall emigrate," said Lord Bullman, very dejectedly, looking sadly into his gardens. "I think I shall become a pilgrim father and emigrate if this ever happens again."

"But where will you go to?" inquired Lady Bullman, with a smile and a little cough.

"To the cannibal islands," replied he, "for there, surely, it would be easy to empty a nobleman's gardens of the rude populace."

Lady Bullman yawned.

There was a knock at the door, and the servant who opened it observed in a careless tone that Mr. Hayhoe, the curate of Dodder, awaited his Lordship's pleasure in the tenants' parlour.

"How long has he been there?" inquired the master.

"About an hour, my lord," replied the man.

Lord Bullman proceeded at once to the little room.

"I have sent for you, Mr. Hayhoe," he said, after coldly greeting his guest, who rose with a happy sigh from his chair, and thrust a book into his pocket, "to tell you that I have heard stories about you. No, do not reply"—for Mr.

Hayhoe was about to say something—"I am unfortunately aware that you know Daisy Huddy too intimately, and surely it is not proper that I should present the living of Dodder to a carnal sinner? I myself have seen you with her, and I am told that Daisy is a wicked young woman."

"My lord," answered Mr. Hayhoe calmly, "your informant has been mistaken. This young woman, through the grace of Jane, is no longer a sinner. She has taken the scarlet thread from the window, and would have made me a waistcoat of it, only Winnie asked for it first. I merely visit the cottage to read books aloud."

"I trust that one of those books is the Bible?" exclaimed Lord Bullman.

"Alas! no," replied Mr. Hayhoe, with a blush, "for after I was unlucky enough to read Joshua to Daisy, I have not ventured upon anything else in those holy pages. I then received a sad lesson that I have taken very deeply to heart, and although the Roman church is very much in the wrong for not allowing their priests to marry—for no man can ever get to heaven without the help of a Priscilla—yet in the matter of Bible reading, the older Church does show more wisdom than we. Daisy knows all about Rosings."

"Then you have certainly corrupted her," cried Lord Bullman.

"I have done my best to make her happy," said Mr. Hayhoe.

"In a country way," answered Lord Bullman, with a short cough.

Lord Bullman moved a chair; he opened the door to see that there was no one behind it, and blew his nose. He scratched his ear, and buttoned his coat. He stood first on one leg and then on another, as if he wished to show his fine trousers. Then he stepped near to his guest.

"You may still keep my favour," he observed, in a low tone, "and be as secure and safe in your benefice as any fox upon Madder Hill when hunting ends. I presume that you believe all laws to be right and just that have been made in Christian times?"

"When they are kind ones and are useful to mankind," replied Mr. Hayhoe.

Lord Bullman struck his knee with his hand.

"There is no kinder or more useful law," he cried, "than the one that gives the right to the lord of the manor to know carnally, within his barony, every maid that is about to be married. But, alas, like so many of our best things"— Lord Bullman took out his gold watch—"this law is said to have been made first in Germany, though I can assure you that we in England were soon converted to it."

Mr. Hayhoe smiled.

"I am aware," continued Lord Bullman, "that at first a little secrecy ought to be used in re-establishing this ancient right, for the opinions of our bench of Bishops, who are lords too, are inclined to be a little uncertain, as well as somewhat contradictory, in matters of sound legislation. Those who are undecided what to write in the Church prayer-book are not likely to understand the proper and rightful desires of the first estate. Alas! these bishops—some of whom are, I suppose, gentlemen—may be unaware that this law, Jus Primæ Noctis, was blessed and sanctified for many ages by the Holy Church."

"Not by mine," said Mr. Hayhoe, stoutly.

"But surely, sir, you will not deny," observed Lord Bullman, "that here in England there is one law for the poor and another for the rich?"

"I know it, to my own sorrow," replied Mr. Hayhoe.

Lord Bullman held himself very proudly.

"A great baron," he exclaimed, "has the right to do with his whole body what a mere plebeian may only accomplish with his smallest finger. You must surely be aware, Mr. Hayhoe—as you have been, I believe, a student of history—that in this country, at least, the ways of the rich and of the great have always been the same. They slay, they ravish, they take large manors with the sword, they build churches and brew beer, they make kings and then despoil their kingdoms, and when all that is done, they begin at the beginning again, as we all have to do, and learn to plant cabbages. They rob when they can, they caper when the Guards' band plays, they see their pictures in the papers attending the races in Dublin, they suffer from the gout, and would willingly sell all their woods for one friendly girl.

"And what, Mr. Hayhoe, is the good of a landowner residing upon his own lands, if he is never permitted to eat of the first and best fruits that grow upon them? I am neither a wine-bibber nor a glutton, but I like to have what is my due.—You are a philosopher, Mr. Hayhoe?"

"Alas! no," replied Mr. Hayhoe, "I am only a Christian."

"All the great teachers of philosophy, as well as the creators of religion," cried Lord Bullman, "tell us that we ought to make happiness, both here and hereafter, the chief aim of our existence, so that each one of us might have restored to him—or to her—the original and innocent joy of life that was lost in the fall of man. I believe I can tell a thief as well as another when I see one. The Devil is the worst of them; 'twas he who put into the mind of the saintly Paul the thought that a man must not enjoy himself in the right and lawful manner with a woman, and so stole our pleasures."

"Marriage is commended by Saint Paul and instituted of God in the time of man's innocency," replied Mr. Hayhoe.

" 'Twas certainly my innocence that caused me to wed Lady Bullman," said my lord. "Surely you must be aware, Mr. Hayhoe, that, as lay Rector of Dodder, and therefore your superior in office, all obedience—as Saint Peter wisely said—must be rendered to me? Your duty, therefore, if you wish to have the living of Dodder, is as clear as the day —but I will now tell you what that duty is.

"A young girl, whose name is Susie Dawe, and who lives upon my estate, is going to be married tomorrow. I have heard a very good account of her from Mr. Pix. She is obedient to her parent, and attends church every Sunday, and, as far as my information goes, she has never run the streets with the boys. I am told, too, that she is very beautiful, and if she answers one question to my satisfaction, we shall be happy. Surely it is not possible that so much loveliness and good behaviour should all go to Farmer Mere, who fastens his gates with barbed wire, and once, upon my sure knowledge, aimed his gun at a fox that was carrying off a prize turkey.

"Mere shall not have all of Susie. It is my duty to restore a proper custom, that has given much pleasure in the past, to its former position. I command and desire that pretty Susie be brought to my bed tonight at a quarter past eleven, for that is the hour, when I stay in the country, that I retire to rest. I assure you that I am able and willing to fulfil this law."

"I do not doubt your word, my lord," answered Mr. Hayhoe, "though I am sorry that you have reminded me of this unlucky wedding, for I do not like to think of it. God pardon me for saying so, but I believe that Mr. Mere is a wicked and a cruel man. My wife and I have both prayed to God to frustrate this wedding."

"Oh, Mr. Hayhoe," cried Lord Bullman, "what has a poor clergyman to do with praying to God in such a manner? and if you pray at all, 'tis for your fee you should ask. You will be sure to find me a better paymaster than Farmer Mere. Do but send Susie to me as the guest of my housekeeper, and the living of Dodder is your own."

Mr. Hayhoe was about to reply to my lord's request when a knock came at the door, and a servant entered holding a coin in his hand.

"Mrs. Mitton," said the man hurriedly, "who keeps the gate open for the populace between the hours of one and six, and is obliged to let any one in who pays a shilling, has received this piece of money from a man who also brought with him a little girl, wearing a pink frock, with bare legs, who shakes her curls naughtily."

"And the man?" inquired Lord Bullman eagerly, "did Mrs. Mitton notice his features?"

"He pulled his hat over his face," replied the servant, "but the girl had the sauciest look that ever Mrs. Mitton had seen."

"Do you know this child?" inquired my lord, turning to Mr. Hayhoe.

"Oh yes," answered Mr. Hayhoe, gladly. "She is Winnie Huddy, and she came with John Death in Mr. Balliboy's car."

Mr. Hayhoe would have added more, only at that moment another person pushed himself into the company. This was none other than Mr. Mitton himself—a short man, but very stout—who brought with him the grandest air of importance.

"The proletariat are behaving themselves, I trust?" asked Lord Bullman, anxiously, "and are keeping to the paths, and have read the notices, about banana skins and sandwich paper?"

Mr. Mitton was unable to reply at once. He was a Baptist and believed in the Devil, and would often talk with Mr. Pix about the sins of the world and of the monstrous immorality of a coloured caterpillar who ate the currant bushes. He had walked faster than was his wont and panted with anger.

Lord Bullman noticed his condition with great concern. He had never seen Mitton more put out, and although he was aware that this high summer tide of the rabble was likely to trouble him, yet the head-gardener's demeanour showed clearly that something more than usually outrageous must have happened.

"A girl has come in," Mr. Mitton exclaimed, as soon as he was able to speak, "who is walking the grounds with a man who is not her husband. I heard him call her Winnie, and she has just been saying that the noble loggia your lordship has built is no better than Farmer Mere's cowhouse. She called the man Johnnie."

Mr. Mitton clenched his fist.

"It's my belief," he shouted, "that this man is Satan, and that he has climbed into these gardens over the wall. He has come to steal your lordship's plums to give to the young angels."

" 'Young devils,' you ought to say," observed Mr. Hayhoe.

Mr. Mitton did not heed the interruption.

"And how do you account for this girl's boldness?" inquired Lord Bullman of his gardener.

"My wife says," replied Mr. Mitton, with a loud groan, "that Winnie never paid for her pink frock."

"Of course she didn't," cried Mr. Hayhoe. "It was Mr. Solly who gave it to her."

Mr. Hayhoe approached the head-gardener.

"Mrs. Mitton," he said happily, "has taken quite a wrong view of the matter. Little Winnie is the saviour of her sex. She is as pretty as the first celandine, and has taken a sad reproach from womankind. She has converted an old infidel in such matters—Mr. Solly—to the true religion. Before he knew Winnie, Mr. Solly saw all women as turnips, but now that Winnie has shown him his error by her loving and modest conduct, he has promised to marry her."

"Tell me when?" cried Lord Bullman eagerly.

"In about nine years' time," replied Mr. Hayhoe.

Lord Bullman sighed.

"I will send for the police," he exclaimed. "We will shut the gardens to all strange people. Whether this John is really the Devil, as Mitton says, I do not know, but I am certain that he is a thief, and before we are aware of what he is up to, he may rob us of our very lives."

"We will catch him in the act," cried Mr. Mitton. "We will go, my lord, and arrest him at once."

"Only let me fetch my hat first," exclaimed Lord Bullman excitedly.

XLVII

A Bed of Begonias

On THEIR way to the part of the grounds where John Death had been seen with Winnie Huddy, Lord Bullman and his company, guided by Mr. Mitton, arrived at a tall box-hedge, upon the other side of which was a smooth green lawn, the beauty of which an unseen person was extolling.

Lord Bullman stopped to listen.

In all the wide world there is no flattery like the flattery of an old servant. An old and faithful servant only praises what he loves, and that for no gain or interest for himself. His love is reverence, and his reverence is love. He retains nothing in his heart to the detriment of his master; he remembers only the happy hours that he spent when in office, the joyful days when he poured wine into my lord's cup.

"It is here," cried the voice, that Mr. Hayhoe recognized as Mr. Titball's, "that my lady, of a summer evening, makes music with her guitar, and my lord composes sonnets to sleep and happiness. How well I remember when both these noble personages returned from the grand tour! The rude peasants were at harvest, and my lord asked me how I did, and what wine there was in the cellar. My lady called for tea."

Then there came a deep sigh from behind the hedge.

"Upon this fair lawn," continued Mr. Titball, as though his feelings almost mastered his tongue, "acts and frolics are done that would surprise the common people to witness. Under the shadow of yonder great plane tree Mary and

Rupert dance and toy. Here, as in heaven itself, is the holy place of beauty, where the best manners in the country are bred and born. For twenty generations noble feet have trod these gravel paths and green pastures. Even the small singing birds have learned to bow to the young ladies, and the finest peacock is not more fine than my lord."

Lord Bullman smiled proudly and passed on.

Presently an under-gardener appeared in the path, whom Mr. Mitton had sent on to discover the suspected persons.

"They are standing beside the large bed of begonias," he whispered to Mr. Mitton. "And she—I mean the girl— is eyeing the blooms most thievingly. You have only to creep round the next corner in order to catch them together."

They were now joined by Mr. Titball, who, having concluded his soliloquy and hearing that my lord was abroad, had come to pay his dutiful respects to him. Mr. Titball approached his old master most humbly. To behold him was enough; he did not expect to be recognized.

But Lord Bullman was not a man to neglect a friend. He shook the honest landlord warmly by the hand, and, desiring him to join the others and keep behind him, he began again to advance cautiously, as though he were stalking a lion, holding his walking-stick like a gun. His position now in his own garden he knew to be dangerous. He had intended to shut himself up in his house all day until the gates were closed and all the mob gone.

There might, he feared, be a murderer amongst the crowd. As he was a large landowner, it was quite possible that he had offended some one. Some person who did not like lords might be prowling there with a knife or loaded pistol in his pocket. And, even if there were no murderer, he had fully persuaded himself that the grounds held only thieves. Perhaps, he considered, the whole plan of letting wild people into a nobleman's gardens was but a trick, cunningly arranged by the supreme contriver of all criminal doings—the Devil himself—who, in some form or other, had gained the King's private ear. Though each one had paid a shilling—except the children, who were admitted for sixpence—all could easily carry something off worth far more than the price of entry.

On his way towards the begonia bed, Lord Bullman had distinctly seen an old man stoop down and pick up something in the path. Perhaps it was a pebble, but in the old happy days of just laws a young woman had been committed to Bridewell for stealing a small twig from a hedge. A lordly pebble was of more value than a twig. In any country village that pebble could be shown with as much pride as if it had come from the temple of Venus at Pompeii. And suppose every one there took away stones, there would soon be no more gravel left!

Fears of this nature made my lord clench his teeth and hurry around the hedge, in his eagerness to catch a thief.

Never had any one been better surprised. Winnie was in the very act of plucking a scarlet begonia to add to her nosegay when Lord Bullman with a loud "Halloo!" came round the corner.

Winnie was in the midst of coloured flowers, looking herself like only another of them and holding a large bunch in her hands. There she was, her hat off and her yellow hair catching the sun, her eyes shining with delight as she culled the spoil. Near to the bed, basking in the sun, and making merry music with two or three knucklebones, was her friend, John.

Lord Bullman advanced upon Winnie, who, giving a little scream of fright, quitted the bed—though not the flowers—and hid herself behind John.

Death laughed.

Lord Bullman strode haughtily up to him.

"Perhaps you do not know who I am?" he shouted fiercely.

"Neither do you, I think, know me," replied John.

"You once measured me for a frock-coat," cried Lord Bullman, whose anger every moment grew hotter, "and I have never seen a coat that fitted me worse."

"I will measure you for another garment one day, my lord," answered Death.

"I should not have been so swindled in Bond Street," Lord Bullman remarked angrily, "and now you steal my flowers. Hell and damnation seize all such thieving tailors!

"Take away the flowers," commanded Lord Bullman of the gardeners.

But no one stirred, for John Death stood between Winnie and the men, and his looks alarmed them.

"I would rather that all this bed of flowers should droop and die," said Lord Bullman, "than that they should be stolen and carried off by such an artful hussy."

"You really wish so?" asked Death in a low tone.

"The flowers are mine," said Lord Bullman, looking proudly at the splendid patch of colour.

"And you wish them dead?" murmured John Death.

"Rather than have them stolen by vagabonds," replied Lord Bullman.

Death stooped down and gathered in his hands a little dust.

" 'Twas but a small miracle," he said, turning to Mr. Hayhoe, "and one that hardly befitted so high and kingly a power, to mix a little spittle with dust in order to give sight to the blind, for who is there that does not know that dust, when directed aright by divine power, can both save and destroy?"

John Death cast the dust over the flowers.

A change came over them. Their beauty waned; as a young girl's who is ravished and spoiled before she be ripe for love, so the lovely flowers drooped sadly, as though parched by excessive heat, or frozen by a January frost. A silent destruction. There was no turmoil of fire or war that, with roar and clamour, blasts and destroys. The flowers could be watched dying. Each plant sickened visibly, show-ing that the sweet juice and colour of life had suddenly been withdrawn.

In one minute every flower was dead. Winnie Huddy looked at them fearfully and held her own nosegay, as though to protect it against a like fate, next to her breast.

"Do not kill mine too," she begged, looking up at Death; "I only picked them to give to Mr. Solly."

Mr. Mitton and Mr. Titball conversed together. Mr. Mitton mentioned ground-lightning, that he believed could be very destructive. Mr. Titball thought that the flowers must be bewitched by one of the visitors, but such a thing, he said, could never have happened had he been at the Hall.

Lord Bullman paid little heed to what had happened. He was looking earnestly at Death's clothes. As to the begonias, Lord Bullman was aware that such low earth-born matters might easily fade away. They were altogether a different thing from landed gentry. Perhaps the gardeners, who had, of course, to keep their eyes upon so many thieves, had forgotten to water them. Or, what was even more likely, the poor flowers, being alarmed by the gaze of so many eyes—and all vulgar—had died from fright!

While Lord Bullman looked closely at Death, he was aware that Winnie Huddy was trying to slip away with her stolen spoils, that grew more lovely the longer she held them. Lord Bullman called her back to him, thinking to make her turn king's evidence.

"I will let you keep the flowers, my dear," he said, in the tone he used when he presided over the children's court in the local town, "if only you will tell me where this man, whom you call Johnnie"—Lord Bullman smiled—"got his clothes. Did he steal them, or were they given to him by a friend?"

"They were given to Johnnie," answered Winnie, readily enough, "by Lady Catherine de Bourgh."

"And who is she?" inquired Lord Bullman, a little nervously.

"Mr. Darcy's aunt," replied Winnie.

Lord Bullman looked none the wiser.

"And from where, young woman," he asked sternly, "does John get the golden coins?"

Winnie puckered her brow and remained thoughtful for a moment.

"Oh, yes, I remember now!" she cried, happily. "He gets them from a prettyish kind of a little wilderness on one side of your lawn."

Lord Bullman hurried away, followed by his gardeners and by Mr. Titball.

XLVIII

Winnie Sees the Policeman

THE Reverend Francis Hayhoe remained beside the garden of dead flowers. He looked very sad; neither did Death appear merry; only Winnie, who, now that she was sure that no one would take away her flowers—that she meant to arrange in vases in Mr. Solly's sitting-room the next day —was the happy one.

Mr. Hayhoe went to the dead flowers and bowed his head. Winnie thought that he wept.

"Why did you destroy them?" Mr. Hayhoe asked of Death, in a low tone. "Why have you made their fair faces blacker than darkness?"

Death pointed to the flowers that Winnie held.

"Those still live," he said. "But ask the Earth, and she shall tell thee, that it is she which ought to mourn for the fall of so many that grow upon her. For out of her came all at the first, and out of her shall all others come, and, behold, they walk almost all into destruction, and a multitude of them is utterly rooted out. Who then should make more mourning than she, that hath lost so great a multitude? Not thou, who art sorry for these few."

Mr. Hayhoe knelt beside the parched bed and prayed aloud:

"Are not the evils which are come to us sufficient? If thou forsake us, how much better had it been for us if we also had been burned like these flowers? For we are not better than they that died here."

"You pray wisely," said Death, looking at the work he

had done. "And surely, did I need an excuse for my conduct, your words provide one. What folly is greater than pride, and what mortal dare be proud when the judgment pronounced upon all living things is that they must become dust and ashes?"

"But why," asked Mr. Hayhoe, "should man, alone of all the creatures—vegetable or animal—be the mock of the firmament? Why should man, in all the universe, be the only living thing that is conscious of his irrevocable doom?"

"When God's finger first stirred the pudding," answered Death, with a smile, "He let a tear fall in by mistake, and the tear became man's consciousness. Then, to preserve man from everlasting sorrow, He put Death in the pot."

Mr. Hayhoe bowed reverently.

Winnie, who had not heeded a word of what was being said—for she knew that men will always talk some kind of nonsense—happened to look behind her and gave a little scream.

"The Shelton policeman be coming," she cried, "whose name be Jimmy, and he be staring up at the top of the boxhedge."

"Come," said Mr. Hayhoe. "I think we had better leave this garden by another way." He began to run.

Death and Winnie followed. Mr. Hayhoe, who appeared to know the way, led them down a secluded path that grew more and more wild and less garden-like as they went on. Presently they came to a broken wall which they easily climbed, and were safe in the open fields.

"I thought I should remember the way," said Mr. Hayhoe, panting a little, "for I used, as a boy, to stay at Madder with my godmother, Mr. Solly's aunt, and sometimes I would climb over this wall, creep into the gardens, and take a few plums."

Death laughed loudly.

"Ha!" he cried, "then Winnie and I are not the only ones who take what is not our own. And I wonder much that Lord Bullman did not notice your nose as well as mine, for I think that they are much the same length."

"I was wrong, of course," replied Mr. Hayhoe, blushing, "but my godmother cured me of stealing by making me eat nothing but plum jam for the rest of my stay."

They were now come to a pleasant field-path that led to Dodder, and that crossed, by the help of two stiles, the very lane in which Mr. Hayhoe had first met John Death.

Only a good man, into whose soul evil hath not entered, is able to look at the dreadful pit, that goes down deeper than the beginning of life, into which he must one day descend, and yet still view the golden colour of a child's hair and the green beauty of the fields with untroubled joy.

Mr. Hayhoe watched Winnie with gladness. She ran here and there, picking moon-daisies. One moment she was in one place, and then in another; her legs danced her everywhere.

Mr. Hayhoe, thinking that Death still walked beside him, turned to speak to him, but found that he was not there.

Mr. Hayhoe shuddered.

Winnie ran to him and gave him her flowers to hold, for, besides the begonias, she had gathered nearly an armful of daisies.

"I am going to Madder tomorrow," she said, proudly, "to wash Mr. Solly's shirts."

Mr. Hayhoe commended her industry.

"Oh, that bain't nothing," she cried, "for Mr. Solly do say that 'e didn't let love into his cottage to be idle, but 'e do always light the copper fire and draw the water before I be come."

Mr. Hayhoe nodded even more approvingly.

"And I am soon going to make a nut pie," boasted Winnie, "and learn to paper a room—all blue and yellow—and cook an omelette—but nine years is a long time to wait for a wedding-cake!"

"I wish you joy when that day comes, Winnie," said Mr. Hayhoe. "Have you loved him for long?"

"It has been coming on so gradually," replied Winnie, "that I hardly know when it began. But I believe I must date it from my first seeing his beautiful grounds at Madder."

Mr. Hayhoe smiled.

"I am sure you will be happy," he said hopefully.

"I am sure I shall," answered Winnie, "for Mr. Solly promises to take me to church every Sunday, and his pew be only one step below where real ladies do sit."

Mr. Hayhoe was meditating.

"Is it wrong to steal?" he asked of Winnie.

"Oh yes," replied Winnie, hurriedly, taking the flowers into her own hands again, "it's certainly very wicked."

"Yes, I think it is," said Mr. Hayhoe, sadly, "and yet, ever since I took those plums, I have longed to steal the peace of God."

"Oh, that's always given away," answered Winnie.

"No," said Mr. Hayhoe, "one has to steal that; one has to take His peace away by force. Whoever wants that peace must rob God of it, for it belongs to Him."

"I would much rather rob Lord Bullman," replied Winnie.

Mr. Hayhoe looked at her and smiled again.

They were now come into Dodder and were close to Joseph Bridle's field. Coming near, they were surprised to see that Mr. Balliboy's car had stopped exactly beside Joe's field gate, and that all the occupants had dismounted and were gazing excitedly into the meadow. Mr. Balliboy alone stood aside, for he was telling Miss Sarah Bridle that he would always honour and love her, if she became his—to which she could only reply that she was but a poor creature and no true woman.

Mr. Balliboy kissed her hand, and she promised to be his animal.

"Something very strange has happened," observed Joe Bridle to Mr. Hayhoe. "In the morning the field was bare, but now the grass is as long and as green as though it grew in the Dodder churchyard."

"Oh, that's nothing," cried Winnie Huddy, "it's only John's silly scythe that makes the grass grow so quickly. He is always telling me about that scythe of his. He says that the faster he cuts with it, the greener and better the grass grows up behind him."

"The Lord created man of the earth," said Mr. Hayhoe, "and turned him into it again. . . . For all things cannot be in men, because the son of man is not immortal."

"I would rather hear you read about Mr. Bingley than talk so," said Winnie.

Mr. Hayhoe sighed deeply.

"*Pride and Prejudice* is finished," he said.

XLIX

The Greed of a Collector

INSTEAD of going home at once to Madder, after stepping out of Mr. Balliboy's car, Mr. Solly returned with the Bridles to tea, and even after that meal was over he was disinclined to leave Dodder. Something dreadful he knew was about to happen, though what that something was he knew not.

Mr. Solly, as is the way with a peaceful and harmless man, was very prone to notice omens. On his way to Dodder that morning he had seen three swans pass over, with necks outstretched, as though they intended a long journey. Mr. Solly, who admired swans more at a distance than near by, watched their flight, and soon, to his surprise, though he heard the bird utter no song, one—the most beautiful of them—fell at his feet, dead. . . .

Was it a mere chance that a yellow leaf, driven before the wind, lifted up and was blown here and there along the lanes, until at last a wilder gust, or a swirl of eddies, carried the leaf into my room and placed it upon the paper beside my pen?

Has the leaf a known purpose? Does it come to ease me of my care, or has it come to say that it loves me? What is it that takes a man, as well as a leaf, out of his path, and bids him follow a road that he has not intended to travel?

A day passes and the evening comes, and we think to return, as Mr. Solly thought, to our garden of nuts—but, instead, we go elsewhere. To where an everlasting battle is fought between Love and Death. Can no shadow come between these two, or a fountain of water, or lonely silence? Will God never be still? . . .

"I would like to step up to the Dodder churchyard before returning to Madder," Solly said to Joseph, when tea was over, "for an odd fancy has come to me that Love is not only content to eat my nuts, but wishes also to catch a butterfly in Dodder."

Joe Bridle said that he would go too, but, before starting off, he loitered for a few moments in the cottage garden. Of late Joe had not troubled to attend to it. Bindweed, nettle and thistle had grown in abundance.

Joseph Bridle looked away from the garden and towards the downs. It was there that he had laboured, though with but small success. Had he kept his hopes there, desiring but the little increase of his fields—the sure content of toil—instead of settling all his thoughts in the curious body of a girl, what happiness might he not have yet had?

Mr. Solly sadly answered his thought.

"Even the thickest grove of nut-bushes," he observed, "cannot keep away Love. All things must go the way of nature. The oldest gods, that moved first in the still waters, must ever rule. Until the seas again become the void, until the hills are emptied into the bowl of eternal darkness, the pains of love must continue. But to us, Madder Hill is the same yesterday, today, and for ever. When the scene of our short vision ends, hardly a stone shall be moved, hardly a root gone. All the turmoil and trouble that love makes for a man, during the few years of his vanity, is of less consequence in the universe than the moving of one small worm from one burrow to another. Trouble Heaven as we will, make all the outcry we may, complain of our care to the wind and to the stars of the sky, nothing—no tittle—shall

be left out of the law of our ways. We run our race blind-
fold, and when all is done, we have but moved one place,
one step lower in degree, down Madder Hill."

Mr. Solly and his friend left the garden; they walked in
silence through the village and came to the church gates.
All seemed silent there, and going in they took a path that
led them around the church.

Dodder village was unusually quiet for a Sunday evening,
but so many had visited Lord Bullman's gardens, and all who
had been there had so much to talk of, that most of the
people were indoors.

Mr. Solly walked the first in the path. Behind the
church and very much to his surprise, he saw a new-dug
grave, and near beside it a heap of earth. Upon this heap of
soil were laid out a girl's clothes, neatly folded. Nearby,
and lying naked upon the grass, was Susie Dawe, with her
head resting upon a grave-mound, and thrown backwards a
little, with her neck ready for the stroke.

Before the body of Susie stood Death, with his arms
stretched back and his sharp scythe ready to strike.

The two had crept together unnoticed into the churchyard, where Death had dug a grave and hidden his scythe
in readiness for the final act. After showing Susie the grave,
he had bid her unclothe, and as she took off her garments,
Death folded them—as a loving mother does a baby's at
night-time—and then bid Susie to lie down and to receive
the blow.

Joe Bridle stood between them. Death laid his scythe
softly upon the ground.

"Love is as strong as death," he said, sadly, "and it is
not given to me now to dispute a man's right to a mortal
girl. My time will come. He, under Whom I have my
dominion and my power, is a dark star. Who can escape

Him? I thought to have enjoyed Susie and to have forsaken for ever the hard task that has been laid upon me, and I almost attained to that freedom."

Susie rose bewildered, but, knowing that she was naked, she dressed herself again, looking like one in a dream.

As soon as she was dressed, Mr. Solly led her to her home. Death and Joseph Bridle faced one another.

Joe stood silently, but Death was by no means abashed. He raised his scythe and looked with pleasure at its sharp edge.

"It is curious to observe," he said to Joseph, "that one is often more pleased than sorry when interrupted in one's pleasures. Although my experience in such affairs must be —for my holiday has been short—somewhat limited, yet I am now sure that, for the sake of one's own happiness, it is better to renounce love. I have often disputed upon this subject with Mr. Hayhoe, who would always affirm that a peaceful hour, spent in reading the *Watsons*, can give a greater happiness than a whole night with a Helen or Laïs, and now I am inclined to agree with him. I remember well that in our conversation we both regretted an act of providence that compelled that book to be so nearly the last of them.

"Alas! Joseph," said Death, sitting down contentedly upon a grave-mound, "some one, whom I will not name, has His own ideas about literature. But, if only my Master had been educated at Benet College in Cambridge instead of in Palestine, perhaps He might have thought a little differently about prose-writers. But, as it is, He always preferred a short story to a novel, viewing a parable and a short story as the same thing. And, though His taste is sometimes sound, yet it is a well-known fact that He often prefers any fool or charlatan to a good writer.

"This is unfortunate, for as He is able to do what He likes with His own, He permits one to write on, when, for the sake of posterity, their lives, as well as their works, had much better have been shortened."

Death chuckled.

"Or else," he said, with a knowing wink, "there may be another reason why so many of the best authors die young. You must be aware, Joseph, that sometimes a valuable manuscript is lost. God is a collector. An author had better look to his wares. There may come a robber, who will open the most hidden drawer, and I can promise you that the Shelton policeman will not catch Him.

"A fire may come, or else a whirlwind may pass through the house upon a sudden and carry off something. If a writer misses anything, he had best beware. Who does not know that Keats was inclined to be careless and to leave things about? Others have done the same, and we know what high price can be made of a few lines of manuscript. This collector, I fear, is a greedy fellow."

Death laughed.

Joe Bridle looked into the grave.

"Give me my parchment," cried Death, "for either you have it, or else you know where it is."

"And suppose I do know," answered Bridle. "You cannot compel me to give it up."

"There is to be a wedding tomorrow in Dodder church," said Death carelessly.

Joe Bridle walked off, leaving Death in the churchyard. Soon the company at the Inn heard a well-known sound —the whetting of a scythe.

L

Droit de Seigneur

OVER certain accidents God draws a natural veil. And, if the accident has not harmed the mind of its subject, all may yet be well. The veil is a woman's longing and it covers much. Under the banner of love a sacrifice that is not killed recovers apace. The veil hides all. A girl may lie naked to death, and yet find her life again, and even forget in a little while what had happened to her.

As soon as Susie reached her home, her father blamed her for being late and for not laying his supper as she was used to do. Had James Dawe spoken kindly to her, Susie might not have gained possession of herself so easily. His rudeness and angry words made things ordinary again, and having once prepared herself for Death's embrace, she did not care now what happened to her. She was quite ready, she told her father, to marry Mr. Mere the next day.

When supper was over and while Susie was washing the plates in the back-house, there came a soft knock at the front door. Susie sighed. She supposed that Mr. Mere was come. Her father would soon call her, and the farmer would wish to use her as countrymen do use the women they are soon to wed. She did not care what he did.

Her father now called to her to come to the parlour, although his tone of voice was quieter than she had expected. Susie went, expecting to see Mr. Mere, but she was welcomed by Lord Bullman.

If ever a man was made to change a dull and musty

atmosphere, charged with dour cruelty, into a lighter kind of fancy, that man was Lord Bullman. Even Mr. Pix could not always regard his master—if his back was turned —without a smile. Lord Bullman's look of ponderous displeasure at all he saw in the country—unless his gaze encountered a fair maid—his almost impossible pride in his own presence, and a simplicity of purpose, that he considered the utmost cunning, could never fail to amuse an onlooker. According to an old established custom in the family, the Bullmans, though a little brusque with their wives, had always been extremely civil and polite to their mistresses.

Lord Bullman bowed low to Susie. Indeed, he had reason to, for he had never in his life seen a young girl look so lovely.

Susie was very pale. Her love for Death had changed her into a creature that hardly seemed to be a being of this world.

James Dawe withdrew.

Lord Bullman bowed to Susie again. But, before he sat with her upon the sofa, he wished, he said, to ask her one question.

Susie smiled and permitted him to whisper.

"I have never," murmured Lord Bullman, eagerly, "been able to pass a happy night of love since a certain fashion of clothes has been used by women in bed. But you, my dear, I know, wear a nightgown."

"I have worn one ever since I can remember," answered Susie gaily, "and I am sure I can be as happy with old fashions as you, my lord."

"And," exclaimed Lord Bullman, sitting joyfully beside Susie on the sofa, "you will not mind my talking to you a little before we go to bed?"

"I will listen to you gladly," observed Susie.

"Even if I talk about thieves and robbers?" cried Lord Bullman.

"Talk as long as you like," replied Susie, "and of anything you many choose."

Never had Lord Bullman been answered so prettily. Those ladies of pleasure that he had been wont to visit sometimes had always, after their first embraces were over, made a mock of him, and even before their playing, did he wish to talk a little seriously, they would not permit it.

But Lord Bullman was not behaving to Susie quite as he intended to. While walking to Dodder, he had made up his mind what he meant to do. He had decided to go to bed with Susie first, and then to talk to her afterwards. But, as soon as he saw her, his feelings took a different turn. He saw her at once as a young woman who would listen to a man's conversation in the most kindly manner, yielding a ready sympathy to the utmost folly. Unless it were Mr. Titball, no one had ever cared to listen to his views upon any local case of the thieving of even a hen-roost.

Did he mention anything of the kind—a little timidly, of course—to his valet, that amiable young man would change the subject to the poetry of Robert Browning. Mr. Dapper, the present butler, would do worse, for when Lord Bullman happened once to be dining alone, and mentioned —in quite a social manner—the case of a man who had broken through one window and three locked doors and then, though he had the house entirely at his mercy, only stole the kitchen-maid's chemise, Mr. Dapper without any reply or word of comment, poured out for his lordship a glass of cold water.

Lord Bullman was now completely at his ease.

"According to a learned lawyer that I have lately consulted," he observed, "there is nothing mentioned in the 'droit de seigneur' about the right to talk. That law, it appears—if the old Latin can be depended upon—only covers certain familiarities that are too common to name, and are often a little too creature-like to do. If you have no objection, my dear, we will, for the present, pass over these country matters, for I have something far more important to talk of."

Lord Bullman sighed and took her hand.

"Ever since," he said, "I heard of the robbery in Merly Wood, I have been busy looking for the thief, and also considering very carefully the motive that could lead a man to undress a poor suicide—hanged and dead—and to steal his clothes."

"Perhaps they were better than his own," suggested Susie.

"I also thought that might be so," said Lord Bullman, "until I met the tailor, John Death, at Daisy Huddy's."

Susie frowned.

"I went there for no harm," said Lord Bullman hastily, "but I had only to look once at that man John to know that he was a thief. I was sure of it the first moment I saw him, and I can assure you, Susie, by my soul, that he is the worst of robbers."

Susie's face coloured, then again grew deadly pale.

"In my own garden," went on Lord Bullman, "near to a few paltry dead flowers, I knew that he was the man who had taken the clothes from the corpse."

Susie shuddered.

"After being put upon a false scent by a girl named Winnie, I interviewed the Shelton policeman."

Susie smiled.

"You have never read lawyer Coke, my dear?"

Susie shook her head. Lord Bullman looked relieved.

"One must," he said, "discover a motive for the crime. This is how I saw the matter. When I was a tiny boy, I very much wished to obtain a doll dressed in the finest hussar uniform, that belonged to my cousin Margaret—"

"You stole it?" cried Susie.

"No, I only tried to," replied my lord. "Margaret discovered me in her bedroom and began to cry. My motive was simple, but who would wish to rob a corpse of clothes that were not paid for?—the bill would follow the thief. I found the case more difficult as I proceeded in it, and soon thought it necessary to consult counsel. This is what I have discovered. It appears that Tailor John had a kind of right to the clothes of the dead man."

"He helped to make them perhaps?" said Susie.

Lord Bullman kissed her hand.

"You have guessed rightly, child," he cried, "and they were not paid for. Mr. Triggle, the man who hanged himself, had always been a very vain person, and when he determined to end his life, he wished to wear his best clothes. He ordered them for the purpose. They were made for him by a jobbing tailor of Maidenbridge, with whom I myself once had dealings"—Lord Bullman blushed—"and who has left the town and cannot be found. He is believed to have changed his name from Love to Death. The clothes were delivered to Mr. Triggle, but the bill was unpaid. I have learned from Mrs. Triggle, who still bemoans the loss of her good man, that her husband had agreed with the tailor, Love, that if the clothes were not paid for by a certain date, he, the tailor, had the right to his own again.

"Though I am but a poor theologian," observed Lord Bullman, "John Death does not appear to have done any more harm to this man than God does to us when we die.

He takes our garment of flesh from us, that is given by Love, and returns it to the proper owner—our Mother Earth. But our laws are not God's."

Lord Bullman smiled.

"Though Death cannot be charged with theft—and there his nose deceived me—yet he shall and can be sent to prison for a common assault. Tomorrow I will make out a warrant for John's arrest."

Susie praised his cleverness.

Lord Bullman rose to go. He bowed low to Susie.

"I only called to wish you every happiness," he said, as he opened the door to go out.

LI

Death No Enemy

A DEEP gloom had settled upon the Dodder Vicarage this Sunday evening. The Sabbath day had not been spent by Mr. Hayhoe or by Priscilla in the way that they liked best to spend it. They had both missed, as all good people do, that pleasant hour—the evensong worship.

When they met at the Vicarage again, after their visit to the grand gardens, Mr. Hayhoe observed unhappily that his talk with Lord Bullman had not been very suitable to the holy day. He had listened politely, of course, as became an inferior, he informed Priscilla, "but," he said, with a deep sigh, "I fear the living of Dodder will never be ours."

After supper was over, Mr. Hayhoe withdrew to his study, where he busied himself for a while in writing a sermon for the next Sunday, hoping that by means of this occupation the gloom that lay upon his own heart as well as upon the village of Dodder might be raised a little.

After writing for about an hour, Mr. Hayhoe—who always doubted his own inspiration—wished to ask his wife whether his treatment of Judith, the heroine of his sermon, was entirely proper, and so he left the study to seek Priscilla. He first sought her in the parlour, but she was not there, neither was she in the kitchen. Then he went softly to her bedroom and opened the door.

To one who had sorrowed much, the kindly relief of soothing tears will never come. Only a deep sadness and one strange hope was left to Priscilla. She sat down close to the open window, and as though she could not take her eyes away from that place, she looked longingly at the grave of her little son.

Mr. Hayhoe watched her in silence, for she had not heard him open the door, and thought that she followed with her eyes the movement of some one in the churchyard. The summer evening was very light. He wondered who it was that she saw.

Mr. Hayhoe withdrew as silently as he had come and went down again to his study.

Sometimes, all unexpectedly, human eyes that have known love and no hate are opened to strange sights.

The shepherds, watching their silly sheep, once saw the heavens open and the winged host descend. A king beheld armed forces in the air, ready to rush upon his enemies that lay before the gates of Samaria, and to many a dying wight has an unexpected joy come.

A great hope can open the heavens, and sorrow too—as well as joy—can sometimes uncover the deep places of darkness, burst the bonds of everlasting night and let the soul free.

Priscilla Hayhoe looked into the churchyard. Some one moved there.

She knew who this was—the gravedigger. But Death did not look the same man. He was become young and beautiful. Susie had seen him thus, because love had uncovered her eyes, and now her own lasting sorrow showed the man, in his true form, to Priscilla.

He moved like a blessed silence in the churchyard. His stature was kingly. He paused and spread out his hands over the holy dead. From a gesture that he made, he seemed to be dividing the living from the dead. Upon this side, the folly of passion, sorrow, suffering, and pain: every moment merged into the next, and all time passing away like the shadow of a swiftly moving cloud over Madder Hill. Upon the other side, the sweet silence of God.

Mr. Hayhoe grew sleepy over his work, until at last he laid his head upon the Bible before him, and fell asleep.

Priscilla softly went downstairs and out into the lane. She hastened into the churchyard. The evening darkened, a cloud of white mist descended upon the village.

Priscilla found Death. She bowed before him.

"I wish to see my boy," she said. "Cannot I behold him, only this once?"

Death looked upon her with compassion, but he shook his head.

"Then kill me," cried Priscilla, and bowed low, waiting for the stroke.

Instead of striking her with his scythe, Death took her into his arms and resumed his human form. His mood just then was a merry one.

"Mr. Hayhoe is lying fast asleep," he said, "with his forehead upon the Holy Bible. Why should we not be happy? Here is your child's grave. I kill, and Love gives life, but in reality we are one and the same. We often exchange our weapons. And then 'tis I that give life, and Love that kills. I have taken upon me, during my holiday, the usual follies that men do to pass the time with, and I have seen that it is truly my presence that all men need to make them glad. The earthly ending, after the brave folly that is called life is ended, is God's largesse to man. And I am the bringer of the gift.

"A sad mistake has been made.

"In the midst of the firmament is set—a tiny mirror—the Earth. And God has seen His own face in this glass. In this mirror God saw Himself as man.

"When a deathly numbness overcomes a body, when the flesh corrupts, and the colour of the face is changed in the grave, then I have done for man more than Love can do, for I have changed a foolish and unnatural craving into everlasting content.

"In all the love feats, I take my proper part. When a new life begins to form in the womb, my seeds are there, as well as Love's. We are bound together in the same knot. I could be happy lying with you now, and one day you will be glad to lie with me.

"And yet, Priscilla"—and Death looked at her strangely —"I begin indeed to grow weary of being a reaper, and that only because of the vanity of some one whom I will not name, and who should never have wished to see himself as Narcissus did. I even wish that you had the power to wield my own scythe against me."

Death stood again before Priscilla as a being of glory.

"But why should men fear me?" he cried. "I do but change a fleeting, futile, and vaporous being into eternal loveliness. I—a king—give crowns. I cloud the mirror, and God sees Himself no more. But I thought that perhaps I might, if I became a man, live and die like one."

Death sighed.

"Alas! I cannot die," he said. "The blessed gift that I give to others I shall never know."

"But I have read in the Bible," said Priscilla softly, "that 'death shall be no more.'"

"Perhaps I am an illusion," said Death, more gaily. "Certainly Love is. But, whether real or no, I am no enemy to man."

"Show me my child," cried Priscilla.

Death drew her under the green boughs of the yew.

"Look!" he said.

She peeped out of her hiding-place, and saw a company of merry children playing amongst the tombs. They were the same children—although a little younger—as those who lived in Shelton and who used sometimes to come and play in Dodder. But, strangely enough, the season of the year was changed. Instead of summer leaves, the signs of autumn were there. Yellow leaves hung from the trees, and the fields were brown and bare. One of the children—a boy—laughed joyously. Priscilla would have run to him, only Death prevented her. Priscilla held out her arms and called her child by name, but he saw her not—and in a few moments the children were gone.

"Though you supposed yourself to be under the yew," said Death, when they stood beside the little grave again, "yet in reality you were a great way off, and saw what has been, as still being. You saw your child alive."

"I do not understand," said Priscilla.

"Neither do I," answered Death.

Priscilla lay down upon the grave, and closed her eyes. Death thought that she slept.

"Love defeated me first," he said, sadly, "and now sleep has robbed me of my happiness. How ungrateful is a woman! I thought certainly to have enjoyed Priscilla. But, instead, I will walk upon Madder Hill, and gather a few mushrooms for my supper."

LII

A Bridal Weapon

A SUMMER's night is soon passed and gone. Susie's wedding-day was come, but no country mind ever accepts anything that has not happened as sure to happen.

Joseph Bridle believed that something unforeseen would prevent the wedding. And why not? Joseph Bridle had not carried that dread parchment in his bosom for so long without feeling sure that the two names written there could never be separated. Though not in life, they must, he knew, be one in death—and perhaps in life too. If Death could not defeat him, how then could Mr. Mere?

Many a girl has changed her mind upon the wedding morn, and until the marriage lines were writ there was hope for him.

After saving Susie from Death, Joe had called his cows from the down and let them into his field. He watched them for a little. They had not browsed there for many moments, in the cool of the evening, before a change came over them. They had before been but meagre creatures—only lean kine, but even after the first few mouthfuls of that green grass they grew fat. And soon the best beasts in Mr. Mere's herd could not match them.

At first Joe feared that they might merely be blown. But no, for within an hour of eating that sweet grass they lay down contentedly to chew the cud.

Joe Bridle slept happily that night, and rose in the morning with hope in his heart. The day was come that must decide his fate. Yet he felt no anxiety. As he dressed himself, he looked through the window at Madder Hill.

Hope came from that hill. Whatever happened to him, whatever happened to Susie, Madder Hill would still look down upon Dodder, and the peace of that hill nothing can destroy.

Never had his cows yielded more milk than they did that morning, and if Susie came to him even at this last moment, all might yet be well. His love was no new creation; it was like the sun. It went back into the far past and reached into the everlasting future. Could such a high matter be set aside and its consummation delayed?

As soon as he had finished milking, and had eaten his breakfast, Joseph Bridle went to Susie's cottage.

She was in the garden tending some late chickens that she had reared from eggs her father had found, for hardly did any hen stray in Dodder that escaped the eye of Mr. Dawe. Susie did not look like a bride; she wore black.

Joe Bridle begged her to come to him. He leaned against the gate, the merry birds sang and chirped in the garden, the bees were busy with the flowers, and the warm summer sun kissed the green earth, but upon Madder Hill the shadow of a cloud rested.

Susie began to tease Joe, as she had often done during their courtship. She told him what Lord Bullman had said, and how friendly that gentleman had been to her. "All know," she said, "of his lordship's wish to revive an old law." Susie counted upon her fingers the possible brides of that year that might be wedded in the neighbourhood, and observed that Lord Bullman would have as busy a time of it as Mr. Hayhoe. Susie laughed and turned up her sleeve. She showed the marks of teeth.

"I know now that it was Mr. Mere who bit me," she said;

and suddenly, without his expecting her, she threw herself into Joe's arms, clung to him, and kissed his lips.

"Oh," she whispered, "if only you had so fine a house, a real drive, and big gates, I would have had you instead of Mr. Mere—but only think how glad Daisy Huddy would be to see me poor!"

She broke away from him, and ran into the house.

Joseph Bridle, hardly knowing how he reached there, found himself beside the pond in the field. A word came into his mind—"Unclay." He was not the only one who had stood there and heard that command spoken. Others had heard the same word. To obey the command was now a simple matter.

The word was not set upon him alone, but upon all flesh. It was writ on the forehead of the unborn babe, it was carved upon the highest mountains, and written in the hidden slime of the lowest valleys. Everywhere was the same word, telling man, telling all matter, of the same awful fate. Unclay!

The word became a monster in Bridle's mind. It grew larger. The terrible letters of it encircled the earth. It was God's writing; no star in the vast firmament could escape it, and no mortal man. Whatsoever be wrapped and clothed in garments of clay shall hear that word spoken.

Bridle uttered a great cry.

He saw in the water of the pond the death-pale face of a girl. He fled in terror. And now he began to wish that he had never found the parchment. Had that paper remained in the right hands, two graves would already have been dug. So why had he not stept into the water when that signature floated there?

The morning passed. Joseph Bridle attended to his work. He cleaned out the cow-stalls, and busied himself for a little in the neglected garden, clearing it of weeds.

The wedding was to be at two o'clock.

Bridle ate his dinner, in silence, at one. Sarah watched him. She wondered that he could eat so well when his young girl was to be taken away from him. But she supposed that, having been a camel for so long, she was not yet human enough to understand the ways of a man. Perhaps Mr. Balliboy would explain.

It has been said that Tinker Jar can give sight to the blind. He now gave sight to Madder Hill. Though Madder Hill had existed for so long, it had never loved before. But, now it was able to see, the Hill loved Bridle's pond. The pond was deep enough for a Hill to look into.

Madder Hill gazed into Joseph's pond and loved it. The Hill looked for God. It had learned from the worms that God dwells in deep places. Madder Hill saw God in the pond.

While the Hill looked into the pond, Farmer Mere was preparing for his wedding. All the night he had dreamed of cruel doings. He wished he could transform himself into the giant, cut in the chalk down near Enmore village. Were he as potent as that giant appeared to be, he could certainly terrify a young bride, but, being an old man, he had not much hope of that.

Of course he could bite Susie, but he wished to frighten her to death, as well as to torture her. A man may do as he likes with his own.

He might, just for the jest, of course, take a loaded gun into the bedroom, and press the cold muzzle between her breasts. Or else carry her in her nightgown into the yard, where the surly bull was kept, and throw her down and goad him at her. But perhaps the bull would pity her distress as his dog had done. Only a man's manners would do for her.

Mr. Mere considered what he could do. His eyes gleamed cruelly, and he laughed aloud.

He had thought of something, he had remembered Death's scythe. Surely no better scourge could be found to terrify a poor, frightened girl. Every man in Dodder had admired the sharpness of its edge, for honest John had always liked to show off the weapon that he was so proud of. Even Mr. Titball had admired the scythe and had observed that he believed the edge to be nearly as keen as Lord Bullman's best razor.

Mere thought that the scythe would be easy to steal. It was said that Death had begun again to search in the fields for his lost property, and also, in talking to his landlord, Card, Death had said that he was growing tired of Dodder and was already beginning to look out for another habitation.

From the garden of the Manor farm, Mr. Mere could look into the churchyard. A few people were already loitering there, waiting for him to come and be married. One old woman—Mrs. Moggs—had a paper bag in her hand—rice! Amongst these waiting people, Mr. Mere noticed John Death.

The farmer walked unconcernedly out of his gate. He went to Death's cottage. The scythe was hung upon a nail in the kitchen.

Mere stole the scythe.

He believed that no one saw him, and entered the Manor house by the back way.

LIII

Joe Bridle Turns to the Wall

THERE is a certain Name that is best let alone. If one meets this Name at any time, when out walking, it is best to go by with one's eyes shut. If any man can forget the Name, so much the better for him. His way of life will be easier.

With the Name forgotten, a man's pleasures may be moderate, and he will be happy. He will never love to excess, as did Joseph Bridle. He will shut out suffering from his mind and close his ears to injustice. A man is wise who lives to himself alone, and forgets that Name.

If this Name, by some unlucky chance, is hidden in thy heart, cast it out. Away with it, away with it! It is a torment, a terrible fang. With that Name within you, uneasy thoughts will trouble you. Hide it, cast it out! Take it into the church, and carry yourself along too, in the robes of a bishop, place the Name upon the Altar, and the old serpent will devour it. Then power, praise and might, goods and honour will come to you; with that Name out of your sight, you will be rich.

But whatever others can do, Joseph Bridle could not forget the Name, for it was written upon the parchment in his bosom. He had never let the signature go from him, neither at night nor in the day. He had kept the parchment for so long that his view of time was altered. He thought that his love for Susie would make her his for all eternity.

Instead of looking forward, according to the ordinary process of time—in which all things move gradually to fruition in a slow measured tread, one season meeting another either in cold shower or warm sunshine, but all moving and passing on—Joseph Bridle saw all things done and ended. By the virtue of the parchment that he carried, he saw his life before him but as a moment. Hours, days, and years came and went with the rapidity of seconds. Children were born, grew to manhood, and found new homes for themselves. Susie and he, together, sank contentedly into the grave.

But neither his life, nor yet hers, were the only things that vanished. All time and all life were ended too. All the rivers of life, with their many waters, were sunk for ever in the great sea. . . .

Joseph Bridle waited in the church porch with John Death. Mr. Mere was in the vestry, with Mr. Hayhoe, awaiting the bride.

Presently Susie Dawe approached the church with her father. As she came up the path, Winnie Huddy ran to her. Winnie whispered to her that, if she would only give up Mr. Mere and go home again, she would present her with Mr. Solly, while she, Winnie, would be the servant.

" 'Tis only money thee do want," said Winnie, knowingly. "But Farmer Mere bain't got so much as Mr. Solly. In his parlour there be golden candlesticks in glass case. And that bain't all, neither. For he have a wide, big drawer full of silver sixpences."

James Dawe drove Winnie away.

In the church porch Joseph Bridle stopped Susie. He begged her to go with him to his home. But she only looked at him strangely, as if she had not heard what he said. Joseph Bridle turned his face to the wall.

Susie knelt to Death. Her look changed. She became like a girl who had just learned to love. She blushed coyly and invited Death to take her into his arms. She told him, in country terms, that she loved him. Death turned from her and hid his face, and James Dawe drew her into the church.

Never had Mr. Hayhoe read any service with a more troubled mind. When he came to the words, "Wilt thou have this woman?" he trembled as if a cold blast had struck him, lost his place, and could only be heard to mutter, "Susie, Susie, my dear Susie, where are you? Here is your tippet. Mrs. Hayhoe begs you to put on your tippet. She says she is afraid there will be draughts in the passage, though everything has been done—one door nailed up—quantities of matting—my dear Susie, indeed you must."

But, even though Mr. Hayhoe may have forgotten himself a little during that part of the service, the wedding was properly concluded, and shortly afterwards Susie was led from the church by Mr. Mere, and through the private gate to the Manor farm.

As soon as the wedding party were gone, Joseph Bridle put his hand into his bosom and drew out a piece of parchment.

This parchment he gave to Death.

LIV

Winnie Brings a Message

WHEN a man who has looked a long time for something that he has lost, and at last has found it, one may well believe that his joy at the happy discovery will be disagreeably lessened if, at that moment, he finds that something else of his is gone too.

Predestination is a strange cat. That all should be arranged from the beginning to go so funnily is a queer concern. One would think almost that at the bottom of the well of being one may discover, instead of a mighty God, only the cap and bells of a mad fool. But, whoever be there, He has a fine fancy, and likes to play a trick upon His friends, and may introduce John Knox to the Devil instead of to Moses.

It is well known that every good workman has a favourite tool. A gardener—and even Wordsworth's Mr. Wilkinson —loves his spade. A carpenter may value his hammer more than its weight in gold. John Death was fond of his scythe. Many a fine swath of grass he had cut with it, besides much that was withered and dry.

When a king's messenger receives a command, he starts at once upon his mission. And, as soon as Death had recovered his parchment, he wished at once to obey the written order, and so, leaving Joseph Bridle, he hurried to his cottage to fetch his scythe.

The scythe was not there.

"Robbers," cried John, "thieves and rascals!" and ran out into the lane. There he met Winnie Huddy.

Perceiving Death's pitiful and scared look—and indeed, he looked like an old witch who has lost her black cat—Winnie could only laugh. She had never seen a man before so utterly defeated by destiny. John knew not what do do. He held up his arm, as though to ward off a blow that he seemed to expect at any moment to descend upon him from the sky. He saw as many thieves about him as ever Lord Bullman could have seen in his gardens. He even looked at Joe Bridle's horse with suspicion.

"I have lost my scythe, Winnie," said Death. "Do you know who has taken it?"

"Of course I do," answered Winnie, carelessly. "Tommy Moggs, who be always peeping, did see Mr. Mere carry 'en off, but 'tain't for a poor servant like thee to call me Winnie —'tis 'Miss Winnie' thee must say now."

"What has made you so proud?" asked Death. "You haven't married Mr. Solly already?"

"Don't 'ee talk so foolish," replied Winnie. "You know a married woman bain't no Miss."

"I beg your pardon," said Death, with a low bow, "but tell me what has happened."

"I have been talking to an angel," observed Winnie haughtily.

"The devil you have!" exclaimed Death.

"Yes, and I be the one to be trusted with a message," she said, holding her head even higher.

"I thought they'd soon miss me," said Death, grimly. "But how came you to talk with an angel?"

"When I told Susie," replied Winnie, "that she might have Mr. Solly—who always does what I tell him—and she would not, I couldn't stay to see the wedding, but ran off to the top of Madder Hill to cry—but the men don't know what crying be."

"Since I have lived at Dodder I have learned to weep," said Death, sadly.

"And there bain't no place," observed Winnie, "like Madder Hill for crying, and some do say that it do a woman good to shed tears."

"They say truly," replied Death.

"As soon as I felt better," said Winnie, "and was wiping my eyes with my frock, a coloured cloud came over me, and and an angel fell out of it."

"What did he say to you?" inquired Death, eagerly.

"That I were a pretty little girl," replied Winnie, "and then 'e did ask I for a flower."

"And you gave him one, I suppose," said Death, a little jealously.

"Oh, no," cried Winnie, "I don't give nothing to strange angels."

"And what did he do then?" asked Death.

"Picked a few for himself," replied Winnie, "and after picking they flowers, he said to me, with his eyes all bright and shining, 'Do you know of a man whose name be Death, who do lodge in these parts?' But I bain't one to like questions from foreigners."

"And how did you answer?" inquired Death.

"I asked what his name was," said Winnie.

"And what did he say?" asked Death.

"That I were a true daughter of Eve, and 'is name were Gabriel."

"I wonder you stayed with him," said Death, smiling.

"Oh, I wasn't frightened," said Winnie.

Death nodded. "And what happened then?" he asked.

"I have a message for you," replied Winnie. " 'Twas like this, the angel said it." Winnie paused. " 'I have a message to Death, but this time the order is not written, for as he has lost one parchment, he is not to be trusted with another. But can I trust you?' he asked rudely. I bain't one to be spoken to like that, so I began to walk away. But he called me back, and asked me again whether I could be relied upon."

"And what did you say?" inquired Death.

"That Mr. Solly do trust I to clean his silver teapot," answered Winnie, "and then I said that I didn't carry no angel's message for nothing, and Gabriel offered me eternal life as a wage."

"And what did you say to that?" asked Death.

"That I would sooner have a packet of Mrs. Moggs's sweets," replied Winnie. " 'Twas then that the angel's look frightened me and I hid my eyes. 'Go to Death,' he said, 'and speak this word to him—Unclay. Say that word after me, Winnie, so that you do not forget it.' I said what I were told.

" 'But that is not all you must remember,' said the angel—and his voice sounded like thunder—'for this is what you must tell Death to do—Unclay George Mere.'

" 'What be the meaning of thik word?' I said, opening my eyes wide, though I partly guessed, from the angel's manner, that nothing was to be given to Farmer but that something was to be taken from him.

" 'You may say also,' said the angel in a terrible voice, 'that this night his soul is required.'

" 'And 'tis time it were,' I replied."

Death smiled.

"They travelling angels do take liberties," Winnie observed. "First he did ruffle me hair the wrong way, then 'e did kiss me cheek, and told I to call at Mrs. Moggs's for they sweets 'e had paid for."

"What happened next?" asked Death.

"I began to go away, but he called me back again.

" 'I forgot half my errand,' he said. 'There's another name to be mentioned.'

" 'Tain't Winnie, I hope,' I said.

" 'No,' he replied, with a gay laugh, ' 'tis only James Dawe.'

" 'They two won't be missed,' I told 'e, and throwing a kiss to Gabriel with me fingers, I ran off.—Will you take a sweet?"

Death took three.

"Was there no one else in the shop when you went in for these?" asked Death.

"Oh, yes," replied Winnie. "Jimmy, the Shelton policeman, was there, and 'e were telling a fine tale about you— and all found out by Lord Bullman because you killed they flowers. 'Tis said you be wanted by Lord Bullman for being a thief."

"Oh, he wants me, does he?" laughed Death.

"He wants to lock you up in prison," cried Winnie.

"He is not the first lord," replied Death, "who has wished to do that, nor will he be the last."

"Don't 'ee be afraid," said Winnie, "for I bain't going to let any one who I've been friendly wi' be taken up by thik Shelton policeman. And who be Lord Bullman to make so much of himself? 'E bain't nothing to Squire Knightley, though 'twouldn't have taken me so long to call 'e George as it did Miss Emma. Thik Shelton policeman do like drink and women."

"Most men do," observed Death, dryly.

"I did tell Jimmy," whispered Winnie, "that sister Daisy will meet him a mile beyond Madder, where the road makes a sudden turn and is deeply shaded by elms on each side and becomes, for a considerable stretch, very retired."

"You little liar!" cried Death.

"I were only repeating words out of a book," said Winnie.

"And what did the policeman do when you told him that?" asked Death.

"He went to Mr. Titball's," replied Winnie. "But whether 'twas beer or Daisy, I bain't the one to know."

"Winnie," observed Death, with a deep sigh, "we must part for a while."

"You promised me a penny when you went away," said Winnie.

"And I will give you two pennies, when we meet again," replied Death, grimly.

.   .   .   .

When, that same night, George Mere was left alone with his wife, he told her that he kept a kind of oddity in his bedroom that could give a bride some pretty pains. It was now hidden, but when she was naked in bed, he promised to show her the shining edge.

Susie gave no heed to him; she only looked at something that was set up against the wall—Death's scythe.

Mere cast her down upon the bed and went to take up the weapon. But Susie was before him. She seized the scythe first. Mere uttered a howl of rage, clutched at her, and fell upon the floor. Death was in the room.

Susie swung the sharp scythe. She was a mower in a fair meadow, who had come upon an ugly thing in the grass—a man. Susie mowed the swath.

"A good stroke," Death said to her. "Dress yourself, go to the pond in Bridle's field, and I will come to you there. . . ."

Joseph Bridle waited beside the pond. He waited there gladly.

The sun that, during a summer's night, only moves a little

way below the rim of the world, gave light to the fields of Dodder. Madder Hill, overweighted by love, looked into the pond. The Shelton church clock struck twelve.

Joseph Bridle had not to wait long for Susie to come to him. A slight figure left the Manor farm, and came into the lane.

A few moments of joy may complete the full circle. The longest life may fade and perish, but one moment can live and become immortal.

Joseph Bridle, holding Susie in his arms, listened. He heard the sharpening of a scythe. He looked towards James Dawe's cottage. A rush of hot wind stirred the waters of the pond. Death opened the cottage door. There was no sound.

Priscilla Hayhoe had awaked and knew the footsteps. She roused her husband, and they knelt to pray.

Leaving Dawe's cottage, Death entered Joe Bridle's field. Susie and Joseph were standing at the farther side of the pond. With gladness they saw Death come, and holding each other by the hand, they stept in.

The dark waters closed over their heads.

Death vanished.